TALES BEFORE MIDNIGHT

CONTENTS

I

INTO EGYPT

IT had finally been decided to let them go and now, for three days, they had been passing. The dust on the road to the frontier had not settled for three days or nights. But the strictest orders had been given and there were very few incidents. There could easily have been more.

Even the concentration camps had been swept clean, for this thing was to be final. After it, the State could say "How fearless we are – we let even known conspirators depart." It is true that, in the case of those in the concentration camps, there had been a preliminary rectification – a weeding, so to speak. But the news of that would not be officially published for some time and the numbers could always be disputed. If you kill a few people, they remain persons with names and identities, but, if you kill in the hundreds, there is simply a number for most of those who read the newspapers. And, once you start arguing about numbers, you begin to wonder if the thing ever happened at all. This too had been foreseen.

In fact, everything had been foreseen – and with great acuteness. There had been the usual diplomatic tension, solved, finally, by the usual firm stand. At the last moment, the other Powers had decided to co-operate. They had done so unwillingly, grudgingly, and with many representations, but they had done so. It was another great victory. And everywhere the trains rolled and the dust rose on the roads, for, at last and at length, the Accursed People were going. Every one of them, man, woman and child, to the third and the fourth generation — every one of them with a drop of that blood in his veins. And this was the end of it all and, by sunset on the third day, the land would know them no more. It was another great victory — perhaps the greatest. There would be a week of celebration after it, with appropriate ceremonies and speeches, and the date would be marked in the new calendar, with the date of the founding of the State and other dates.

Nevertheless, and even with the noteworthy efficiency of which the State was so proud, any mass evacuation is bound to be a complicated and fatiguing affair. The lieutenant stationed at the crossroads found it so — he was young and in the best of health but the strain was beginning to tell on him, though he would never have admitted it. He had been a little nervous at first — a little nervous and exceedingly anxious that everything should go according to plan. After all, it was an important post, the last crossroads before the frontier. A minor road, of course — they'd be busier on the main highways and at the ports of embarkation — but a last crossroads, nevertheless. He couldn't flatter himself it was worth a decoration — the bigwigs would get those. But, all the same, he was expected to evacuate so many thousands — he knew the figures by heart. Easy enough to say one had only to follow the plan! That might do for civilians — an officer was an officer. Would he show himself enough of an officer, would he make a fool of himself in front of his men? Would he even, perhaps, by some horrible, unforeseen mischance, get his road clogged with fleeing humanity till they had to send somebody over from Staff to straighten the tangle out? The thought was appalling.

He could see it happening in his mind – as a boy, he had been imaginative. He could hear the staff officer's words while he stood at attention, eyes front. One's first real command and a black mark on one's record! Yes, even if it was only police work – that didn't matter – a citizen of the State, a member of the Party must be held to an unflinching standard. If one failed to meet that standard there was nothing left in life. His throat had been dry and his movements a little jerky as he made his last dispositions and saw the first black specks begin to straggle toward the crossroads.

He could afford to laugh at that now, if he had had time. He could even afford to remember old Franz, his orderly, trying to put the brandy in his coffee, that first morning. "It's a chilly morning, Lieutenant," but there had been a question in Franz's eyes. He'd refused the brandy, of course, and told Franz off properly, too. The new State did not depend on Dutch courage but on the racial valor of its citizens. And the telling-off had helped – it had made his own voice firmer and given a little fillip of anger to his pulse. But Franz was an old soldier and imperturbable. What was it he had said, later? "The lieutenant must not worry. Civilians are always sheep – it is merely a matter of herding them." An improper remark, of course, to one's lieutenant, but it had helped settle his mind and make it cooler. Yes, an orderly like Franz was worth something, once one learned the knack of keeping him in his place.

Then they had begun to come, slowly, stragglingly, not like soldiers. He couldn't remember who had been the first. It was strange but he could not – he had been sure that he would remember. Perhaps a plodding family, with the scared children looking at him – perhaps one of the old men with long beards and burning eyes. But, after three days, they all mixed, the individual faces. As Franz had said, they became civilian sheep – sheep that one must herd and keep moving, keep moving always through day and night, moving on to the frontier. As they went, they wailed. When the wailing grew too loud, one took measures; but, sooner or later it always began again. It would break out down the road, die down as it came toward the post. It seemed to come out of their mouths without their knowledge – the sound of broken wood, of wheat ground between stones. He had tried to stop it completely at first, now he no longer bothered. And yet there were many – a great many – who did not wail.

At first, it had been interesting to see how many different types there were. He had not thought to find such variety among the Accursed People – one had one's own mental picture, reinforced by the pictures in the newspapers. But, seeing them was different. They were not all like the picture. They were tall and short, plump and lean, black-haired, yellow-haired, red-haired. It was obvious, even under the film of dust, that some had been rich, others poor, some thoughtful, others active. Indeed, it was often hard to tell them, by the looks. But that was not his affair — his affair was to keep them moving. All the same, it gave you a shock, sometimes, at first.

Perhaps the queerest thing was that they all looked so ordinary, so much a part of everyday. That was because one had been used to seeing them — it could be no more than that. But, under the film of dust and heat, one would look at a face. And then one think, unconsciously, "Why, what is that fellow doing, so far from where he lives? Why, for heaven's sake, is he straggling along this road? He doesn't look happy." Then the mind would resume control and one would remember. But the thought would come, now and then, without orders from the mind.

He had seen very few that he knew. That was natural — he came from the South. He had seen Willi Schneider, to be sure — that had been the second day and it was very dusty. When he was a little boy, very young, he had played in Willi's garden with Willi, in the summers, and, as they had played, there had come to them, through the open window, the ripple of a piano and the clear, rippling flow of Willi's mother's voice. It was not a great voice — not a Brunhild voice — but beautiful in *lieder* and beautifully sure. She had sung at their own house; that was odd to remember. Of course, her husband had not been one of them — a councilor, in fact. Needless to say, that had been long before the discovery that even the faintest trace of that blood tainted. As for Willi and himself, they had been friends — yes, even through the first year or so at school.

Both of them had meant to run away and be cowboys, and they had had a secret password. Naturally, things had changed, later on.

For a horrible moment, he had thought that Willi would speak to him — recall the warm air of summer and the smell of linden and those young, unmanly days. But Willi did not. Their eyes met, for an instant, then both had looked away. Willi was helping an old woman along, an old woman who muttered fretfully as she walked, like a cat with sore paws. They were both of them covered with dust and the old woman went slowly. Willi's mother had walked with a quick step and her voice had not been cracked or fretful. After play, she had given them both cream buns, laughing and moving her hands, in a bright green dress. It was not permitted to think further of Willi Schneider.

That was the only real acquaintance but there were other, recognizable faces. There was the woman who had kept the newsstand, the brisk little waiter at the summer hotel, the taxi chauffeur with the squint and the heart specialist. Then there was the former scientist — one could still tell him from his pictures — and the actor one had often seen. That was all that one knew and not all on the same day. That was enough. He had not imagined the taxi chauffeur with a wife and children and that the youngest child should be lame. That had surprised him — surprised him almost as much as seeing the heart specialist walking along the road like any man. It had surprised him, also, to see the scientist led along between two others and to recognize the fact that he was mad.

But that also mixed with the dust — the endless, stifling cloud of the dust, the endless, moving current. The dust got in one's throat and one's eyes — it was hard to cut, even with brandy, from one's throat. It lay on the endless bundles people carried; queer bundles, bulging out at the ends, with here a ticking clock, and there a green bunch of carrots. It lay on the handcarts a few of them pushed — the handcarts bearing the sort of goods that one would snatch, haphazard, from a burning house. It rose and whirled and penetrated — it was never still. At night, slashed by the efficient searchlights that made the night bright as day, it was still a mist above the road. As for sleep — well, one slept when one could, for a couple of hours after midnight, when they too slept, ungracefully, in heaps and clumps by the road. But, except for the first night, he could not even remember Franz pulling his boots off.

His men had been excellent, admirable, indefatigable. That was, of course, due to the Leader and the State, but still, he would put it in his report. They had kept the stream moving, always. The attitude had been the newly prescribed one — not that of punishment, richly as that was deserved, but of complete aloofness, as if the Accursed People did not even exist. Naturally, now and then, the men had had their fun. One could not blame them for that — some of the incidents had been extremely comic. There had been the old woman with the hen — a comedy character. Of course, she had not been permitted to keep the hen. They should have taken it away from her at the inspection point. But she had looked very funny, holding on to the squawking chicken by the tail feathers, with the tears running down her face.

Yes, the attitude of the men would certainly go in his report. He would devote a special paragraph to the musicians also — they had been indefatigable. They had played the prescribed tunes continually, in spite of the dust and the heat. One would hope that those tunes would sink into the hearts of the Accursed People, to be forever a warning and a memory. Particularly if they happened to know the words. But one could never be sure about people like that.

Staff cars had come four times, the first morning, and once there had been a general. He had felt nervous, when they came, but there had been no complaint. After that, they had let him alone, except for an occasional visit — that must mean they thought him up to his work. Once, even, the road had been almost clear, for a few minutes — he was moving them along faster than they did at the inspection point. The thought had gone to his head for an instant, but he kept cool — and, soon enough, the road had been crowded again.

As regarded casualties — he could not keep the exact figure in his head, but it was a minor one. A couple of heart attacks — one the man who had been a judge, or so the others said. Unpleasant but valuable to see the life drain out of a face like that. He had made himself watch it — one must harden oneself. They had wanted to remove the body — of course, that had not been allowed. The women taken in childbirth had been adequately dealt with — one could do nothing to assist. But he had insisted, for decency's sake, on a screen, and

Franz had been very clever at rigging one up. Only two of those had died, the rest had gone on — they showed a remarkable tenacity. Then there were the five executions, including the man suddenly gone crazy, who had roared and foamed. A nasty moment, that — for a second the whole current had stopped flowing. But his men had jumped in at once — he himself had acted quickly. The others were merely incorrigible stragglers and of no account.

And now, it was almost over and soon the homeland would be free. Free as it never had been — for, without the Accursed People, it would be unlike any other country on earth. They were gone, with their books and their music, their false, delusive science and their quick way of thinking. They were gone, all the people like Willi Schneider and his mother, who had spent so much time in talking and being friendly. They were gone, the willful people, who clung close together and yet so willfully supported the new and the untried. The men who haggled over pennies, and the others who gave — the sweater, the mimic, the philosopher, the discoverer — all were gone. Yes, and with them went their slaves' religion, the religion of the weak and the humble, the religion that fought so bitterly and yet exalted the prophet above the armed man.

One could be a whole man, with them gone, without their doubts and their mockery and their bitter, self-accusing laughter, their melancholy, deep as a well, and their endless aspiration for something that could not be touched with the hand. One could be solid and virile and untroubled, virile and huge as the old, thunderous gods. It was so that the Leader had spoken, so it must be true. And the countries who weakly received them would be themselves corrupted into warm unmanliness and mockery, into a desire for peace and a search for things not tangible. But the homeland would stand still and listen to the beat of its own heart — not even listen, but stand like a proud fierce animal, a perfect, living machine. To get children, to conquer others, to die gloriously in battle — that was the end of man. It had been a long time forgotten, but the Leader had remembered it. And, naturally, one could not do that completely with them in the land, for they had other ideas.

He thought of these things dutifully because it was right to think of them. They had been repeated and repeated in his ears till they had occupied his mind. But, meanwhile, he was very tired and the dust still rose. They were coming by clumps and groups, now — the last stragglers — they were no longer a solid, flowing current. The afternoon had turned hot — unseasonably hot. He didn't want any more brandy — the thought of it sickened his stomach. He wanted a glass of beer — iced beer, cold and dark, with foam on it — and a chance to unbutton his collar. He wanted to have the thing done and sit down and have Franz pull off his boots. If it were only a little cooler, a little quieter — if even these last would not wail so, now and then — if only the dust would not rise! He found himself humming, for comfort, a Christmas hymn — it brought a little, frail coolness to his mind.

"Silent night, holy night,
All is calm, all is bright. . . ."

The old gods were virile and thunderous, but, down in the South, they would still deck the tree, in kindliness. Call it a custom – call it anything you like – it still came out of the heart. And it was a custom of the homeland – it could not be wrong. Oh, the beautiful, crisp snow of Christmas Day, the greetings between friends, the bright, lighted tree! Well, there'd be a Christmas to come. Perhaps he'd be married, by then – he had thought of it, often. If he were, they would have a tree – young couples were sentimental, in the South. A tree and a small manger beneath it, with the animals and the child. They carved the figures out of wood, in his country, with loving care – the thought of them was very peaceful and cool. In the old days, he had always given Willi Schneider part of his almond cake – one knew it was not Willi's festival but one was friendly, for all that. And that must be forgotten. He had had no right to give Willi part of his almond cake – it was the tree that mattered, the tree and the tiny candles, the smell of the fresh pine and the clear, frosty sweetness of the day. They would keep that, he and his wife, keep it with rejoicing, and Willi would not look in through the window, with his old face or his new face. He would not look in at all, ever any more. For now the homeland was released, after many years.

Now the dust was beginning to settle – the current in the road had dwindled to a straggling trickle. He was able to think, for the first time, of the land to which that trickle was going – a hungry land, the papers said, in spite of its boastful ways. The road led blankly into it, beyond the rise of ground – hard to tell what it was like. But they would be dispersed, not only here, but over many lands. Of course, the situation was not comparable – all the same, it must be a queer feeling. A queer feeling, yes, to start out anew, with nothing but the clothes on your back and what you could push in a handcart, if you had a handcart. For an instant the thought came, unbidden, "It must be a great people that can bear such things." But they were the Accursed People – the thought should not have come.

He sighed and turned back to his duty. It was really wonderful – even on the third day there was such order, such precision. It was something to be proud of – something to remember long. The Leader would speak of it, undoubtedly. The ones who came now were the very last stragglers, the weakest, but they were being moved along as promptly as if they were strong. The dust actually no longer rose in a cloud – it was settling, slowly but surely.

He did not quite remember when he had last eaten. It did not matter, for the sun was sinking fast, in a red warm glow. In a moment, in an hour, it would be done – he could rest and undo his collar, have some beer. There was nobody on the road now – nobody at all. He stood rigidly at his post – the picture of an officer, though somewhat dusty – but he knew that his eyes were closing. Nobody on the road – nobody for a whole five minutes . . . for eight . . . for ten.

He was roused by Franz's voice in his ear — he must have gone to sleep, standing up. He had heard of that happening to soldiers on the march — he felt rather proud that, now, it had happened to him. But there seemed to be a little trouble on the road — he walked forward to it, stiffly, trying to clear his throat.

It was a commonplace grouping — he had seen dozens like it in the course of the three days — an older man, a young woman, and, of course, the child that she held. No doubt about them, either — the man's features were strongly marked, the woman had the liquid eyes. As for the child, that was merely a wrapped bundle. They should have started before — stupid people — the man looked strong enough. Their belongings were done up like all poor people's belongings.

He stood in front of them, now, erect and a soldier. "Well," he said. "Don't you know the orders? No livestock to be taken. Didn't they examine you, down the road?" ("And a pretty fool I'll look like, reporting one confiscated donkey to Headquarters," he thought, with irritation. "We've been able to manage, with the chickens, but this is really too much! What can they be thinking of at the inspection point? Oh, well, they're tired too, I suppose, but it's my responsibility.")

He put a rasp in his voice — he had to, they looked at him so stupidly. "Well?" he said. "Answer me! Don't you know an officer when you see one?"

"We have come a long way," said the man, in a low voice. "We heard there was danger to the child. So we are going. May we pass?" The voice was civil enough, but the eyes were dark and large, the face tired and worn. He was resting one hand on his staff, in a peasant gesture. The woman said nothing at all and one felt that she would say nothing. She sat on the back of the gray donkey and the child in her arms, too, was silent, though it moved.

The lieutenant tried to think rapidly. After all, these were the last. But the thoughts buzzed around his head and would not come out of his mouth. That was fatigue. It should be easy enough for a lieutenant to give an order.

He found himself saying, conversationally, "There are just the three of you?"

"That is all," said the man and looked at him with great simplicity. "But we heard there was danger to the child. So we could not stay any more. We could not stay at all."

"Indeed," said the lieutenant and then said again, "indeed."

"Yes," said the man. "But we shall do well enough – we have been in exile before." He spoke patiently and yet with a certain authority. When the lieutenant did not answer, he laid his other hand on the rein of the gray donkey. It moved forward a step and with it, also, the child stirred and moved. The lieutenant, turning, saw the child's face now, and its hands, as it turned and moved its small hands to the glow of the sunset.

"If the lieutenant pleases – " said an eager voice, the voice of the Northern corporal.

"The lieutenant does not please," said the lieutenant. He nodded at the man. "You may proceed."

"But Lieutenant – " said the eager voice.

"Swine and dog," said the lieutenant, feeling something snap in his mind, "are we to hinder the Leader's plans because of one gray donkey? The order says—all out of the country by sunset. Let them go. You will report to me, Corporal, in the morning."

He turned on his heel and walked a straight line to the field hut, not looking back. When Franz, the orderly, came in a little later, he found him sitting in a chair.

"If the lieutenant would take some brandy—" he said, respectfully.

"The lieutenant has had enough brandy," said the lieutenant, in a hoarse, dusty voice. "Have my orders been obeyed?"

"Yes, Lieutenant."

"They are gone—the very last of them?"

"Yes, Lieutenant."

"They did not look back?"

"No, Lieutenant."

The lieutenant said nothing, for a while, and Franz busied himself with boots. After some time, he spoke.

"The lieutenant should try to sleep," he said. "We have carried out our orders. And now, they are gone."

"Yes," said the lieutenant, and, suddenly, he saw them again, the whole multitude, dispersed among every country—the ones who had walked his road, the ones at the points of embarkation. There were a great many of them, and that he had expected. But they were not dispersed as he had thought. They were not dispersed as he had thought, for, with each one went shame, like a visible burden. And the shame was not theirs, though they carried it — the shame belonged to the land that had driven them forth — his own land. He could see it growing and spreading like a black blot — the shame of his country spread over the whole earth.

"The lieutenant will have some brandy," he said. "Quickly, Franz."

When the brandy was brought, he stared at it for a moment, in the cup.

"Tell me, Franz," he said. "Did you know them well? Any of them? Before?"

"Oh yes, Lieutenant," said Franz, in his smooth, orderly's voice. "In the last war, I was billeted — well, the name of the town does not matter, but the woman was one of them. Of course that was before we knew about them," he said, respectfully. "That was more than twenty years ago. But she was very kind to me — I used to make toys for her children. I have often wondered what happened to her — she was very considerate and kind. Doubtless I was wrong, Lieutenant? But that was in another country."

"Yes, Franz," said the lieutenant. "There were children, you say?"

"Yes, Lieutenant."

"You saw the child today? The last one?"

"Yes, Lieutenant."

"Its hands had been hurt," said the lieutenant. "In the middle. Right through. I saw them. I wish I had not seen that. I wish I had not seen its hands."

II

JOHNNY PYE AND THE FOOL-KILLER

YOU don't hear so much about the Fool-Killer these days, but when Johnny Pye was a boy there was a good deal of talk about him. Some said he was one kind of person, and some said another, but most people agreed that he came around fairly regular. Or, it seemed so to Johnny Pye. But then, Johnny was an adopted child, which is, maybe, why he took it so hard.

The miller and his wife had offered to raise him, after his own folks died, and that was a good deed on their part. But, as soon as he lost his baby teeth and started acting the way most boys act, they began to come down on him like thunder, which wasn't so good. They were good people, according to their lights, but their lights were terribly strict ones, and they believed that the harder you were on a youngster, the better and brighter he got. Well, that may work with some children, but it didn't with Johnny Pye.

He was sharp enough and willing enough — as sharp and willing as most boys in Martinsville. But, somehow or other, he never seemed to be able to do the right things or say the right words — at least when he was home. Treat a boy like a fool and he'll act like a fool, I say, but there's some folks need convincing. The miller and his wife thought the way to smarten Johnny was to treat him like a fool, and finally they got so he pretty much believed it himself.

And that was hard on him, for he had a boy's imagination, and maybe a little more than most. He could stand the beatings and he did. But what he couldn't stand was the way things went at the mill. I don't suppose the miller intended to do it. But, as long as Johnny Pye could remember, whenever he heard of the death of somebody he didn't like, he'd say, "Well, the Fool-Killer's come for so-and-so," and sort of smack his lips. It was, as you might say, a family joke, but the miller was a big man with a big red face, and it made a strong impression on Johnny Pye. Till, finally, he got a picture of the Fool-Killer, himself. He was a big man, too, in a checked shirt and corduroy trousers, and he went walking the ways of the world, with a hickory club that had a lump of lead in the end of it. I don't know how Johnny Pye got that picture so clear, but, to him, it was just as plain as the face of any human being in Martinsville. And, now and then, just to test it, he'd ask a grown-up person, kind of timidly, if that was the way the Fool-Killer looked. And, of course, they'd generally laugh and tell him it was. Then Johnny would wake up at night, in his room over the mill, and listen for the Fool-Killer's step on the road and wonder when he was coming. But he was brave enough not to tell anybody that.

Finally, though, things got a little more than he could bear. He'd done some boy's trick or other – let the stones grind a little fine, maybe, when the miller wanted the meal ground coarse – just carelessness, you know. But he'd gotten two whippings for it, one from the miller and one from his wife, and, at the end of it, the miller had said, "Well, Johnny Pye, the Fool-Killer ought to be along for you most any day now. For I never did see a boy that was such a fool." Johnny looked to the miller's wife to see if she believed it, too, but she just shook her head and looked serious. So he went to bed that night, but he couldn't sleep, for every time a bough rustled or the mill wheel creaked, it seemed to him it must be the Fool-Killer. And, early next morning, before anybody was up, he packed such duds as he had in a bandanna handkerchief and ran away.

He didn't really expect to get away from the Fool-Killer very long — as far as he knew, the Fool-Killer got you wherever you went. But he thought he'd give him a run for his money, at least. And when he got on the road, it was a bright spring morning, and the first peace and quiet he'd had in some time. So his spirits rose, and he chunked a stone at a bullfrog as he went along, just to show he was Johnny Pye and still doing business.

He hadn't gone more than three or four miles out of Martinsville, when he heard a buggy coming up the road behind him. He knew the Fool-Killer didn't need a buggy to catch you, so he wasn't afraid of it, but he stepped to the side of the road to let it pass. But it stopped, instead, and a black-whiskered man with a stovepipe hat looked out of it.

"Hello, bub," he said. "Is this the road for East Liberty?"

"My name's John Pye and I'm eleven years old,"

said Johnny, polite but firm, "and you take the next left fork for East Liberty. They say it's a pretty town — I've never been there myself." And he sighed a little, because he thought he'd like to see the world before the Fool-Killer caught up with him.

"H'm," said the man. "Stranger here, too, eh? And what brings a smart boy like you on the road so early in the morning?"

"Oh," said Johnny Pye, quite honestly, "I'm running away from the Fool-Killer. For the miller says I'm a fool and his wife says I'm a fool and almost everybody in Martinsville says I'm a fool except little Susie Marsh. And the miller says the Fool-Killer's after me — so I thought I'd run away before he came."

The black-whiskered man sat in his buggy and wheezed for a while. When he got his breath back, "Well, jump in, bub," he said. "The miller may say you're a fool, but I think you're a right smart boy to be running away from the Fool-Killer all by yourself. And I don't hold with small-town prejudices and I need a right smart boy, so I'll give you a lift on the road."

"But, will I be safe from the Fool-Killer, if I'm with you?" said Johnny. "For, otherwise, it don't signify."

"Safe?" said the black-whiskered man, and wheezed again. "Oh, you'll be safe as houses. You see, I'm a herb doctor — and some folks think, a little in the Fool-Killer's line of business, myself. And I'll teach you a trade worth two of milling. So jump in, bub."

"Sounds all right the way you say it," said Johnny, "but my name's John Pye," and he jumped into the buggy. And they went rattling along toward East Liberty with the herb doctor talking and cutting jokes till Johnny thought he'd never met a pleasanter man. About half a mile from East Liberty, the doctor stopped at a spring.

"What are we stopping here for?" said Johnny Pye.

"Wait and see," said the doctor, and gave him a wink. Then he got a haircloth trunk full of empty bottles out of the back of the buggy and made Johnny fill them with spring water and label them. Then he added a pinch of pink powder to each bottle and shook them up and corked them and stowed them away.

"What's that?" said Johnny, very interested.

"That's Old Doctor Waldo's Unparalleled Universal Remedy," said the doctor, reading from the label. "Made from the purest snake oil and secret Indian herbs, it cures rheumatism, blind staggers, headache, malaria, five kinds of fits, and spots in front of the eyes. It will also remove oil or grease stains, clean knives and silver, polish brass, and is strongly recommended as a general tonic and blood purifier. Small size, one dollar – family bottle, two dollars and a half."

"But I don't see any snake oil in it," said Johnny, puzzled, "or any secret Indian herbs."

"That's because you're not a fool," said the doctor, with another wink. "The Fool-Killer wouldn't, either. But most folks will."

And, that very same night, Johnny saw. For the doctor made his pitch in East Liberty and he did it handsome. He took a couple of flaring oil torches and stuck them on the sides of the buggy; he put on a diamond stickpin and did card tricks and told funny stories till he had the crowd goggle-eyed. As for Johnny, he let him play on the tambourine. Then he started talking about Doctor Waldo's Universal Remedy, and, with Johnny to help him, the bottles went like hot cakes. Johnny helped the doctor count the money afterward, and it was a pile.

"Well," said Johnny, "I never saw money made easier. You've got a fine trade, Doctor."

"It's cleverness does it," said the doctor, and slapped him on the back.

"Now a fool's content to stay in one place and do one thing, but the Fool-Killer never caught up with a good pitchman yet."

"Well, it's certainly lucky I met up with you," said Johnny, "and, if it's cleverness does it, I'll learn the trade or bust."

So he stayed with the doctor quite a while – in fact, till he could make up the remedy and do the card tricks almost as good as the doctor. And the doctor liked Johnny, for Johnny was a biddable boy. But one night they came into a town where things didn't go as they usually did. The crowd gathered as usual, and the doctor did his tricks. But, all the time, Johnny could see a sharp-faced little fellow going through the crowd and whispering to one man and another. Till, at last, right in the middle of the doctor's spiel, the sharp-faced fellow gave a shout of "That's him all right! I'd know them whiskers anywhere!" and, with that, the crowd growled once and began to tear slats out of the nearest fence. Well, the next thing Johnny knew, he and the doctor were being ridden out of town on a rail, with the doctor's long coattails flying at every jounce.

They didn't hurt Johnny particular – him only being a boy. But they warned 'em both never to show their faces in that town again, and then they heaved the doctor into a thistle patch and went their ways.

"Owoo!" said the doctor, "ouch!" as Johnny was helping him out of the thistle patch. "Go easy with those thistles! And why didn't you give me the office, you blame little fool?"

"Office?" said Johnny. "What office?"

"When that sharp-nosed man started snooping around," said the doctor. "I thought that infernal main street looked familiar – I was through there two years ago, selling solid gold watches for a dollar apiece."

"But the works to a solid gold watch would be worth more than that," said Johnny.

"There weren't any works," said the doctor, with a groan, "but there was a nice lively beetle inside each case and it made the prettiest tick you ever heard."

"Well, that certainly was a clever idea," said Johnny. "I'd never have thought of that."

"Clever?" said the doctor. "Ouch – it was ruination! But who'd have thought the fools would bear a grudge for two years? And now we've lost the horse and buggy, too – not to speak of the bottles and the money. Well, there's lots more tricks to be played and we'll start again."

But, though he liked the doctor, Johnny began to feel dubious. For it occurred to him that, if all the doctor's cleverness got him was being ridden out of town on a rail, he couldn't be so far away from the Fool-Killer as he thought. And, sure enough, as he was going to sleep that night, he seemed to hear the Fool-Killer's footsteps coming after him – step, step, step. He pulled his jacket up over his ears, but he couldn't shut it out. So, when the doctor had got in the way of starting business over again, he and Johnny parted company. The doctor didn't bear any grudge; he shook hands with Johnny and told him to remember that cleverness was power. And Johnny went on with his running away.

He got to a town, and there was a store with a sign in the window, BOY WANTED, so he went in. There, sure enough, was the merchant, sitting at his desk, and a fine, important man he looked, in his black broadcloth suit.

Johnny tried to tell him about the Fool-Killer, but the merchant wasn't interested in that. He just looked Johnny over and saw that he looked biddable and strong for his age. "But, remember, no fooling around, boy!" said the merchant sternly, after he'd hired him.

"No fooling around?" said Johnny, with the light of hope in his eyes.

"No," said the merchant, meaningly. "We've no room for fools in this business, I can tell you! You work hard, and you'll rise. But, if you've got any foolish notions, just knock them on the head and forget them."

Well, Johnny was glad enough to promise that, and he stayed with the merchant a year and a half. He swept out the store, and he put the shutters up and took them down; he ran errands and wrapped up packages and learned to keep busy twelve hours a day. And, being a biddable boy and an honest one, he rose, just like the merchant had said. The merchant raised his wages and let him begin to wait on customers and learn accounts. And then, one night, Johnny woke up in the middle of the night. And it seemed to him he heard, far away but getting nearer, the steps of the Fool-Killer after him — tramping, tramping.

He went to the merchant next day and said, "Sir, I'm sorry to tell you this, but I'll have to be moving on."

"Well, I'm sorry to hear that, Johnny," said the merchant, "for you've been a good boy. And, if it's a question of salary —"

"It isn't that," said Johnny, "but tell me one thing, sir, if you don't mind my asking. Supposing I did stay with you — where would I end?"

The merchant smiled. "That's a hard question to answer," he said, "and I'm not much given to compliments. But I started, myself, as a boy, sweeping out the store. And you're a bright youngster with lots of go-ahead. I don't see why, if you stuck to it, you shouldn't make the same kind of success that I have."

"And what's that?" said Johnny.

The merchant began to look irritated, but he kept his smile.

"Well," he said, "I'm not a boastful man, but I'll tell you this. Ten years ago I was the richest man in town. Five years ago, I was the richest man in the county. And five years from now — well, I aim to be the richest man in the state."

His eyes kind of glittered as he said it, but Johnny

was looking at his face. It was sallow-skinned and pouchy, with the jaw as hard as a rock. And it came upon Johnny that moment that, though he'd known the merchant a year and a half, he'd never really seen him enjoy himself except when he was driving a bargain.

"Sorry, sir," he said, "but, if it's like that, I'll certainly have to go. Because, you see, I'm running away from the Fool-Killer, and if I stayed here and got to be like you, he'd certainly catch up with me in no –"

"Why, you impertinent young cub!" roared the merchant, with his face gone red all of a sudden. "Get your money from the cashier!" and Johnny was on the road again before you could say "Jack Robinson." But, this time, he was used to it, and walked off whistling.

Well, after that, he hired out to quite a few different people, but I won't go into all of his adventures. He worked for an inventor for a while, and they split up because Johnny happened to ask him what would be the good of his patent, self-winding, perpetual-motion machine, once he did get it invented. And, while the inventor talked big about improving the human race and the beauties of science, it was plain he didn't know. So that night, Johnny heard the steps of the Fool-Killer, far off but coming closer, and, next morning, he went away. Then he stayed with a minister for a while, and he certainly hated to leave him, for the minister was a good man. But they got talking one evening and, as it chanced, Johnny asked him what happened to people who didn't believe in his particular religion. Well, the minister was broad-minded, but there's only one answer to that. He admitted they might be good folks – he even admitted they mightn't exactly go to hell – but he couldn't let them into heaven, no, not the best and the wisest of them, for there were the specifications laid down by creed and church, and, if you didn't fulfill them, you didn't.

So Johnny had to leave him, and, after that, he went with an old drunken fiddler for a while. He wasn't a good man, I guess, but he could play till the tears ran down your cheeks. And, when he was playing his best, it seemed to Johnny that the Fool-Killer was very far away. For, in spite of his faults and his weaknesses, while he played, there was might in the man. But he died drunk in a ditch, one night, with Johnny to hold his head, and, while he left Johnny his fiddle, it didn't do Johnny much good. For, while Johnny could play a tune, he couldn't play like the fiddler – it wasn't in his fingers.

Then it chanced that Johnny took up with a company of soldiers. He was still too young to enlist, but they made a kind of pet of him, and everything went swimmingly for a while. For the captain was the bravest man Johnny had ever seen, and he had an answer for everything, out of regulations and the Articles of War. But then they went West to fight Indians and the same old trouble cropped up again. For one night the captain said to him, "Johnny, we're going to fight the enemy tomorrow, but you'll stay in camp."

"Oh, I don't want to do that," said Johnny; "I want to be in on the fighting."

"It's an order," said the captain, grimly. Then he

gave Johnny certain instructions and a letter to take to his wife.

"For the colonel's a copper-plated fool," he said, "and we're walking straight into an ambush."

"Why don't you tell him that?" said Johnny.

"I have," said the captain, "but he's the colonel."

"Colonel or no colonel," said Johnny, "if he's a fool, somebody ought to stop him."

"You can't do that, in an army," said the captain. "Orders are orders." But it turned out the captain was wrong about it, for, next day, before they could get moving, the Indians attacked and got badly licked. When it was all over, "Well, it was a good fight," said the captain, professionally. "All the same, if they'd waited and laid an ambush, they'd have had our hair. But, as it was, they didn't stand a chance."

"But why didn't they lay an ambush?" said Johnny.

"Well," said the captain, "I guess they had their orders too. And now, how would you like to be a soldier?"

"Well, it's a nice outdoors life, but I'd like to think it over," said Johnny. For he knew the captain was brave and he knew the Indians had been brave — you couldn't find two braver sets of people. But, all the same, when he thought the whole thing over, he seemed to hear steps in the sky. So he soldiered to the end of the campaign and then he left the army, though the captain told him he was making a mistake.

By now, of course, he wasn't a boy any longer; he was getting to be a young man with a young man's thoughts and feelings. And, half the time, nowadays, he'd forget about the Fool-Killer except as a dream he'd had when he was a boy. He could even laugh at it now and then, and think what a fool he'd been to believe there was such a man.

But, all the same, the desire in him wasn't satisfied, and something kept driving him on. He'd have called it ambitiousness, now, but it came to the same thing. And with every new trade he tried, sooner or later would come the dream — the dream of the big man in the checked shirt and corduroy pants, walking the ways of the world with his hickory stick in one hand. It made him angry to have that dream, now, but it had a singular power over him. Till, finally, when he was turned twenty or so, he got scared.

"Fool-Killer or no Fool-Killer," he said to himself. "I've got to ravel this matter out. For there must be some one thing a man could tie to, and be sure he wasn't a fool. I've tried cleverness and money and half a dozen other things, and they don't seem to be the answer. So now I'll try book learning and see what comes of that."

So he read all the books he could find, and whenever he'd seem to hear the steps of the Fool-Killer coming for the authors — and that was frequent — he'd try and shut his ears. But some books said one thing was best and some another, and he couldn't rightly decide.

"Well," he said to himself, when he'd read and read till his head felt as stuffed with book learning as a sausage with meat, "it's interesting, but it isn't exactly contemporaneous. So I think I'll go down to Washington and ask the wise men there. For it must take a lot of wisdom to run a country like the United States, and if there's people who can answer my questions, it's there they ought to be found."

So he packed his bag and off to Washington he went. He was modest for a youngster, and he didn't intend to try and see the President right away. He thought probably a congressman was about his size. So he saw a congressman, and the congressman told him the thing to be was an upstanding young American and vote the Republican ticket—which sounded all right to Johnny Pye, but not exactly what he was after.

Then he went to a senator, and the senator told him to be an upstanding young American and vote the Democratic ticket—which sounded all right, too, but not what he was after, either. And, somehow, though both men had been impressive and affable, right in the middle of their speeches he'd seemed to hear steps—you know.

But a man has to eat, whatever else he does, and Johnny found he'd better buckle down and get himself a job. It happened to be with the first congressman he struck, for that one came from Martinsville, which is why Johnny went to him in the first place. And, in a little while, he forgot his search entirely and the Fool-Killer, too, for the congressman's niece came East to visit him, and she was the Susie Marsh that Johnny had sat next in school. She'd been pretty then, but she was prettier now, and as soon as Johnny Pye saw her, his heart gave a jump and a thump.

"And don't think we don't remember you in Martinsville, Johnny Pye," she said, when her uncle had explained who his new clerk was. "Why, the whole town'll be excited when I write home. We've heard all about your killing Indians and inventing perpetual motion and traveling around the country with a famous doctor and making a fortune in dry goods and—oh, it's a wonderful story!"

"Well," said Johnny, and coughed, "some of that's just a little bit exaggerated. But it's nice of you to be interested. So they don't think I'm a fool any more, in Martinsville?"

"I never thought you were a fool," said Susie with a little smile, and Johnny felt his heart give another bump.

"And I always knew you were pretty, but never how pretty till now," said Johnny, and coughed again. "But, speaking of old times, how's the miller and his wife? For I did leave them right sudden, and while there were faults on both sides, I must have been a trial to them too."

"They've gone the way of all flesh," said Susie Marsh, "and there's a new miller now. But he isn't very well-liked, to tell the truth, and he's letting the mill run down."

"That's a pity," said Johnny, "for it was a likely mill." Then he began to ask her more questions and she began to remember things too. Well, you know how the time can go when two youngsters get talking like that.

Johnny Pye never worked so hard in his life as he did that winter. And it wasn't the Fool-Killer he thought about—it was Susie Marsh. First he thought she loved him and then he was sure she didn't, and then he was betwixt and between, and all perplexed and confused. But, finally, it turned out all right and he had her promise, and Johnny Pye knew he was the happiest man in the world. And that night, he waked up in the night and heard the Fool-Killer coming after him — step, step, step.

He didn't sleep much after that, and he came down to breakfast hollow-eyed. But his uncle-to-be didn't notice that — he was rubbing his hands and smiling.

"Put on your best necktie, Johnny!" he said, very cheerful, "for I've got an appointment with the President today, and, just to show I approve of my niece's fiancé, I'm taking you along."

"The President!" said Johnny, all dumfounded.

"Yes," said Congressman Marsh, "you see, there's a little bill — well, we needn't go into that. But slick down your back hair, Johnny — we'll make Martinsville proud of us this day!"

Then a weight seemed to go from Johnny's shoulders and a load from his heart. He wrung Mr. Marsh's hand.

"Thank you, Uncle Eben!" he said. "I can't thank you enough." For, at last, he knew he was going to look upon a man that was bound to be safe from the Fool-Killer — and it seemed to him if he could just once do that, all his troubles and searchings would be ended.

Well, it doesn't signify which President it was — you can take it from me that he was President and a fine-looking man. He'd just been elected, too, so he was lively as a trout, and the saddle galls he'd get from Congress hadn't even begun to show. Anyhow, there he was, and Johnny feasted his eyes on him. For if there was anybody in the country the Fool-Killer couldn't bother, it must be a man like this.

The President and the congressman talked politics for a while, and then it was Johnny's turn.

"Well, young man," said the President, affably, "and what can I do for you – for you look to me like a fine, upstanding young American."

The congressman cut in quick before Johnny could open his mouth.

"Just a word of advice, Mr. President," he said. "Just a word in season. For my young friend's led an adventurous life, but now he's going to marry my niece and settle down. And what he needs most of all is a word of ripe wisdom from you."

"Well," said the President, looking at Johnny rather keenly, "if that's all he needs, a short horse is soon curried. I wish most of my callers wanted as little."

But, all the same, he drew Johnny out, as such men can, and before Johnny knew it, he was telling his life story.

"Well," said the President, at the end, "you certainly have been a rolling stone, young man. But there's nothing wrong in that. And, for one of your varied experience there's one obvious career. Politics!" he said, and slapped his fist in his hand.

"Well," said Johnny, scratching his head, "of course, since I've been in Washington, I've thought of that. But I don't know that I'm rightly fitted."

"You can write a speech," said Congressman Marsh,

quite thoughtful, "for you've helped me with mine. You're a likeable fellow too. And you were born poor and worked up — and you've even got a war record — why, hell! Excuse me, Mr. President! — he's worth five hundred votes just as he stands!"

"I — I'm more than honored by you two gentlemen," said Johnny, abashed and flattered, "but supposing I did go into politics — where would I end up?"

The President looked sort of modest.

"The Presidency of the United States," said he, "is within the legitimate ambition of every American citizen. Provided he can get elected, of course."

"Oh," said Johnny, feeling dazzled, "I never thought of that. Well, that's a great thing. But it must be a great responsibility too."

"It is," said the President, looking just like his pictures on the campaign buttons.

"Why, it must be an awful responsibility!" said Johnny. "I can't hardly see how a mortal man can bear it. Tell me, Mr. President," he said, "may I ask you a question?"

"Certainly," said the President, looking prouder and more responsible and more and more like his picture on the campaign buttons every minute.

"Well," said Johnny, "it sounds like a fool question, but it's this: This is a great big country of ours, Mr. President, and it's got the most amazing lot of different people in it. How can any President satisfy all those people at one time? Can you yourself, Mr. President?"

The President looked a bit taken aback for a minute. But then he gave Johnny Pye a statesman's glance.

"With the help of God," he said, solemnly, "and in accordance with the principles of our great party, I intend . . ."

But Johnny didn't even hear the end of the sentence. For, even as the President was speaking, he heard a step outside in the corridor and he knew, somehow, it wasn't the step of a secretary or a guard. He was glad the President had said "with the help of God" for that sort of softened the step. And when the President finished, Johnny bowed.

"Thank you, Mr. President," he said; "that's what I wanted to know. And now I'll go back to Martinsville, I guess."

"Go back to Martinsville?" said the President, surprised.

"Yes, sir," said Johnny. "For I don't think I'm cut out for politics."

"And is that all you have to say to the President of the United States?" said his uncle-to-be, in a fume.

But the President had been thinking, meanwhile, and he was a bigger man than the congressman.

"Wait a minute, Congressman," he said. "This young man's honest, at least, and I like his looks. Moreover, of all the people who've come to see me in the last six months, he's the only one who hasn't wanted something – except the White House cat, and I guess she wanted something, too, because she meowed. You don't want to be President, young man – and, confidentially, I don't blame you. But how would you like to be postmaster at Martinsville?"

"Postmaster at Martinsville?" said Johnny. "But –"

"Oh, it's only a tenth-class post office," said the President, "but, for once in my life, I'll do something because I want to, and let Congress yell its head off. Come – is it yes or no?"

Johnny thought of all the places he'd been and all the trades he'd worked at. He thought, queerly enough, of the old drunk fiddler dead in the ditch, but he knew he couldn't be that. Mostly, though, he thought of Martinsville and Susie Marsh. And, though he'd just heard the Fool-Killer's step, he defied the Fool-Killer.

"Why, it's yes, of course, Mr. President," he said, "for then I can marry Susie."

"That's as good a reason as you'll find," said the President. "And now, I'll just write a note."

Well, he was as good as his word, and Johnny and his Susie were married and went back to live in Martinsville. And, as soon as Johnny learned the ways of postmastering, he found it as good a trade as most. There wasn't much mail in Martinsville, but, in between whiles, he ran the mill, and that was a good trade too. And all the time, he knew, at the back of his mind, that he hadn't quite settled accounts with the Fool-Killer. But he didn't much care about that, for he and Susie were happy. And after a while they had a child, and that was the most remarkable experience that had ever happened to any young couple, though the doctor said it was a perfectly normal baby.

One evening, when his son was about a year old, Johnny Pye took the river road, going home. It was a mite longer than the hill road, but it was the cool of the evening, and there's times when a man likes to walk by himself, fond as he may be of his wife and family.

He was thinking of the way things had turned out for him, and they seemed to him pretty astonishing and singular, as they do to most folks, when you think them over. In fact, he was thinking so hard that, before he knew it, he'd almost stumbled over an old scissors grinder who'd set up his grindstone and tools by the side of the road. The scissors grinder had his cart with him, but he'd turned the horse out to graze – and a lank, old, white horse it was, with every rib showing. And he was very busy, putting an edge on a scythe.

"Oh, sorry," said Johnny Pye. "I didn't know anybody was camping here. But you might come around to my house tomorrow – my wife's got some knives that need sharpening."

Then he stopped, for the old man gave him a long, keen look.

"Why, it's you, Johnny Pye," said the old man. "And how do you do, Johnny Pye! You've been a long time coming – in fact, now and then, I thought I'd have to fetch you. But you're here at last."

Johnny Pye was a grown man now, but he began to tremble.

"But it isn't you!" he said, wildly. "I mean you're not him! Why, I've known how he looks all my life! He's a big man, with a checked shirt, and he carries a hickory stick with a lump of lead in one end."

"Oh, no," said the scissors grinder, quite quiet. "You may have thought of me that way, but that's not the way I am." And Johnny Pye heard the scythe go whet-whet-whet on the stone. The old man ran some water on it and looked at the edge. Then he shook his head as if the edge didn't quite satisfy him. "Well, Johnny, are you ready?" he said, after a while.

"Ready?" said Johnny, in a hoarse voice. "Of course I'm not ready."

"That's what they all say," said the old man, nodding his head, and the scythe went whet-whet on the stone.

Johnny wiped his brow and started to argue it out. "You see, if you'd found me earlier," he said, "or later. I don't want to be unreasonable, but I've got a wife and a child."

"Most has wives and many has children," said the old man, grimly, and the scythe went whet-whet on the stone as he pushed the treadle. And a shower of sparks flew, very clear and bright, for the night had begun to fall.

"Oh, stop that damn racket and let a man think for a minute!" said Johnny, desperate. "I can't go, I tell you. I won't. It isn't time. It's – "

The old man stopped the grindstone and pointed with the scythe at Johnny Pye.

"Tell me one good reason," he said. "There's men would be missed in the world, but are you one of them? A clever man might be missed, but are you a clever man?"

"No," said Johnny, thinking of the herb doctor. "I had a chance to be clever, but I gave it up."

"One," said the old man, ticking off on his fingers. "Well, a rich man might be missed – by some. But you aren't rich, I take it."

"No," said Johnny, thinking of the merchant, "nor wanted to be."

"Two," said the old man. "Cleverness – riches – they're done. But there's still martial bravery and being a hero. There might be an argument to make, if you were one of those."

Johnny Pye shuddered a little, remembering the way that battlefield had looked, out West, when the Indians were dead and the fight over.

"No," he said, "I've fought, but I'm not a hero."

"Well, then, there's religion," said the old man, sort of patient, "and science, and – but what's the use? We know what you did with those. I might feel a trifle of compunction if I had to deal with a President of the United States. But – "

"Oh, you know well enough I ain't President," said Johnny, with a groan. "Can't you get it over with and be done?"

"You're not putting up a very good case," said the old man, shaking his head. "I'm surprised at you, Johnny. Here you spend your youth running away from being a fool. And yet, what's the first thing you do, when you're man grown? Why, you marry a girl, settle down in your home town, and start raising children when you don't know how they'll turn out. You might have known I'd catch up with you, then – you just put yourself in my way."

"Fool I may be," said Johnny Pye in his agony, "and if you take it like that, I guess we're all fools. But Susie's my wife, and my child's my child. And, as for work in the world – well, somebody has to be postmaster, or folks wouldn't get the mail."

"Would it matter much if they didn't?" said the old man, pointing his scythe.

"Well, no, I don't suppose it would, considering what's on the post cards," said Johnny Pye. "But while it's my business to sort it, I'll sort it as well as I can."

The old man whetted his scythe so hard that a long shower of sparks flew out on the grass.

"Well," he said, "I've got my job, too, and I do it likewise. But I'll tell you what I'll do. You're coming my way, no doubt of it, but, looking you over, you don't look quite ripe yet. So I'll let you off for a while. For that matter," said he, "if you'll answer one question of mine – how a man can be a human being and not be a fool – I'll let you off permanent. It'll be the first time in history," he said, "but you've got to do something on your own hook, once in a while. And now you can walk along, Johnny Pye."

With that he grounded the scythe till the sparks flew out like the tail of a comet and Johnny Pye walked along. The air of the meadow had never seemed so sweet to him before.

All the same, even with his relief, he didn't quite forget, and sometimes Susie had to tell the children not to disturb father because he was thinking. But time went ahead, as it does, and pretty soon Johnny Pye found he was forty. He'd never expected to be forty, when he was young, and it kind of surprised him. But there it was, though he couldn't say he felt much different, except now and then when he stooped over. And he was a solid citizen of the town, well-liked and well-respected, with a growing family and a stake in the community, and when he thought those things over, they kind of surprised him too. But, pretty soon, it was as if things had always been that way.

It was after his eldest son had been drowned out fishing that Johnny Pye met the scissors grinder again. But this time he was bitter and distracted, and, if he could have got to the old man, he'd have done him a mortal harm. But, somehow or other, when he tried to come to grips with him, it was like reaching for air and mist. He could see the sparks fly from the ground scythe, but he couldn't even touch the wheel.

"You coward!" said Johnny Pye. "Stand up and fight like a man!" But the old man just nodded his head and the wheel kept grinding and grinding.

"Why couldn't you have taken me?" said Johnny Pye, as if those words had never been said before. "What's the sense in all this? Why can't you take me now?"

Then he tried to wrench the scythe from the old man's hands, but he couldn't touch it. And then he fell down and lay on the grass for a while.

"Time passes," said the old man, nodding his head. "Time passes."

"It will never cure the grief I have for my son," said Johnny Pye.

"It will not," said the old man, nodding his head. "But time passes. Would you leave your wife a widow and your other children fatherless for the sake of your grief?"

"No, God help me!" said Johnny Pye. "That wouldn't be right for a man."

"Then go home to your house, Johnny Pye," said the old man. And Johnny Pye went, but there were lines in his face that hadn't been there before.

And time passed, like the flow of the river, and Johnny Pye's children married and had houses and children of their own. And Susie's hair grew white, and her back grew bent, and when Johnny Pye and his children followed her to her grave, folks said she'd died in the fullness of years, but that was hard for Johnny Pye to believe. Only folks didn't talk as plain as they used to, and the sun didn't heat as much, and sometimes, before dinner, he'd go to sleep in his chair.

And once, after Susie had died, the President of those days came through Martinsville and Johnny Pye shook hands with him and there was a piece in the paper about his shaking hands with two Presidents, fifty years apart. Johnny Pye cut out the clipping and kept it in his pocketbook. He liked this President all right, but, as he told people, he wasn't a patch on the other one fifty years ago. Well, you couldn't expect it – you didn't have Presidents these days, not to call them Presidents. All the same, he took a lot of satisfaction in the clipping.

He didn't get down to the river road much any more – it wasn't too long a walk, of course, but he just didn't often feel like it. But, one day, he slipped away from the granddaughter that was taking care of him, and went. It was kind of a steep road, really – he didn't remember its being so steep.

"Well," said the scissors grinder, "and good afternoon to you, Johnny Pye."

"You'll have to talk a little louder," said Johnny Pye. "My hearing's perfect, but folks don't speak as plain as they used to. Stranger in town?"

"Oh, so that's the way it is," said the scissors grinder.

"Yes, that's the way it is," said Johnny Pye. He knew he ought to be afraid of this fellow, now he'd put on his spectacles and got a good look at him, but for the life of him, he couldn't remember why.

"I know just who you are," he said, a little fretfully. "Never forgot a face in my life, and your name's right on the tip of my tongue — "

"Oh, don't bother about names," said the scissors grinder. "We're old acquaintances. And I asked you a question, years ago — do you remember that?"

"Yes," said Johnny Pye, "I remember." Then he began to laugh — a high, old man's laugh. "And of all the fool questions I ever was asked," he said, "that certainly took the cake."

"Oh?" said the scissors grinder.

"Uh-huh," said Johnny Pye. "For you asked me how a man could be a human being and yet not be a fool. And the answer is — when he's dead and gone and buried. Any fool would know that."

"That so?" said the scissors grinder.

"Of course," said Johnny Pye. "I ought to know. I'll be ninety-two next November, and I've shook hands with two Presidents. The first President I shook — "

"I'll be interested to hear about that," said the scissors grinder, "but we've got a little business, first. For, if all human beings are fools, how does the world get ahead?"

"Oh, there's lots of other things," said Johnny Pye, kind of impatient. "There's the brave and the wise and the clever – and they're apt to roll it ahead as much as an inch. But it's all mixed in together. For, Lord, it's only some fool kind of creature that would have crawled out of the sea to dry land in the first place – or got dropped from the Garden of Eden, if you like it better that way. You can't depend on the kind of folks people think they are – you've got to go by what they do. And I wouldn't give much for a man that some folks hadn't thought was a fool, in his time."

"Well," said the scissors grinder, "you've answered my question – at least as well as you could, which is all you can expect of a man. So I'll keep my part of the bargain."

"And what was that?" said Johnny. "For, while it's all straight in my head, I don't quite recollect the details."

"Why," said the scissors grinder, rather testy, "I'm to let you go, you old fool! You'll never see me again till the Last Judgment. There'll be trouble in the office about it," said he, "but you've got to do what you like, once in a while."

"Phew!" said Johnny Pye. "That needs thinking over!" And he scratched his head.

"Why?" said the scissors grinder, a bit affronted. "It ain't often I offer a man eternal life."

"Well," said Johnny Pye, "I take it very kind, but, you see, it's this way." He thought for a moment. "No," he said, "you wouldn't understand. You can't have touched seventy yet, by your looks, and no young man would."

"Try me," said the scissors grinder.

"Well," said Johnny Pye, "it's this way," and he scratched his head again. I'm not saying – if you'd made the offer forty years ago, or even twenty. But, well, now, let's just take one detail. Let's say 'teeth.' "

"Well, of course," said the scissors grinder, "naturally – I mean you could hardly expect me to do anything about that."

"I thought so," said Johnny Pye. "Well, you see, these are good, bought teeth, but I'm sort of tired of hearing them click. And spectacles, I suppose, the same?"

"I'm afraid so," said the scissors grinder. "I can't interfere with time, you know – that's not my department. And, frankly, you couldn't expect, at a hundred and eighty, let's say, to be quite the man you was at ninety. But still, you'd be a wonder!"

"Maybe so," said Johnny Pye, "but, you see – well, the truth is, I'm an old man now. You wouldn't think it to look at me, but it's so. And my friends – well, they're gone – and Susie and the boy – and somehow you don't get as close to the younger people, except the children. And to keep on just going and going till Judgment Day, with nobody around to talk to that had real horse sense – well, no, sir, it's a handsome offer but I just don't feel up to accepting it. It may not be patriotic of me, and I feel sorry for Martinsville. It'd do wonders for the climate and the chamber of commerce to have a leading citizen live till Judgment Day. But a man's got to do as he likes, at least once in his life." He stopped and looked at the scissors grinder. "I'll admit, I'd kind of like to beat out Ike Leavis," he said. "To hear him talk, you'd think nobody had ever pushed ninety before. But I suppose – "

"I'm afraid we can't issue a limited policy," said the scissors grinder.

"Well," said Johnny Pye, "I just thought of it. And Ike's all right." He waited a moment. "Tell me," he said, in a low voice. "Well, you know what I mean. Afterwards. I mean, if you're likely to see" – he coughed –"your friends again. I mean, if it's so – like some folks believe."

"I can't tell you that," said the scissors grinder. "I only go so far."

"Well, there's no harm in asking," said Johnny Pye, rather humbly. He peered into the darkness; a last shower of sparks flew from the scythe, then the whir of the wheel stopped.

"H'm," said Johnny Pye, testing the edge. "That's a well-ground scythe. But they used to grind 'em better in the old days." He listened and looked, for a moment, anxiously. "Oh, Lordy!" he said, "there's Helen coming to look for me. She'll take me back to the house."

"Not this time," said the scissors grinder. "Yes, there isn't bad steel in that scythe. Well, let's go, Johnny Pye."

O'HALLORAN'S LUCK

THEY were strong men built the Big Road, in the early days of America, and it was the Irish did it.

My grandfather, Tim O'Halloran, was a young man then, and wild. He could swing a pick all day and dance all night, if there was a fiddler handy; and if there was a girl to be pleased he pleased her, for he had the tongue and the eye. Likewise, if there was a man to be stretched, he could stretch him with the one blow.

I saw him later on in years when he was thin and white-headed, but in his youth he was not so. A thin, white-headed man would have had little chance, and they driving the Road to the West. It was two-fisted men cleared the plains and bored through the mountains. They came in the thousands to do it from every county in Ireland; and now the names are not known. But it's over their graves you pass, when you ride in the Pullmans. And Tim O'Halloran was one of them, six feet high and solid as the Rock of Cashel when he stripped to the skin.

He needed to be all of that, for it was not easy labor. 'Twas a time of great booms and expansions in the railroad line, and they drove the tracks north and south, east and west, as if the devil was driving behind. For this they must have the boys with shovel and pick, and every immigrant ship from Ireland was crowded with bold young men. They left famine and England's rule behind them – and it was the thought of many they'd pick up gold for the asking in the free States of America, though it's little gold that most of them ever saw. They found themselves up to their necks in the water of the canals, and burnt black by the suns of the prairie – and that was a great surprise to them. They saw their sisters and their mothers made servants that had not been servants in Ireland, and that was a strange change too. Eh, the death and the broken hopes it takes to make a country! But those with the heart and the tongue kept the tongue and the heart.

Tim O'Halloran came from Clonmelly, and he was the fool of the family and the one who listened to tales. His brother Ignatius went for a priest and his brother James for a sailor, but they knew he could not do those things. He was strong and biddable and he had the O'Halloran tongue; but there came a time of famine, when the younger mouths cried for bread and there was little room in the nest. He was not entirely wishful to emigrate, and yet, when he thought of it, he was wishful. 'Tis often enough that way, with a younger son. Perhaps he was the more wishful because of Kitty Malone.

'Tis a quiet place, Clonmelly, and she'd been the light of it to him. But now the Malones had gone to the States of America – and it was well known that Kitty had a position there the like of which was not to be found in all Dublin Castle. They called her a hired girl, to be sure, but did not she eat from gold plates, like all the citizens of America? And when she stirred her tea, was not the spoon made of gold? Tim O'Halloran thought of this, and of the chances and adventures that a bold young man might find, and at last he went to the boat. There were many from Clonmelly on that boat, but he kept himself to himself and dreamed his own dreams.

The more disillusion it was to him, when the boat landed him in Boston and he found Kitty Malone there, scrubbing the stairs of an American house with a pail and brush by her side. But that did not matter, after the first, for her cheeks still had the rose in them and she looked at him in the same way. 'Tis true there was an Orangeman courting her — conductor he was on the horsecars, and Tim did not like that. But after Tim had seen her, he felt himself the equal of giants; and when the call came for strong men to work in the wilds of the West, he was one of the first to offer. They broke a sixpence between them before he left — it was an English sixpence, but that did not matter greatly to them. And Tim O'Halloran was going to make his fortune, and Kitty Malone to wait for him, though her family liked the Orangeman best.

Still and all, it was cruel work in the West, as such work must be, and Tim O'Halloran was young. He liked the strength and the wildness of it — he'd drink with the thirstiest and fight with the wildest — and that he knew how to do. It was all meat and drink to him — the bare tracks pushing ahead across the bare prairie and the fussy cough of the wood-burning locomotives and the cold blind eyes of a murdered man, looking up at the prairie stars. And then there was the cholera and the malaria – and the strong man you'd worked on the grade beside, all of a sudden gripping his belly with the fear of death on his face and his shovel falling to the ground.

Next day he would not be there and they'd scratch a name from the pay roll. Tim O'Halloran saw it all.

He saw it all and it changed his boyhood and hardened it. But, for all that, there were times when the black fit came upon him, as it does to the Irish, and he knew he was alone in a strange land. Well, that's a hard hour to get through, and he was young. There were times when he'd have given all the gold of the Americas for a smell of Clonmelly air or a glimpse of Clonmelly sky. Then he'd drink or dance or fight or put a black word on the foreman, just to take the aching out of his mind. It did not help him with his work and it wasted his pay; but it was stronger than he, and not even the thought of Kitty Malone could stop it. 'Tis like that, sometimes.

Well, it happened one night he was coming back from the place where they sold the potheen, and perhaps he'd had a trifle more of it than was advisable. Yet he had not drunk it for that, but to keep the queer thoughts from his mind. And yet, the more that he drank, the queerer were the thoughts in his head. For he kept thinking of the Luck of the O'Hallorans and the tales his granda had told about it in the old country – the tales about pookas and banshees and leprechauns with long white beards.

"And that's a queer thing to be thinking and myself

at labor with a shovel on the open prairies of America," he said to himself. "Sure, creatures like that might live and thrive in the old country — and I'd be the last to deny it — but 'tis obvious they could not live here. The first sight of Western America would scare them into conniptions. And as for the Luck of the O'Hallorans, 'tis little good I've had of it, and me not even able to rise to foreman and marry Kitty Malone. They called me the fool of the family in Clonmelly, and I misdoubt but they were right. Tim O'Halloran, you're a worthless man, for all your strong back and arms." It was with such black, bitter thoughts as these that he went striding over the prairie. And it was just then that he heard the cry in the grass.

'Twas a strange little piping cry, and only the half of it human. But Tim O'Halloran ran to it, for in truth he was spoiling for a fight. "Now this will be a beautiful young lady," he said to himself as he ran, "and I will save her from robbers; and her father, the rich man, will ask me — but, wirra, 'tis not her I wish to marry, 'tis Kitty Malone. Well, he'll set me up in business, out of friendship and gratitude, and then I will send for Kitty — "

But by then he was out of breath, and by the time he had reached the place where the cry came from he could see that it was not so. It was only a pair of young wolf cubs, and they chasing something small and helpless and playing with it as a cat plays with a mouse. Where the wolf cub is the old wolves are not far, but Tim O'Halloran felt as bold as a lion. "Be off with you!" he cried and he threw a stick and a stone. They ran away into the night, and he could hear them howling—a lonesome sound. But he knew the camp was near, so he paid small attention to that but looked for the thing they'd been chasing.

It scuttled in the grass but he could not see it. Then he stooped down and picked something up, and when he had it in his hand he stared at it unbelieving. For it was a tiny shoe, no bigger than a child's. And more than that, it was not the kind of shoe that is made in America. Tim O'Halloran stared and stared at it—and at the silver buckle upon it—and still he could not believe.

"If I'd found this in the old country," he said to himself, half aloud, "I'd have sworn that it was a leprechaun's and looked for the pot of gold. But here, there's no chance of that—"

"I'll trouble you for the shoe," said a small voice close by his feet.

Tim O'Halloran stared round him wildly. "By the piper that played before Moses!" he said. "Am I drunk beyond comprehension? Or am I mad? For I thought that I heard a voice."

"So you did, silly man," said the voice again, but irritated, "and I'll trouble you for my shoe, for it's cold in the dewy grass."

"Honey," said Tim O'Halloran, beginning to believe his ears, "honey dear, if you'll but show yourself—"

"I'll do that and gladly," said the voice; and with that the grasses parted, and a little old man with a long white beard stepped out. He was perhaps the size of a well-grown child, as O'Halloran could see clearly by the moonlight on the prairie; moreover, he was dressed in the clothes of antiquity, and he carried cobbler's tools in the belt at his side.

"By faith and belief, but it *is* a leprechaun!" cried O'Halloran, and with that he made a grab for the apparition. For you must know, in case you've been ill brought up, that a leprechaun is a sort of cobbler fairy and each one knows the whereabouts of a pot of gold. Or it's so they say in the old country. For they say you can tell a leprechaun by his long white beard and his cobbler's tools; and once you have the possession of him, he must tell you where his gold is hid.

The little old man skipped out of reach as nimbly as a cricket. "Is this Clonmelly courtesy?" he said with a shake in his voice, and Tim O'Halloran felt ashamed.

"Sure, I didn't mean to hurt your worship at all," he said, "but if you're what you seem to be, well, then, there's the little matter of a pot of gold – "

"Pot of gold!" said the leprechaun, and his voice was hollow and full of scorn. "And would I be here today if I had that same? Sure, it all went to pay my sea passage, as you might expect."

"Well," said Tim O'Halloran, scratching his head, for that sounded reasonable enough, "that may be so or again it may not be so. But – "

"Oh, 'tis bitter hard," said the leprechaun, and his voice was weeping, "to come to the waste, wild prairies all alone, just for the love of Clonmelly folk – and then to be disbelieved by the first that speaks to me! If it had been an Ulsterman now, I might have expected it. But the O'Hallorans wear the green."

"So they do," said Tim O'Halloran, "and it shall not be said of an O'Halloran that he denied succor to the friendless. I'll not touch you."

"Do you swear it?" said the leprechaun.

"I swear it," said Tim O'Halloran.

"Then I'll just creep under your coat," said the leprechaun, "for I'm near destroyed by the chills and damps of the prairie. Oh, this weary emigrating!" he said, with a sigh like a furnace. " 'Tis not what it's cracked up to be."

Tim O'Halloran took off his own coat and wrapped it around him. Then he could see him closer — and it could not be denied that the leprechaun was a pathetic sight. He'd a queer little boyish face, under the long white beard, but his clothes were all torn and ragged and his cheeks looked hollow with hunger.

"Cheer up!" said Tim O'Halloran and patted him on the back. "It's a bad day that beats the Irish. But tell me first how you came here — for that still sticks in my throat."

"And would I be staying behind with half Clonmelly on the water?" said the leprechaun stoutly. "By the bones of Finn, what sort of a man do you think I am?"

"That's well said," said Tim O'Halloran. "And yet I never heard of the Good People emigrating before."

"True for you," said the leprechaun. "The climate here's not good for most of us and that's a fact. There's a boggart or so that came over with the English, but then the Puritan ministers got after them and they had to take to the woods. And I had a word or two, on my way West, with a banshee that lives by Lake Superior — a decent woman she was, but you could see she'd come down in the world. For even the bits of children wouldn't believe in her; and when she let out a screech, sure they thought it was a steamboat. I misdoubt she's died since then — she was not in good health when I left her.

"And as for the native spirits — well, you can say what you like, but they're not very comfortable people. I was captive to some of them a week and they treated me well enough, but they whooped and danced too much for a quiet man, and I did not like the long, sharp knives on them. Oh, I've had the adventures on my way here," he said, "but they're over now, praises be, for I've found a protector at last," and he snuggled closer under O'Halloran's coat.

"Well," said O'Halloran, somewhat taken aback, "I did not think this would be the way of it when I found O'Halloran's Luck that I'd dreamed of so long. For, first I save your life from the wolves; and now, it seems, I must be protecting you further. But in the tales it's always the other way round."

"And is the company and conversation of an ancient and experienced creature like myself nothing to you?" said the leprechaun fiercely. "Me that had my own castle at Clonmelly and saw O'Sheen in his pride? Then St. Patrick came — wirra, wirra! — and there was an end to it all. For some of us — the Old Folk of Ireland — he baptized, and some of us he chained with the demons of hell. But I was Lazy Brian, betwixt and between, and all I wanted was peace and a quiet life. So he changed me to what you see – me that had six tall harpers to harp me awake in the morning – and laid a doom upon me for being betwixt and between. I'm to serve Clonmelly folk and follow them wherever they go till I serve the servants of servants in a land at the world's end. And then, perhaps, I'll be given a Christian soul and can follow my own inclinations."

"Serve the servants of servants?" said O'Halloran. "Well, that's a hard riddle to read."

"It is that," said the leprechaun, "for I never once met the servant of a servant in Clonmelly, all the time I've been looking. I doubt but that was in St. Patrick's mind."

"If it's criticizing the good saint you are, I'll leave you here on the prairie," said Tim O'Halloran.

"I'm not criticizing him," said the leprechaun with a sigh, "but I could wish he'd been less hasty. Or more specific. And now, what do we do?"

"Well," said O'Halloran, and he sighed, too, " 'tis a great responsibility, and one I never thought to shoulder. But since you've asked for help, you must have it. Only there's just this to be said. There's little money in my pocket."

"Sure, 'tis not for your money I've come to you," said the leprechaun joyously. "And I'll stick closer than a brother."

"I've no doubt of that," said O'Halloran with a wry laugh. "Well, clothes and food I can get for you – but if you stick with me, you must work as well. And perhaps the best way would be for you to be my young nephew, Rory, run away from home to work on the railroad."

"And how would I be your young nephew, Rory, and me with a long white beard?"

"Well," said Tim O'Halloran with a grin, "as it happens, I've got a razor in my pocket."

And with that you should have heard the leprechaun. He stamped and he swore and he pled – but it was no use at all. If he was to follow Tim O'Halloran, he must do it on Tim O'Halloran's terms and no two ways about it. So O'Halloran shaved him at last, by the light of the moon, to the leprechaun's great horror, and when he got him back to the construction camp and fitted him out in some old duds of his own – well, it wasn't exactly a boy he looked, but it was more like a boy than anything else. Tim took him up to the foreman the next day and got him signed on for a water boy, and it was a beautiful tale he told the foreman. As well, too, that he had the O'Halloran tongue to tell it with, for when the foreman first looked at young Rory you could see him gulp like a man that's seen a ghost.

"And now what do we do?" said the leprechaun to Tim when the interview was over.

"Why, you work," said Tim with a great laugh, "and Sundays you wash your shirt."

"Thank you for nothing," said the leprechaun with an angry gleam in his eye. "It was not for that I came here from Clonmelly."

"Oh, we've all come here for great fortune," said

Tim, "but it's hard to find that same. Would you rather be with the wolves?"

"Oh, no," said the leprechaun.

"Then drill, ye tarrier, drill!" said Tim O'Halloran and shouldered his shovel, while the leprechaun trailed behind.

At the end of the day the leprechaun came to him.

"I've never done mortal work before," he said, "and there's no bone in my body that's not a pain and an anguish to me."

"You'll feel better after supper," said O'Halloran. "And the night's made for sleep."

"But where will I sleep?" said the leprechaun.

"In the half of my blanket," said Tim, "for are you not young Rory, my nephew?"

It was not what he could have wished, but he saw he could do no otherwise. Once you start a tale, you must play up to the tale.

But that was only the beginning, as Tim O'Halloran soon found out. For Tim O'Halloran had tasted many things before, but not responsibility, and now responsibility was like a bit in his mouth. It was not so bad the first week, while the leprechaun was still ailing. But when, what with the food and the exercise, he began to recover his strength, 'twas a wonder Tim O'Halloran's hair did not turn gray overnight. He was not a bad creature, the leprechaun, but he had all the natural mischief of a boy of twelve and, added to that, the craft and knowledge of generations.

There was the three pipes and the pound of shag the leprechaun stole from McGinnis—and the dead frog he slipped in the foreman's tea – and the bottle of potheen he got hold of one night when Tim had to hold his head in a bucket of water to sober him up. A fortunate thing it was that St. Patrick had left him no great powers, but at that he had enough to put the jumping rheumatism on Shaun Kelly for two days – and it wasn't till Tim threatened to deny him the use of his razor entirely that he took off the spell.

That brought Rory to terms, for by now he'd come to take a queer pleasure in playing the part of a boy and he did not wish to have it altered.

Well, things went on like this for some time, and Tim O'Halloran's savings grew; for whenever the drink was running he took no part in it, for fear of mislaying his wits when it came to deal with young Rory. And as it was with the drink, so was it with other things – till Tim O'Halloran began to be known as a steady man. And then, as it happened one morning, Tim O'Halloran woke up early. The leprechaun had finished his shaving and was sitting cross-legged, chuckling to himself.

"And what's your source of amusement so early in the day?" said Tim sleepily.

"Oh," said the leprechaun, "I'm just thinking of the rare hard work we'll have when the line's ten miles farther on."

"And why should it be harder there than it is here?" said Tim.

"Oh, nothing," said the leprechaun, "but those fools of surveyors have laid out the line where there's hidden springs of water. And when we start digging, there'll be the devil to pay."

"Do you know that for a fact?" said Tim.

"And why wouldn't I know it?" said the leprechaun. "Me that can hear the waters run underground."

"Then what should we do?" said Tim.

"Shift the line half a mile to the west and you'd have a firm roadbed," said the leprechaun.

Tim O'Halloran said no more at the time. But for all that, he managed to get to the assistant engineer in charge of construction at the noon hour. He could not have done it before, but now he was known as a steady man. Nor did he tell where he got the information – he put it on having seen a similar thing in Clonmelly.

Well, the engineer listened to him and had a test made – and sure enough, they struck the hidden spring. "That's clever work, O'Halloran," said the engineer. "You've saved us time and money. And now how would you like to be foreman of a gang?"

"I'd like it well," said Tim O'Halloran.

"Then you boss Gang Five from this day forward," said the engineer. "And I'll keep my eye on you. I like a man that uses his head."

"Can my nephew come with me," said Tim, "for, 'troth, he's my responsibility?"

"He can," said the engineer, who had children of his own.

So Tim got promoted and the leprechaun along with him. And the first day on the new work, young Rory stole the gold watch from the engineer's pocket, because he liked the tick of it, and Tim had to threaten him with fire and sword before he'd put it back.

Well, things went on like this for another while, till finally Tim woke up early on another morning and heard the leprechaun laughing.

"And what are you laughing at?" he said.

"Oh, the more I see of mortal work, the less reason there is to it," said the leprechaun. "For I've been watching the way they get the rails up to us on the line. And they do it thus and so. But if they did it so and thus, they could do it in half the time with half the work."

"Is that so indeed?" said Tim O'Halloran, and he made him explain it clearly. Then, after he'd swallowed his breakfast, he was off to his friend the engineer.

"That's a clever idea, O'Halloran," said the engineer. "We'll try it." And a week after that, Tim O'Halloran found himself with a hundred men under him and more responsibility than he'd ever had in his life. But it seemed little to him beside the responsibility of the leprechaun, and now the engineer began to lend him books to study and he studied them at nights while the leprechaun snored in its blanket.

A man could rise rapidly in those days – and it was then Tim O'Halloran got the start that was to carry him far. But he did not know he was getting it, for his heart was near broken at the time over Kitty Malone. She'd written him a letter or two when he first came West, but now there were no more of them and at last he got a word from her family telling him he should not be disturbing Kitty with letters from a laboring man.

That was bitter for Tim O'Halloran, and he'd think about Kitty and the Orangeman in the watches of the night and groan. And then, one morning, he woke up after such a night and heard the leprechaun laughing.

"And what are you laughing at now?" he said sourly. "For my heart's near burst with its pain."

"I'm laughing at a man that would let a cold letter keep him from his love, and him with pay in his pocket and the contract ending the first," said the leprechaun.

Tim O'Halloran struck one hand in the palm of the other.

"By the piper, but you've the right of it, you queer little creature!" he said. "'Tis back to Boston we go when this job's over."

It was laborer Tim O'Halloran that had come to the West, but it was Railroadman Tim O'Halloran that rode back East in the cars like a gentleman, with a free pass in his pocket and the promise of a job on the railroad that was fitting a married man. The leprechaun, I may say, gave some trouble in the cars, more particularly when he bit a fat woman that called him a dear little boy; but what with giving him peanuts all the way, Tim O'Halloran managed to keep him fairly quieted.

When they got to Boston he fitted them both out in new clothes from top to toe. Then he gave the leprechaun some money and told him to amuse himself for an hour or so while he went to see Kitty Malone.

He walked into the Malones' flat as bold as brass, and there sure enough, in the front room, were Kitty Malone and the Orangeman. He was trying to squeeze her hand, and she refusing, and it made Tim O'Halloran's blood boil to see that. But when Kitty saw Tim O'Halloran she let out a scream.

"Oh, Tim!" she said. "Tim! And they told me you were dead in the plains of the West!"

"And a great pity that he was not," said the Orangeman, blowing out his chest with the brass buttons on it, "but a bad penny always turns up."

"Bad penny is it, you brass-buttoned son of iniquity," said Tim O'Halloran. "I have but the one question to put you. Will you stand or will you run?"

"I'll stand as we stood at Boyne Water," said the Orangeman, grinning ugly. "And whose backs did we see that day?"

"Oh, is that the tune?" said Tim O'Halloran. "Well, I'll give you a tune to match it. Who fears to speak of Ninety-Eight?"

With that he was through the Orangeman's guard and stretched him at the one blow, to the great consternation of the Malones. The old woman started to screech and Pat Malone to talk of policemen, but Tim O'Halloran silenced the both of them.

"Would you be giving your daughter to an Orangeman that works on the horsecars, when she might be marrying a future railroad president?" he said. And with that he pulled his savings out of his pocket and the letter that promised the job for a married man. That quieted the Malones a little and, once they got a good look at Tim O'Halloran, they began to change their tune. So, after they'd got the Orangeman out of the house – and he did not go willing, but he went as a whipped man must – Tim O'Halloran recounted all of his adventures.

The tale did not lose in the telling, though he did not speak of the leprechaun, for he thought that had better be left to a later day; and at the end Pat Malone was offering him a cigar. "But I find I have none upon me," said he with a wink at Tim, "so I'll just run down to the corner."

"And I'll go with you," said Kitty's mother, "for if Mr. O'Halloran stays to supper – and he's welcome – there's a bit of shopping to be done."

So the old folks left Tim O'Halloran and his Kitty alone. But just as they were in the middle of their planning and contriving for the future, there came a knock on the door.

"What's that?" said Kitty, but Tim O'Halloran knew well enough and his heart sank within him. He opened the door – and sure enough, it was the leprechaun.

"Well, Uncle Tim," said the creature, grinning, "I'm here."

Tim O'Halloran took a look at him as if he saw him for the first time. He was dressed in new clothes, to be sure, but there was soot on his face and his collar had thumbmarks on it already. But that wasn't what made the difference. New clothes or old, if you looked at him for the first time, you could see he was an unchancy thing, and not like Christian souls.

"Kitty," he said, "Kitty darlint, I had not told you. But this is my young nephew, Rory, that lives with me."

Well, Kitty welcomed the boy with her prettiest

manners, though Tim O'Halloran could see her giving him a side look now and then. All the same, she gave him a slice of cake, and he tore it apart with his fingers; but in the middle of it he pointed to Kitty Malone.

"Have you made up your mind to marry my Uncle Tim?" he said. "Faith, you'd better, for he's a grand catch."

"Hold your tongue, young Rory," said Tim O'Halloran angrily, and Kitty blushed red. But then she took the next words out of his mouth.

"Let the gossoon be, Tim O'Halloran," she said bravely. "Why shouldn't he speak his mind? Yes, Rory-een – it's I that will be your aunt in the days to come – and a proud woman too."

"Well, that's good," said the leprechaun, cramming the last of the cake in his mouth, "for I'm thinking you'll make a good home for us, once you're used to my ways."

"Is that to be the way of it, Tim?" said Kitty Malone very quietly, but Tim O'Halloran looked at her and knew what was in her mind. And he had the greatest impulse in the world to deny the leprechaun and send him about his business. And yet, when he thought of it, he knew that he could not do it, not even if it meant the losing of Kitty Malone.

"I'm afraid that must be the way of it, Kitty," he said with a groan.

"Then I honor you for it," said Kitty, with her eyes like stars. She went up to the leprechaun and took his hard little hand. "Will you live with us, young Rory?" she said. "For we'd be glad to have you."

"Thank you kindly, Kitty Malone – O'Halloran to be," said the leprechaun. "And you're lucky, Tim O'Halloran – lucky yourself and lucky in your wife. For if you had denied me then, your luck would have left you – and if she had denied me then, 'twould be but half luck for you both. But now the luck will stick to you the rest of your lives. And I'm wanting another piece of cake," said he.

"Well, it's a queer lad you are," said Kitty Malone, but she went for the cake. The leprechaun swung his legs and looked at Tim O'Halloran. "I wonder what keeps my hands off you," said the latter with a groan.

"Fie!" said the leprechaun, grinning, "and would you be lifting the hand to your one nephew? But tell me one thing, Tim O'Halloran, was this wife you're to take ever in domestic service?"

"And what if she was?" said Tim O'Halloran, firing up. "Who thinks the worse of her for that?"

"Not I," said the leprechaun, "for I've learned about mortal labor since I came to this country – and it's an honest thing. But tell me one thing more. Do you mean to serve this wife of yours and honor her through the days of your wedded life?"

"Such is my intention," said Tim, "though what business it is of – "

"Never mind," said the leprechaun. "Your shoelace is undone, bold man. Command me to tie it up."

"Tie up my shoe, you black-hearted, villainous little anatomy!" thundered Tim O'Halloran, and the leprechaun did so. Then he jumped to his feet and skipped about the room.

"Free! Free!" he piped. "Free at last! For I've served the servants of servants and the doom has no power on me longer. Free, Tim O'Halloran! O'Halloran's Luck is free!"

Tim O'Halloran stared at him, dumb; and even as he stared, the creature seemed to change. He was small, to be sure, and boyish – but you could see the unchancy look leave him and the Christian soul come into his eyes. That was a queer thing to be seen, and a great one too.

"Well," said Tim O'Halloran in a sober voice, "I'm glad for you, Rory. For now you'll be going back to Clonmelly, no doubt – and faith, you've earned the right."

The leprechaun shook his head.

"Clonmelly's a fine, quiet place," said he, "but this country's bolder. I misdoubt it's something in the air – you will not have noticed it, but I've grown two inches and a half since first I met you, and I feel myself growing still. No, it's off to the mines of the West I am, to follow my natural vocation – for they say there are mines out there you could mislay all Dublin Castle in – and wouldn't I like to try! But speaking of that, Tim O'Halloran," he said, "I was not quite honest with you about the pot of gold. You'll find your share behind the door when I've gone. And now good day and long life to you!"

"But, man dear," said Tim O'Halloran, " 'tis not good-by!" For it was then he realized the affection that was in him for the queer little creature.

"No, 'tis not good-by," said the leprechaun. "When

you christen your first son, I'll be at his cradle, though you may not see me — and so with your sons' sons and their sons, for O'Halloran's luck's just begun. But we'll part for the present now. For now I'm a Christian soul, I've work to do in the world."

"Wait a minute," said Tim O'Halloran. "For you would not know, no doubt, and you such a new soul. And no doubt you'll be seeing the priest — but a layman can do it in an emergency and I think this is one. I dare not have you leave me — and you not even baptized."

And with that he made the sign of the cross and baptized the leprechaun. He named him Rory Patrick.

" 'Tis not done with all the formalities," he said at the end, "but I'll defend the intention."

"I'm grateful to you," said the leprechaun. "And if there was a debt to be paid, you've paid it back and more."

And with that he was gone somehow, and Tim O'Halloran was alone in the room. He rubbed his eyes. But there was a little sack behind the door, where the leprechaun had left it — and Kitty was coming in with a slice of cake on a plate.

"Well, Tim," she said, "and where's that young nephew of yours?"

So he took her into his arms and told her the whole story. And how much of it she believed, I do not know. But there's one remarkable circumstance. Ever since then, there's always been one Rory O'Halloran in the family, and that one luckier than the lave. And when Tim O'Halloran got to be a railroad president, why, didn't he call his private car "The Leprechaun"? For that matter, they said, when he took his business trips there'd be a small boyish-looking fellow would be with him now and again. He'd turn up from nowhere, at some odd stop or other, and he'd be let in at once, while the great of the railroad world were kept waiting in the vestibule. And after a while, there'd be singing from inside the car.

JACOB AND THE INDIANS

IT goes back to the early days — may God profit all who lived then — and the ancestors.

Well, America, you understand, in those days was different. It was a nice place, but you wouldn't believe it if you saw it today. Without busses, without trains, without states, without Presidents, nothing!

With nothing but colonists and Indians and wild woods all over the country and wild animals to live in the wild woods. Imagine such a place! In these days, you children don't even think about it; you read about it in the schoolbooks, but what is that? And I put in a call to my daughter, in California, and in three minutes I am saying "Hello, Rosie," and there it is Rosie and she is telling me about the weather, as if I wanted to know! But things were not always that way. I remember my own days, and they were different. And in the times of my grandfather's grandfather, they were different still. Listen to the story.

My grandfather's grandfather was Jacob Stein, and he came from Rettelsheim, in Germany. To Philadelphia he came, an orphan in a sailing ship, but not a common man. He had learning — he had been to the *chedar* — he could have been a scholar among the scholars. Well, that is the way things happen in this bad world. There was a plague and a new grand duke — things are always so. He would say little of it afterward — they had left his teeth in his mouth, but he would say little of it. He did not have to say — we are children of the Dispersion — we know a black day when it comes.

Yet imagine — a young man with fine dreams and learning, a scholar with a pale face and narrow shoulders, set down in those early days in such a new country. Well, he must work, and he did. It was very fine, his learning, but it did not fill his mouth. He must carry a pack on his back and go from door to door with it. That was no disgrace; it was so that many began. But it was not expounding the Law, and at first he was very homesick. He would sit in his room at night, with the one candle, and read the preacher Koheleth, till the bitterness of the preacher rose in his mouth. Myself, I am sure that Koheleth was a great preacher, but if he had had a good wife he would have been a more cheerful man. They had too many wives in those old days — it confused them. But Jacob was young.

As for the new country where he had come, it was to him a place of exile, large and frightening. He was glad to be out of the ship, but, at first, that was all. And when he saw his first real Indian in the street — well, that was a day! But the Indian, a tame one, bought a ribbon from him by signs, and after that he felt better. Nevertheless, it seemed to him at times that the straps of the pack cut into his very soul, and he longed for the smell of the *chedar* and the quiet streets of Rettelsheim and the good smoked goose-breast pious housewives keep for the scholar. But there is no going back — there is never any going back.

All the same, he was a polite young man, and a hardworking. And soon he had a stroke of luck—or at first it seemed so. It was from Simon Ettelsohn that he got the trinkets for his pack, and one day he found Simon Ettelsohn arguing a point of the Law with a friend, for Simon was a pious man and well thought of in the Congregation Mikveh Israel. Our grandfather's grandfather stood by very modestly at first—he had come to replenish his pack and Simon was his employer. But finally his heart moved within him, for both men were wrong, and he spoke and told them where they erred. For half an hour he spoke, with his pack still upon his shoulders, and never has a text been expounded with more complexity, not even by the great Reb Samuel. Till, in the end, Simon Ettelsohn threw up his hands and called him a young David and a candle of learning. Also, he allowed him a more profitable route of trade. But, best of all, he invited young Jacob to his house, and there Jacob ate well for the first time since he had come to Philadelphia. Also he laid eyes upon Miriam Ettelsohn for the first time, and she was Simon's youngest daughter and a rose of Sharon.

After that, things went better for Jacob, for the protection of the strong is like a rock and a well. But yet things did not go altogether as he wished. For, at first, Simon Ettelsohn made much of him, and there was stuffed fish and raisin wine for the young scholar, though he was a peddler. But there is a look in a man's eyes that says "H'm? Son-in-law?" and that look Jacob did not see. He was modest—he did not expect to win the maiden overnight, though he longed for her. But gradually it was borne in upon him what he was in the Ettelsohn house—a young scholar to be shown before Simon's friends, but a scholar whose learning did not fill his mouth. He did not blame Simon for it, but it was not what he had intended. He began to wonder if he would ever get on in the world at all, and that is not good for any man.

Nevertheless, he could have borne it, and the aches and pains of his love, had it not been for Meyer Kappelhuist. Now, there was a pushing man! I speak no ill of anyone, not even of your Aunt Cora, and she can keep the De Groot silver if she finds it in her heart to do so; who lies down in the straw with a dog, gets up with fleas. But this Meyer Kappelhuist! A big, red-faced fellow from Holland with shoulders the size of a barn door and red hair on the backs of his hands. A big mouth for eating and drinking and telling schnorrer stories—and he talked about the Kappelhuists, in Holland, till you'd think they were made of gold. The crane says, "I am really a peacock—at least on my mother's side." And yet, a thriving man—that could not be denied. He had started with a pack, like our grandfather's grandfather. and now he was trading with the Indians and making money hand over fist. It seemed to Jacob that he could never go to the Ettelsohn house without meeting Meyer and hearing about those Indians. And it dried the words in Jacob's mouth and made his heart burn.

For, no sooner would our grandfather's grandfather begin to expound a text or a proverb, than he would see Meyer Kappelhuist looking at the maiden. And when Jacob had finished his expounding, and there should have been a silence, Meyer Kappelhuist would take it upon himself to thank him, but always in a tone that said: "The Law is the Law and the Prophets are the Prophets, but prime beaver is also prime beaver, my little scholar!" It took the pleasure from Jacob's learning and the joy of the maiden from his heart. Then he would sit silent and burning, while Meyer told a great tale of Indians, slapping his hands on his knees. And in the end he was always careful to ask Jacob how many needles and pins he had sold that day; and when Jacob told him, he would smile and say very smoothly that all things had small beginnings, till the maiden herself could not keep from a little smile. Then, desperately, Jacob would rack his brains for more interesting matter. He would tell of the wars of the Maccabees and the glory of the Temple. But even as he told them, he felt they were far away. Whereas Meyer and his accursed Indians were there, and the maiden's eyes shone at his words.

Finally he took his courage in both hands and went to Simon Ettelsohn. It took much for him to do it, for he had not been brought up to strive with men, but with words. But it seemed to him now that everywhere he went he heard of nothing but Meyer Kappelhuist and his trading with the Indians, till he thought it would drive him mad. So he went to Simon Ettelsohn in his shop.

"I am weary of this narrow trading in pins and needles," he said, without more words.

Simon Ettelsohn looked at him keenly; for while he was an ambitious man, he was kindly as well.

"*Nu,*" he said. "A nice little trade you have and the people like you. I myself started in with less. What would you have more?"

"I would have much more," said our grandfather's grandfather stiffly. "I would have a wife and a home in this new country. But how shall I keep a wife? On needles and pins?"

"*Nu,* it has been done," said Simon Ettelsohn, smiling a little. "You are a good boy, Jacob, and we take an interest in you. Now, if it is a question of marriage, there are many worthy maidens. Asher Levy, the baker, has a daughter. It is true that she squints a little, but her heart is of gold." He folded his hands and smiled.

"It is not of Asher Levy's daughter I am thinking," said Jacob, taken aback. Simon Ettelsohn nodded his head and his face grew grave.

"*Nu,* Jacob," he said. "I see what is in your heart. Well, you are a good boy, Jacob, and a fine scholar. And if it were in the old country, I am not saying. But here, I have one daughter married to a Seixas and one to a Da Silva. You must see that makes a difference." And he smiled the smile of a man well pleased with his world.

"And if I were such a one as Meyer Kappelhuist?" said Jacob bitterly.

"Now—well, that is a little different," said Simon Ettelsohn sensibly. "For Meyer trades with the Indians. It is true, he is a little rough. But he will die a rich man."

"I will trade with the Indians too," said Jacob, and trembled.

Simon Ettelsohn looked at him as if he had gone out of his mind. He looked at his narrow shoulders and his scholar's hands.

"Now, Jacob," he said soothingly, "do not be foolish. A scholar you are, and learned, not an Indian trader. Perhaps in a store you would do better. I can speak to Aaron Copras. And sooner or later we will find you a nice maiden. But to trade with Indians — well, that takes a different sort of man. Leave that to Meyer Kappelhuist."

"And your daughter, that rose of Sharon? Shall I leave her, too, to Meyer Kappelhuist?" cried Jacob.

Simon Ettelsohn looked uncomfortable.

"Nu, Jacob," he said. "Well, it is not settled, of course. But — "

"I will go forth against him as David went against Goliath," said our grandfather's grandfather wildly. "I will go forth into the wilderness. And God should judge the better man!"

Then he flung his pack on the floor and strode from the shop. Simon Ettelsohn called out after him, but he did not stop for that. Nor was it in his heart to go and seek the maiden. Instead, when he was in the street, he counted the money he had. It was not much. He had meant to buy his trading goods on credit from Simon Ettelsohn, but now he could not do that. He stood in the sunlit street of Philadelphia, like a man bereft of hope.

Nevertheless, he was stubborn — though how stubborn he did not yet know. And though he was bereft of hope, he found his feet taking him to the house of Raphael Sanchez.

Now, Raphael Sanchez could have bought and sold Simon Ettelsohn twice over. An arrogant old man he was, with fierce black eyes and a beard that was whiter than snow. He lived apart, in his big house with his granddaughter, and men said he was very learned, but also very disdainful, and that to him a Jew was not a Jew who did not come of the pure sephardic strain.

Jacob had seen him, in the Congregation Mikveh Israel, and to Jacob he had looked like an eagle, and fierce as an eagle. Yet now, in his need, he found himself knocking at that man's door.

It was Raphael Sanchez himself who opened. "And what is for sale today, peddler?" he said, looking scornfully at Jacob's jacket where the pack straps had worn it.

"A scholar of the Law is for sale," said Jacob in his bitterness, and he did not speak in the tongue he had learned in this country, but in Hebrew.

The old man stared at him a moment.

"Now am I rebuked," he said. "For you have the tongue. Enter, my guest," and Jacob touched the scroll by the doorpost and went in.

They shared the noon meal at Raphael Sanchez's table. It was made of dark, glowing mahogany, and the light sank into it as sunlight sinks into a pool. There were many precious things in that room, but Jacob had no eyes for them. When the meal was over and the blessing said, he opened his heart and spoke, and

Raphael Sanchez listened, stroking his beard with one hand. When the young man had finished, he spoke.

"So, Scholar," he said, though mildly, "you have crossed an ocean that you might live and not die, and yet all you see is a girl's face."

"Did not Jacob serve seven years for Rachel?" said our grandfather's grandfather.

"Twice seven, Scholar," said Raphael Sanchez dryly, "but that was in the blessed days." He stroked his beard again. "Do you know why I came to this country?" he said.

"No," said Jacob Stein.

"It was not for the trading," said Raphael Sanchez. "My house has lent money to kings. A little fish, a few furs — what are they to my house? No, it was for the promise — the promise of Penn — that this land should be an habitation and a refuge, not only for the Gentiles. Well, we know Christian promises. But so far, it has been kept. Are you spat upon in the street here, Scholar of the Law?"

"No," said Jacob. "They call me Jew, now and then. But the Friends, though Gentile, are kind."

"It is not so in all countries," said Raphael Sanchez, with a terrible smile.

"No," said Jacob quietly, "it is not."

The old man nodded. "Yes, one does not forget that," he said. "The spittle wipes off the cloth, but one does not forget. One does not forget the persecutor or the persecuted. That is why they think me mad, in the Congregation Mikveh Israel, when I speak what is in my mind. For, look you" — and he pulled a map from a drawer — "here is what we know of these colonies, and here and here our people make a new beginning, in another air. But here is New France — see it? — and down the great river come the French traders and their Indians."

"Well?" said Jacob in puzzlement.

"Well?" said Raphael Sanchez. "Are you blind? I do not trust the King of France — the king before him drove out the Huguenots, and who knows what he may do? And if they hold the great rivers against us, we shall never go westward."

"We?" said Jacob in bewilderment.

"We," said Raphael Sanchez. He struck his hand on the map. "Oh, they cannot see it in Europe — not even their lords in parliament and their ministers of state," he said. "They think this is a mine, to be worked as the Spaniards worked Potosi, but it is not a mine. It is something beginning to live, and it is faceless and nameless yet. But it is our lot to be part of it — remember that in the wilderness, my young scholar of the Law. You think you are going there for a girl's face, and that is well enough. But you may find something there you did not expect to find."

He paused and his eyes had a different look.

"You see, it is the trader first," he said. "Always the trader, before the settled man. The Gentiles will forget that, and some of our own folk too. But one pays for the land of Canaan; one pays in blood and sweat."

Then he told Jacob what he would do for him and dismissed him, and Jacob went home to his room with his head buzzing strangely. For at times it seemed to him that the Congregation Mikveh Israel was right in thinking Raphael Sanchez half mad. And at other times it seemed to him that the old man's words were a veil, and behind them moved and stirred some huge and unguessed shape. But chiefly he thought of the rosy cheeks of Miriam Ettelsohn.

It was with the Scotchman, McCampbell, that Jacob made his first trading journey. A strange man was McCampbell, with grim features and cold blue eyes, but strong and kindly, though silent, except when he talked of the Ten Lost Tribes of Israel. For it was his contention that they were the Indians beyond the Western Mountains, and on this subject he would talk endlessly.

Indeed, they had much profitable conversation, McCampbell quoting the doctrines of a rabbi called John Calvin, and our grandfather's grandfather replying with Talmud and Torah till McCampbell would almost weep that such a honey-mouthed scholar should be destined to eternal damnation. Yet he did not treat our grandfather's grandfather as one destined to eternal damnation, but as a man, and he, too, spoke of cities of refuge as a man speaks of realities, for his people had also been persecuted.

First they left the city behind them, and then the outlying towns and, soon enough, they were in the wilderness. It was very strange to Jacob Stein. At first he would wake at night and lie awake listening, while his heart pounded, and each rustle in the forest was the step of a wild Indian, and each screech of an owl in the forest the whoop before the attack. But gradually this passed. He began to notice how silently the big man, McCampbell, moved in the woods; he began to imitate him. He began to learn many things that even a scholar of the Law, for all his wisdom, does not know – the girthing of a packsaddle and the making of fires, the look of dawn in the forest and the look of evening. It was all very new to him, and sometimes he thought he would die of it, for his flesh weakened. Yet always he kept on.

When he saw his first Indians – in the woods, not in the town – his knees knocked together. They were there as he had dreamt of them in dreams, and he thought of the spirit, Iggereth-beth-Mathlan, and her seventy-eight dancing demons, for they were painted and in skins. But he could not let his knees knock together, before heathens and a Gentile, and the first fear passed. Then he found they were grave men, very ceremonious and silent at first, and then when the silence had been broken, full of curiosity. They knew McCampbell, but him they did not know, and they discussed him and his garments with the frankness of children, till Jacob felt naked before them, and yet not afraid. One of them pointed to the bag that hung at Jacob's neck – the bag in which, for safety's sake, he carried his phylactery – then McCampbell said something and the brown hand dropped quickly, but there was a buzz of talk.

Later on, McCampbell explained to him that they, too, wore little bags of deerskin and inside them sacred objects – and they thought, seeing his, that he must be a person of some note. It made him wonder. It made him wonder more to eat deer meat with them, by a fire.

It was a green world and a dark one that he had fallen in — dark with the shadow of the forest, green with its green. Through it ran trails and paths that were not yet roads or highways — that did not have the dust and smell of the cities of men, but another scent, another look. These paths Jacob noted carefully, making a map, for that was one of the instructions of Raphael Sanchez. It seemed a great labor and difficult and for no purpose; yet, as he had promised, so he did. And as they sank deeper and deeper into the depths of the forest, and he saw pleasant streams and wide glades, untenanted but by the deer, strange thoughts came over him. It seemed to him that the Germany he had left was very small and crowded together; it seemed to him that he had not known there was so much width to the world.

Now and then he would dream back — dream back to the quiet fields around Rettelsheim and the red-brick houses of Philadelphia, to the stuffed fish and the raisin wine, the chanting in the *chedar* and the white twisted loaves of calm Sabbath, under the white cloth. They would seem very close for the moment, then they would seem very far away. He was eating deer's meat in a forest and sleeping beside embers in the open night. It was so that Israel must have slept in the wilderness. He had not thought of it as so, but it was so.

Now and then he would look at his hands — they seemed tougher and very brown, as if they did not belong to him any more. Now and then he would catch a glimpse of his own face, as he drank at a stream. He had a beard, but it was not the beard of a scholar – it was wild and black. Moreover, he was dressed in skins, now; it seemed strange to be dressed in skins at first, and then not strange.

Now all this time, when he went to sleep at night, he would think of Miriam Ettelsohn. But, queerly enough, the harder he tried to summon up her face in his thoughts, the vaguer it became.

He lost track of time – there was only his map and the trading and the journey. Now it seemed to him that they should surely turn back, for their packs were full. He spoke of it to McCampbell, but McCampbell shook his head. There was a light in the Scotchman's eyes now – a light that seemed strange to our grandfather's grandfather – and he would pray long at night, sometimes too loudly. So they came to the banks of the great river, brown and great, and saw it, and the country beyond it, like a view across Jordan. There was no end to that country – it stretched to the limits of the sky and Jacob saw it with his eyes. He was almost afraid at first, and then he was not afraid.

It was there that the strong man, McCampbell, fell sick, and there that he died and was buried. Jacob buried him on a bluff overlooking the river and faced the grave to the west. In his death sickness, McCampbell raved of the Ten Lost Tribes again and swore they were just across the river and he would go to them. It took all Jacob's strength to hold him – if it had been at the beginning of the journey, he would not have had the strength. Then he turned back, for he, too, had seen a Promised Land, not for his seed only, but for nations yet to come.

Nevertheless, he was taken by the Shawnees, in a season of bitter cold, with his last horse dead. At first, when misfortune began to fall upon him, he had wept for the loss of the horses and the good beaver. But, when the Shawnees took him, he no longer wept; for it seemed to him that he was no longer himself, but a man he did not know.

He was not concerned when they tied him to the stake and piled the wood around him, for it seemed to him still that it must be happening to another man. Nevertheless he prayed, as was fitting, chanting loudly; for Zion in the wilderness he prayed. He could smell the smell of the *chedar* and hear the voices that he knew – Reb Moses and Reb Nathan, and through them the curious voice of Raphael Sanchez, speaking in riddles. Then the smoke took him and he coughed. His throat was hot. He called for drink, and though they could not understand his words, all men know the sign of thirst, and they brought him a bowl filled. He put it to his lips eagerly and drank, but the stuff in the bowl was scorching hot and burned his mouth. Very angry then was our grandfather's grandfather, and without so much as a cry he took the bowl in both hands and flung it straight in the face of the man who had brought it, scalding him. Then there was a cry and a murmur from the Shawnees and, after some moments, he felt himself unbound and knew that he lived.

It was flinging the bowl at the man while yet he stood at the stake that saved him, for there is an etiquette about such matters. One does not burn a madman, among the Indians; and to the Shawnees, Jacob's flinging the bowl proved that he was mad, for a sane man would not have done so. Or so it was explained to him later, though he was never quite sure that they had not been playing cat-and-mouse with him, to test him. Also they were much concerned by his chanting his death song in an unknown tongue and by the phylactery that he had taken from its bag and bound upon brow and arm for his death hour, for these they thought strong medicine and uncertain. But in any case they released him, though they would not give him back his beaver, and that winter he passed in the lodges of the Shawnees, treated sometimes like a servant and sometimes like a guest, but always on the edge of peril. For he was strange to them, and they could not quite make up their minds about him, though the man with the scalded face had his own opinion, as Jacob could see.

Yet when the winter was milder and the hunting better than it had been in some seasons, it was he who got the credit of it, and the holy phylactery also; and by the end of the winter he was talking to them of trade, though diffidently at first. Ah, our grandfather's grandfather, *selig,* what woes he had! And yet it was not all woe, for he learned much woodcraft from the Shawnees and began to speak in their tongue.

Yet he did not trust them entirely; and when spring came and he could travel, he escaped. He was no longer a scholar then, but a hunter. He tried to think what day it was by the calendar, but he could only remember the Bee Moon and the Berry Moon. Yet when he thought of a feast he tried to keep it, and always he prayed for Zion. But when he thought of Zion, it was not as he had thought of it before – a white city set on a hill – but a great and open landscape, ready for nations. He could not have said why his thought had changed, but it had.

I shall not tell all, for who knows all? I shall not tell of the trading post he found deserted and the hundred and forty French louis in the dead man's money belt. I shall not tell of the half-grown boy, McGillvray, that he found on the fringes of settlement – the boy who was to be his partner in the days to come – and how they traded again with the Shawnees and got much beaver. Only this remains to be told, for this is true.

It was a long time since he had even thought of Meyer Kappelhuist – the big pushing man with red hairs on the backs of his hands. But now they were turning back toward Philadelphia, he and McGillvray, their packhorses and their beaver; and as the paths began to grow familiar, old thoughts came into his mind. Moreover, he would hear now and then, in the outposts of the wilderness, of a red-haired trader. So when he met the man himself, not thirty miles from Lancaster, he was not surprised.

Now, Meyer Kappelhuist had always seemed a big man to our grandfather's grandfather. But he did not seem such a big man, met in the wilderness by chance, and at that Jacob was amazed. Yet the greater surprise was Meyer Kappelhuist's, for he stared at our grandfather's grandfather long and puzzledly before he cried out, "But it's the little scholar!" and clapped his hand on his knee. Then they greeted each other civilly and Meyer Kappelhuist drank liquor because of the meeting, but Jacob drank nothing. For, all the time, they were talking, he could see Meyer Kappelhuist's eyes fixed greedily upon his packs of beaver, and he did not like that. Nor did he like the looks of the three tame Indians who traveled with Meyer Kappelhuist and, though he was a man of peace, he kept his hand on his arms, and the boy, McGillvray, did the same.

Meyer Kappelhuist was anxious that they should travel on together, but Jacob refused, for, as I say, he did not like the look in the red-haired man's eyes. So he said he was taking another road and left it at that.

"And the news you have of Simon Ettelsohn and his family — it is good, no doubt, for I know you are close to them," said Jacob, before they parted.

"Close to them?" said Meyer Kappelhuist, and he looked black as thunder. Then he laughed a forced laugh. "Oh, I see them no more," he said. "The old rascal has promised his daughter to a cousin of the Seixas, a greeny, just come over, but rich, they say. But to tell you the truth, I think we are well out of it, Scholar — she was always a little too skinny for my taste," and he laughed coarsely.

"She was a rose of Sharon and a lily of the valley," said Jacob respectfully, and yet not with the pang he would have expected at such news, though it made him more determined than ever not to travel with Meyer Kappelhuist. And with that they parted and Meyer Kappelhuist went his way. Then Jacob took a fork in the trail that McGillvray knew of and that was as well for him. For when he got to Lancaster, there was news of the killing of a trader by the Indians who traveled with him; and when Jacob asked for details, they showed him something dried on a willow hoop. Jacob looked at the thing and saw the hairs upon it were red.

"Sculped all right, but we got it back," said the frontiersman, with satisfaction. "The red devil had it on him when we caught him. Should have buried it, too, I guess, but we'd buried him already and it didn't seem feasible. Thought I might take it to Philadelphy, sometime – might make an impression on the governor. Say, if you're going there, you might – after all, that's where he come from. Be a sort of memento to his folks."

"And it might have been mine, if I had traveled with him," said Jacob. He stared at the thing again, and his heart rose against touching it. Yet it was well the city people should know what happened to men in the wilderness, and the price of blood. "Yes, I will take it," he said.

Jacob stood before the door of Raphael Sanchez, in Philadelphia. He knocked at the door with his knuckles, and the old man himself peered out at him.

"And what is your business with me, Frontiersman?" said the old man, peering.

"The price of blood for a country," said Jacob Stein. He did not raise his voice, but there was a note in it that had not been there when he first knocked at Raphael Sanchez's door.

The old man stared at him soberly. "Enter, my son,"

he said at last, and Jacob touched the scroll by the doorpost and went in.

He walked through the halls as a man walks in a dream. At last he was sitting by the dark mahogany table. There was nothing changed in the room — he wondered greatly that nothing in it had changed.

"And what have you seen, my son?" said Raphael Sanchez.

"I have seen the land of Canaan, flowing with milk and honey," said Jacob, Scholar of the Law. "I have brought back grapes from Eshcol, and other things that are terrible to behold," he cried, and even as he cried he felt the sob rise in his throat. He choked it down. "Also there are eighteen packs of prime beaver at the warehouse and a boy named McGillvray, a Gentile, but very trusty," he said. "The beaver is very good and the boy under my protection. And McCampbell died by the great river, but he had seen the land and I think he rests well. The map is not made as I would have it, but is shows new things. And we must trade with the Shawnees. There are three posts to be established — I have marked them on the map — and later, more. And beyond the great river there is country that stretches to the end of the world. That is where my friend McCampbell lies, with his face turned west. But what is the use of talking? You would not understand."

He put his head on his arms, for the room was too quiet and peaceful, and he was very tired. Raphael Sanchez moved around the table and touched him on the shoulder.

"Did I not say, my son, that there was more than a girl's face to be found in the wilderness?" he said.

"A girl's face?" said Jacob. "Why, she is to be married and, I hope, will be happy, for she was a rose of Sharon. But what are girls' faces beside this?" and he flung something on the table. It rattled dryly on the table, like a cast snakeskin, but the hairs upon it were red.

"It was Meyer Kappelhuist," said Jacob childishly, "and he was a strong man. And I am not strong, but a scholar. But I have seen what I have seen. And we must say Kaddish for him."

"Yes, yes," said Raphael Sanchez. "It will be done. I will see to it."

"But you do not understand," said Jacob. "I have eaten deer's meat in the wilderness and forgotten the month and the year. I have been a servant to the heathen and held the scalp of my enemy in my hand. I will never be the same man."

"Oh, you will be the same," said Sanchez. "And no worse a scholar, perhaps. But this is a new country."

"It must be for all," said Jacob. "For my friend McCampbell died also, and he was a Gentile."

"Let us hope," said Raphael Sanchez and touched him again upon the shoulder. Then Jacob lifted his head and he saw that the light had declined and the evening was upon him. And even as he looked, Raphael Sanchez's granddaughter came in to light the candles for Sabbath. And Jacob looked upon her, and she was a dove, with dove's eyes.

THE DIE-HARD

THERE was a town called Shady, Georgia, and a time that's gone, and a boy named Jimmy Williams who was curious about things. Just a few years before the turn of the century it was, and that seems far away now. But Jimmy Williams was living in it, and it didn't seem far away to him.

It was a small town, Shady, and sleepy, though it had two trains a day and they were putting through a new spur to Vickery Junction.

They'd dedicated the War Memorial in the Square, but, on market days, you'd still see oxcarts on Main Street. And once, when Jimmy Williams was five, there'd been a light fall of snow and the whole town had dropped its business and gone out to see it. He could still remember the feel of the snow in his hands, for it was the only snow he'd ever touched or seen.

He was a bright boy – maybe a little too bright for his age. He'd think about a thing till it seemed real to him – and that's a dangerous gift. His father was the town doctor, and his father would try to show him the difference, but Doctor Williams was a right busy man. And the other Williams children were a good deal younger and his mother was busy with them. So Jimmy had more time to himself than most boys – and youth's a dreamy time.

I reckon it was that got him interested in Old Man Cappalow, in the first place. Every town has its legends and characters, and Old Man Cappalow was one of Shady's. He lived out of town, on the old Vincey place, all alone except for a light-colored Negro named Sam that he'd brought from Virginia with him; and the local Negroes wouldn't pass along that road at night. That was partly because of Sam, who was supposed to be a conjur, but mostly on account of Old Man Cappalow. He'd come in the troubled times, right after the end of the war, and ever since then he'd kept himself to himself. Except that once a month he went down to the bank and drew money that came in a letter from Virginia. But how he spent it, nobody knew. Except that he had a treasure – every boy in Shady knew that.

Now and then, a gang of them would get bold and they'd rattle sticks along the sides of his fence and yell, "Old Man Cappalow! Where's your money?" But then the light-colored Negro, Sam, would come out on the porch and look at them, and they'd run away. They didn't want to be conjured, and you couldn't be sure. But on the way home, they'd speculate and wonder about the treasure, and each time they speculated and wondered, it got bigger to them.

Some said it was the last treasure of the Confederacy, saved right up to the end to build a new *Alabama*, and that Old Man Cappalow had sneaked it out of Richmond when the city fell and kept it for himself; only now he didn't dare spend it, for the mark of Cain was on every piece. And some said it came from the sea islands, where the pirates had left it, protected by h'ants and devils, and Old Man Cappalow had had to fight devils for it six days and six nights before he could take it away. And if you looked inside his shirt, you could see the long white marks where the devils had clawed him. Well, sir, some said one thing and some said another. But they all agreed it was there, and it got to be a byword among the boys of the town.

It used to bother Jimmy Williams tremendously. Because he knew his father worked hard, and yet sometimes he'd only get fifty cents a visit, and often enough he'd get nothing. And he knew his mother worked hard, and that most folks in Shady weren't rich. And yet, all the time, there was that treasure, sitting out at Old Man Cappalow's. He didn't mean to steal it exactly. I don't know just what he did intend to do about it. But the idea of it bothered him and stayed at the back of his mind. Till, finally, one summer when he was turned thirteen, he started making expeditions to the Cappalow place.

He'd go in the cool of the morning or the cool of the afternoon, and sometimes he'd be fighting Indians and Yankees on the way, because he was still a boy, and sometimes he was thinking what he'd be when he grew up, for he was starting to be a man. But he never told the other boys what he was doing – and that was the mixture of both. He'd slip from the road, out of sight of the house, and go along by the fence. Then he'd lie down in the grass and the weeds, and look at the house.

It had been quite a fine place once, but now the porch was sagging and there were mended places in the roof and paper pasted over broken windowpanes. But that didn't mean much to Jimmy Williams; he was used to houses looking like that. There was a garden patch at the side, neat and well-kept, and sometimes he'd see the Negro, Sam, there, working. But what he looked at mostly was the side porch. For Old Man Cappalow would be sitting there.

He sat there, cool and icy-looking, in his white linen suit, on his cane chair, and now and then he'd have a leather-bound book in his hand, though he didn't often read it. He didn't move much, but he sat straight, his hands on his knees and his black eyes alive. There was something about his eyes that reminded Jimmy Williams of the windows of the house. They weren't blind, indeed they were bright, but there was something living behind them that wasn't usual. You didn't expect them to be so black, with his white hair. Jimmy Williams had seen a governor once, on Memorial Day, but the governor didn't look half as fine. This man was like a man made of ice – ice in the heat of the South. You could see he was old, but you couldn't tell how old, or whether he'd ever die.

Once in a great while he'd come out and shoot at a mark. The mark was a kind of metal shield, nailed up on a post, and it had been painted once, but the paint had worn away. He'd hold the pistol very steady, and the bullets would go "whang, whang" on the metal, very loud in the stillness. Jimmy Williams would watch him and wonder if that was the way he'd fought with his devils, and speculate about all kinds of things.

All the same, he was only a boy, and though it was fun and scary, to get so near Old Man Cappalow without being seen, and he'd have a grand tale to tell the others, if he ever decided to tell it, he didn't see any devils or any treasure. And probably he'd have given the whole business up in the end, boylike, if something hadn't happened.

He was lying in the weeds by the fence, one warm afternoon, and, boylike, he fell asleep. And he was just in the middle of a dream where Old Man Cappalow was promising him a million dollars if he'd go to the devil to get it, when he was wakened by a rustle in the weeds and a voice that said, "White boy."

Jimmy Williams rolled over and froze. For there, just half a dozen steps away from him, was the light-colored Negro, Sam, in his blue jeans, the way he worked in the garden patch, but looking like the butler at the club for all that.

I reckon if Jimmy Williams had been on his feet, he'd have run. But he wasn't on his feet. And he told himself he didn't mean to run, though his heart began to pound.

"White boy," said the light-colored Negro, "Marse John see you from up at the house. He send you his obleegances and say will you step that way." He spoke in a light, sweet voice, and there wasn't a thing in his manners you could have objected to. But just for a minute, Jimmy Williams wondered if he was being conjured. And then he didn't care. Because he was going to do what no boy in Shady had ever done. He was going to walk into Old Man Cappalow's house and not be scared. He wasn't going to be scared, though his heart kept pounding.

He scrambled to his feet and followed the line of the fence till he got to the driveway, the light-colored Negro just a little behind him. And when they got near the porch, Jimmy Williams stopped and took a leaf and wiped off his shoes, though he couldn't have told you why. The Negro stood watching while he did it, perfectly at ease. Jimmy Williams could see that the Negro thought better of him for wiping off his shoes, but not much. And that made him mad, and he wanted to say, "I'm no white trash. My father's a doctor," but he knew better than to say it. He just wiped his shoes and the Negro stood and waited. Then the Negro took him around to the side porch, and there was Old Man Cappalow, sitting in his cane chair.

"White boy here, Marse John," said the Negro in his low, sweet voice.

The old man lifted his head, and his black eyes looked at Jimmy Williams. It was a long stare and it went to Jimmy Williams' backbone.

"Sit down, boy," he said, at last, and his voice was friendly enough, but Jimmy Williams obeyed it. "You can go along, Sam," he said, and Jimmy Williams sat on the edge of a cane chair and tried to feel comfortable. He didn't do very well at it, but he tried.

"What's your name, boy?" said the old man, after a while.

"Jimmy Williams, sir," said Jimmy Williams. "I mean James Williams, Junior, sir."

"Williams," said the old man, and his black eyes glowed. "There was a Colonel Williams with the Sixty-fifth Virginia – or was it the Sixty-third? He came from

Fairfax County and was quite of my opinion that we should have kept to primogeniture, in spite of Thomas Jefferson. But I doubt if you are kin."

"No, sir," said Jimmy Williams. "I mean, Father was with the Ninth Georgia. And he was a private. They were aiming to make him a corporal, he says, but they never got around to it. But he fit – he fought lots of Yankees. He fit tons of 'em. And I've seen his uniform. But now he's a doctor instead."

The old man seemed to look a little queer at that. "A doctor?" he said. "Well, some very reputable gentlemen have practiced medicine. There need be no loss of standing."

"Yes, sir," said Jimmy Williams. Then he couldn't keep it back any longer: "Please, sir, were you ever clawed by the devil?" he said.

"Ha-hrrm!" said the old man, looking startled. "You're a queer boy. And suppose I told you I had been?"

"I'd believe you," said Jimmy Williams, and the old man laughed. He did it as if he wasn't used to it, but he did it.

"Clawed by the devil!" he said. "Ha-hrrm! You're a bold boy. I didn't know they grew them nowadays. I'm surprised." But he didn't look angry, as Jimmy Williams had expected him to.

"Well," said Jimmy Williams, "if you had been, I thought maybe you'd tell me about it. I'd be right interested. Or maybe let me see the clawmarks. I mean, if they're there."

"I can't show you those," said the old man, "though

they're deep and wide." And he stared fiercely at Jimmy Williams. "But you weren't afraid to come here and you wiped your shoes when you came. So I'll show you something else." He rose and was tall. "Come into the house," he said.

So Jimmy Williams got up and went into the house with him. It was a big, cool, dim room they went into, and Jimmy Williams didn't see much at first. But then his eyes began to get used to the dimness.

Well, there were plenty of houses in Shady where the rooms were cool and dim and the sword hung over the mantelpiece and the furniture was worn and old. It wasn't that made the difference. But stepping into this house was somehow like stepping back into the past, though Jimmy Williams couldn't have put it that way. He just knew it was full of beautiful things and grand things that didn't quite fit it, and yet all belonged together. And they knew they were grand and stately, and yet there was dust in the air and a shadow on the wall. It was peaceful enough and handsome enough, yet it didn't make Jimmy Williams feel comfortable, though he couldn't have told you why.

"Well," said the old man, moving about among shadows, "how do you like it, Mr. Williams?"

"It's—I never saw anything like it," said Jimmy Williams.

The old man seemed pleased. "Touch the things, boy," he said. "Touch the things. They don't mind being touched."

So Jimmy Williams went around the room, staring at the miniatures and the pictures, and picking up one thing or another and putting it down. He was very careful and he didn't break anything. And there were some wonderful things. There was a game of chess on a table – carved-ivory pieces – a game that people had started, but hadn't finished. He didn't touch those, though he wanted to, because he felt the people might not like it when they came back to finish their game. And yet, at the same time, he felt that if they ever did come back, they'd be dead, and that made him feel queerer. There were silver-mounted pistols, long-barreled, on a desk by a big silver inkwell; there was a quill pen made of a heron's feather, and a silver sand-box beside it – there were all sorts of curious and interesting things. Finally Jimmy Williams stopped in front of a big, tall clock.

"I'm sorry, sir," he said, "but I don't think that's the right time."

"Oh, yes, it is." said the old man. "It's always the right time."

"Yes, sir," said Jimmy Williams, "but it isn't running."

"Of course not," said the old man. "They say you can't put the clock back, but you can. I've put it back and I mean to keep it back. The others can do as they please. I warned them – I warned them in 1850, when they accepted the Compromise. I warned them there could be no compromise. Well, they would not be warned."

"Was that bad of them, sir?" asked Jimmy Williams.

"It was misguided of them," said the old man. "Misguided of them all." He seemed to be talking more to himself than to Jimmy, but Jimmy Williams couldn't help listening. "There can be no compromise with one's class or one's breeding or one's sentiments," the old man said. "Afterwards – well, there were gentlemen I knew who went to Guatemala or elsewhere. I do not blame them for it. But mine is another course." He paused and glanced at the clock. Then he spoke in a different voice. "I beg your pardon," he said. "I fear I was growing heated. You will excuse me. I generally take some refreshment around this time in the afternoon. Perhaps you will join me, Mr. Williams?"

It didn't seem to Jimmy Williams as if the silver hand bell in the old man's hand had even stopped ringing before the Negro, Sam, came in with a tray. He had a queer kind of old-fashioned long coat on now, and a queer old-fashioned cravat, but his pants were the pants of his blue jeans. Jimmy Williams noticed that, but Old Man Cappalow didn't seem to notice.

"Yes," he said, "there are many traitors. Men I held in the greatest esteem have betrayed their class and their system. They have accepted ruin and domination in the name of advancement. But we will not speak of them now." He took the frosted silver cup from the tray and motioned to Jimmy Williams that the small fluted glass was for him. "I shall ask you to rise, Mr. Williams," he said. "We shall drink a toast." He paused for a moment, standing straight. "To the Confederate States of America and damnation to all her enemies!" he said.

Jimmy Williams drank. He'd never drunk any wine before, except blackberry cordial, and this wine seemed to him powerfully thin and sour. But he felt grown up as he drank it, and that was a fine feeling.

"Every night of my life," said the old man, "I drink that toast. And usually I drink it alone. But I am glad of your company, Mr. Williams."

"Yes, sir," said Jimmy Williams, but all the same, he felt queer. For drinking the toast, somehow, had been very solemn, almost like being in church. But in church you didn't exactly pray for other people's damnation, though the preacher might get right excited over sin.

Well, then the two of them sat down again, and Old Man Cappalow began to talk of the great plantation days and the world as it used to be. Of course, Jimmy Williams had heard plenty of talk of that sort. But this was different. For the old man talked of those days as if they were still going on, not as if they were past. And as he talked, the whole room seemed to join in, with a thousand, sighing, small voices, stately and clear, till Jimmy Williams didn't know whether he was on his head or his heels and it seemed quite natural to him to look at the fresh, crisp Richmond newspaper on the desk and see it was dated "June 14, 1859" instead of "June 14, 1897." Well, maybe it was the wine, though he'd only had a thimbleful. But when Jimmy Williams went out into the sun again, he felt changed, and excited too. For he knew about Old Man Cappalow now, and he was just about the grandest person in the world.

The Negro went a little behind him, all the way to the gate, on soft feet. When they got there, the Negro opened the gate and spoke.

"Young marster," he said, "I don't know why Marse John took in his head to ask you up to the house. But we lives private, me and Marse John. We lives very private." There was a curious pleading in his voice.

"I don't tell tales," said Jimmy Williams, and kicked at the fence.

"Yes, sir," said the Negro, and he seemed relieved. "I knew you one of the right ones. I knew that. But we'se living very private till the big folks come back. We don't want no tales spread before. And then we'se going back to Otranto, the way we should."

"I know about Otranto. He told me," said Jimmy Williams, catching his breath.

"Otranto Marse John's plantation in Verginny," said the Negro, as if he hadn't heard. "He owns the river and the valley, the streams and the hills. We got four hundred field hands at Otranto and stables for sixty horses. But we can't go back there till the big folks come back. Marse John say so, and he always speak the truth. But they's goin' to come back, a-shootin' and pirootin', they pistols at they sides. And every day I irons his Richmond paper for him and he reads about the old times. We got boxes and boxes of papers down in the cellar." He paused. "And if he say the old days come back, it bound to be so," he said. Again his voice held that curious pleading. "You remember, young marster," he said. "You remember, white boy."

"I told you I didn't tell tales," said Jimmy Williams. But after that, things were different for him. Because there's one thing about a boy that age that most grown people forget. A boy that age can keep a secret in a way that's perfectly astonishing. And he can go through queer hells and heavens you'll never hear a word about, not even if you got him or bore him.

It was that way with Jimmy Williams; it mightn't have been for another boy. It began like a game, and then it stopped being a game. For, of course, he went back to Old Man Cappalow's. And the Negro, Sam, would show him up to the house and he'd sit in the dim room with the old man and drink the toast in the wine. And it wasn't Old Man Cappalow any more; it was Col. John Leonidas Cappalow, who'd raised and equipped his own regiment and never surrendered. Only, when the time was ripe, he was going back to Otranto, and the old days would bloom again, and Jimmy Williams would be part of them.

When he shut his eyes at night, he could see Otranto and its porches, above the rolling river, great and stately; he could hear the sixty horses stamping in their stalls. He could see the pretty girls, in their wide skirts, coming down the glassy, proud staircases; he could see the fine, handsome gentlemen who ruled the earth and the richness of it without a thought of care. It was all like a storybook to Jimmy Williams — a storybook come true. And more than anything he'd ever wanted in his life, he wanted to be part of it.

The only thing was, it was hard to fit the people he really knew into the story. Now and then Colonel Cappalow would ask him gravely if he knew anyone else in Shady who was worthy of being trusted with the secret. Well, there were plenty of boys like Bob Miller and Tommy Vine, but somehow you couldn't see them in the dim room. They'd fit in, all right, when the great days came back – they'd have to – but meanwhile – well, they might just take it for a tale. And then there was Carrie, the cook. She'd have to be a slave again, of course, and though Jimmy Williams didn't imagine that she'd mind, now and then he had just a suspicion that she might. He didn't ask her about it, but he had the suspicion.

It was even hard to fit Jimmy's father in, with his little black bag and his rumpled clothes and his laugh. Jimmy couldn't quite see his father going up the front steps of Otranto – not because he wasn't a gentleman or grand enough, but because it just didn't happen to be his kind of place. And then, his father didn't really hate anybody, as far as Jimmy knew. But you had to hate people a good deal, if you wanted to follow Colonel Cappalow. You had to shoot at the mark and feel you were really shooting the enemy's colors down. You had to believe that even people like General Lee had been wrong, because they hadn't held out in the mountains and fought till everybody died. Well, it was hard to believe a wrong thing of General Lee, and Jimmy Williams didn't quite manage it. He was willing to hate the Yankees and the Republicans – hate them hot and hard – but there weren't any of them in Shady. Well, come to think of it, there was Mr. Rosen, at the dry-goods store, and Mr. Ailey, at the mill. They didn't look very terrible and he was used to them, but he tried to hate them all he could. He got hold of the Rosen boy one day and rocked him home, but the Rosen boy cried, and Jimmy felt mean about it. But if he'd ever seen a real live Republican, with horns and a tail, he'd have done him a mortal injury — he felt sure he would.

And so the summer passed, and by the end of the summer Jimmy didn't feet quite sure which was real — the times now or the times Colonel Cappalow talked about. For he'd dream about Otranto at night and think of it during the day. He'd ride back there on a black horse, at Colonel Cappalow's left, and his saber would be long and shining. But if there was a change in him, there was a change in Colonel Cappalow too. He was a lot more excitable than he used to be, and when he talked to Jimmy sometimes, he'd call him by other names, and when he shot at the mark with the enemy's colors on it, his eyes would blaze. So by that, and by the news he read out of the old papers, Jimmy suddenly got to know that the time was near at hand. They had the treasure all waiting, and soon they'd be ready to rise. And Colonel Cappalow filled out Jimmy Williams' commission as captain in the army of the New Confederate States of America and presented it to him, with a speech. Jimmy Williams felt very proud of that commission, and hid it under a loose brick in his fireplace chimney, where it would be safe.

Well, then it came to the plans, and when Jimmy Williams first heard about them, he felt a little surprised. There were maps spread all over the big desk in the dim room now, and Colonel Cappalow moved pins and showed Jimmy strategy. And that was very exciting, and like a game. But first of all, they'd have to give a signal and strike a blow. You had to do that first, and then the country would rise. Well, Jimmy Williams could see the reason in that.

They were going into Shady and capture the post office first, and then the railroad station and, after that, they'd dynamite the railroad bridge to stop the trains, and Colonel Cappalow would read a proclamation from the steps of the courthouse. The only part Jimmy Williams didn't like about it was killing the postmaster and the station agent, in case they resisted. Jimmy Williams felt pretty sure they would resist, particularly the station agent, who was a mean customer. And, somehow, killing people you knew wasn't quite like killing Yankees and Republicans. The thought of it shook something in Jimmy's mind and made it waver. But after that they'd march on Washington, and everything would be all right.

All the same, he'd sworn his oath and he was a commissioned officer in the army of the New Confederate States. So, when Colonel Cappalow gave him the pistol that morning, with the bullets and the powder, and explained how he was to keep watch at the door of the post office and shoot to kill if he had to, Jimmy said, "I shall execute the order, sir," the way he'd been taught. After that, they'd go for the station agent and he'd have a chance for a lot more shooting. And it was all going to be for noon the next day.

Somehow, Jimmy Williams couldn't quite believe it was going to be for noon the next day, even when he was loading the pistol in the woodshed of the Williams house, late that afternoon. And yet he saw, with a kind of horrible distinctness, that it was going to be. It might sound crazy to some, but not to him — Colonel Cappalow was a sure shot; he'd seen him shoot at the mark. He could see him shooting, now, and he wondered if a bullet went "whang" when it hit a man. And, just as he was fumbling with the bullets, the woodshed door opened suddenly and there was his father.

Well, naturally, Jimmy dropped the pistol and jumped. The pistol didn't explode, for he'd forgotten it needed a cap. But with that moment something seemed to break inside Jimmy Williams. For it was the first time he'd really been afraid and ashamed in front of his father, and now he was ashamed and afraid. And then it was like waking up out of an illness, for his father saw his white face and said, "What's the matter, son?" and the words began to come out of his mouth.

"Take it easy, son," said his father, but Jimmy couldn't take it easy. He told all about Otranto and Old Man Cappalow and hating the Yankees and killing the postmaster, all jumbled up and higgledy-piggledy. But Doctor Williams made sense of it. At first he smiled a little as he listened, but after a while he stopped smiling, and there was anger in his face. And when Jimmy was quite through, "Well, son," he said, "I reckon we've let you run wild. But I never thought . . ." He asked Jimmy a few quick questions, mostly about the dynamite, and he seemed relieved when Jimmy told him they were going to get it from the men who were blasting for the new spur track.

"And now, son," he said, "when did you say this massacre was going to start?"

"Twelve o'clock at the post office." said Jimmy.

"But we weren't going to massacre. It was just the folks that resisted — "

Doctor Williams made a sound in his throat. "Well," he said, "you and I are going to take a ride in the country, Jimmy. No, we won't tell your mother, I think."

It was the last time Jimmy Williams went out to Old Man Cappalow's, and he remembered that. His father didn't say a word all the way, but once he felt in his back pocket for something he'd taken out of the drawer of his desk, and Jimmy remembered that too.

When they drove up in front of the house, his father gave the reins to Jimmy. "Stay in the buggy, Jimmy," he said. "I'll settle this."

Then he got out of the buggy, a little awkwardly, for he was a heavy man, and Jimmy heard his feet scrunch on the gravel. Jimmy knew again, as he saw him go up the steps, that he wouldn't have fitted in Otranto, and somehow he was glad.

The Negro, Sam, opened the door.

"Tell Colonel Cappalow Doctor Williams wishes to speak with him," said Jimmy's father, and Jimmy could see that his father's neck was red.

"Colonel Cappalow not receivin'," said Sam, in his light sweet voice, but Jimmy's father spoke again.

"Tell Colonel Cappalow," he said. He didn't raise his voice, but there was something in it that Jimmy had never heard in that voice before. Sam looked for a moment and went inside the house.

Then Colonel Cappalow came to the door himself. There was red from the evening sun on his white suit and his white hair, and he looked tall and proud. He looked first at Jimmy's father and then at Jimmy. And his voice said, quite coldly, and reasonably and clearly, "Traitor! All traitors!"

"You'll oblige me by leaving the boy out of it," said Jimmy's father heavily. "This is 1897, sir, not 1860," and for a moment there was something light and heady and dangerous in the air between them. Jimmy knew what his father had in his pocket then, and he sat stiff in the buggy and prayed for time to change and things to go away.

Then Colonel Cappalow put his hand to his forehead. "I beg your pardon, sir," he said, in an altered voice. "You mentioned a date?"

"I said it was 1897," said Doctor Williams, standing square and stocky, "I said Marse Robert's dead – God bless him! – and Jefferson Davis too. And before he died, Marse Robert said we ought to be at peace. The ladies can keep up the war as long as they see fit – that's their privilege. But men ought to act like men."

He stared for a moment at the high-chinned, sculptural face.

"Why, damn your soul!" he said, and it was less an oath than a prayer. "I was with the Ninth Georgia; I went through three campaigns. We fought till the day of Appomattox and it was we-uns' fight." Something rough and from the past had slipped back into his speech – something, too, that Jimmy Williams had never heard in it before. "We didn't own niggers or plantations – the men I fought with. But when it was over, we reckoned it was over and we'd build up the land. Well, we've had a hard time to do it, but we're hoeing corn. We've got something better to do than fill up a boy with a lot of magnolious notions and aim to shoot up a postmaster because there's a Republican President. My God," he said, and again it was less an oath than a prayer, "it was bad enough getting licked when you thought you couldn't be – but when I look at you – well, hate stinks when it's kept too long in the barrel, no matter how you dress it up and talk fine about it. I'm warning you. You keep your hands off my boy. Now, that's enough."

"Traitors," said the old man vaguely, "all traitors." Then a change came over his face and he stumbled forward as if he had stumbled over a stone. The Negro and the white man both sprang to him, but it was the Negro who caught him and lowered him to the ground. Then Jimmy Williams heard his father calling for his black bag, and his limbs were able to move again.

Doctor Williams came out of the bedroom, drying his hands on a towel. His eyes fell upon Jimmy Williams, crouched in front of the chessboard.

"He's all right, son," he said. "At least – he's not all right. But he wasn't in pain."

Jimmy Williams shivered a little. "I heard him talking," he said difficultly. "I heard him calling people things."

"Yes," said his father. "Well, you mustn't think too much of that. You see, a man – " He stopped and began again, "Well, I've no doubt he was considerable of a man once. Only – well, there's a Frenchman calls it a fixed idea. You let it get a hold of you . . . and the way he was brought up. He got it in his head, you see – he couldn't stand it that he might have been wrong about anything. And the hate – well, it's not for a man. Not when it's like that. Now, where's that Nigra?"

Jimmy Williams shivered again; he did not want Sam back in the room. But when Sam came, he heard the Negro answer, politely.

"H'm," said Doctor Williams. "Twice before. He should have had medical attention."

"Marse John don't believe in doctors," said the low, sweet voice.

"He wouldn't," said Doctor Williams briefly. "Well, I'll take the boy home now. But I'll have to come back. I'm coroner for this county. You understand about that?"

"Yes, sir," said the low, sweet voice, "I understand about that." Then the Negro looked at the doctor. "Marse Williams," he said, "I wouldn't have let him do it. He thought he was bound to. But I wouldn't have let him do it."

"Well," said the doctor. He thought, and again said, "Well." Then he said, "Are there any relatives?"

"I take him back to Otranto," said the Negro. "It belongs to another gentleman now, but Marse John got a right to lie there. That's Verginny law, he told me."

"So it is," said the doctor. "I'd forgotten that."

"He don't want no relatives," said the Negro. "He got nephews and nieces and all sorts of kin. But they went against him and he cut them right out of his mind. He don't want no relatives." He paused. "He cut everything out of his mind but the old days," he said.

"He start doing it right after the war. That's why we come here. He don't want no part nor portion of the present days. And they send him money from Verginny, but he only spend it the one way – except when we buy this place." He smiled as if at a secret.

"But how?" said the doctor, staring at furniture and pictures.

"Jus' one muleload from Otranto," said the Negro, softly. "And I'd like to see anybody cross Marse John in the old days." He coughed. "They's just one thing, Marse Williams," he said, in his suave voice. "I ain't skeered of sittin' up with Marse John. I always been with him. But it's the money."

"What money?" said Doctor Williams. "Well, that will go through the courts – "

"No, sir," said the Negro patiently. "I mean Marse John's special money that he spend the other money for. He got close to a millyum dollars in that blind closet under the stairs. And nobody dare come for it, as long as he's strong and spry. But now I don't know. I don't know."

"Well," said Doctor Williams, receiving the incredible fact, "I suppose we'd better see."

It was as the Negro had said – a blind closet under the stairs, opened by an elementary sliding catch.

"There's the millyum dollars," said the Negro as the door swung back. He held the cheap glass lamp high – the wide roomy closet was piled from floor to ceiling with stacks of printed paper.

"H'm," said Doctor Williams. "Yes, I thought so . . . . Have you ever seen a million dollars, son?"

"No, sir," said Jimmy Williams.

"Well, take a look," said his father. He slipped a note from a packet, and held it under the lamp.

"It says 'One Thousand Dollars,'" said Jimmy Williams. "Oh!"

"Yes," said his father gently. "And it also says 'Confederate States of America'. . . . You don't need to worry, Sam. The money's perfectly safe. Nobody will come for it. Except, maybe, museums."

"Yes, Marse Williams," said Sam unquestioningly, accepting the white man's word, now he had seen and judged the white man. He shut the closet.

On his way out, the doctor paused for a moment and looked at the Negro. He might have been thinking aloud — it seemed that way to Jimmy Williams.

"And why did you do it?" he said. "Well, that's something we'll never know. And what are you going to do, once you've taken him back to Otranto?"

"I got my arrangements, thank you, sir," said the Negro.

"I haven't a doubt of it," said Jimmy Williams' father. "But I wish I knew what they were."

"I got my arrangements, gentlemen," the Negro repeated, in his low, sweet voice. Then they left him, holding the lamp, with his tall shadow behind him.

"Maybe I oughtn't to have left him," said Jimmy Williams' father, after a while, as the buggy jogged along. "He's perfectly capable of setting fire to the place and burning it up as a sort of a funeral pyre. And maybe that wouldn't be a bad thing," he added, after a pause. Then he said, "Did you notice the chessmen? I wonder who played that game. It was stopped in the middle." Then, after a while, he said, "I remember the smell of the burning woods in the Wilderness. And I remember Reconstruction. But Marse Robert was right, all the same. You can't go back to the past. And hate's the most expensive commodity in the world. It's never been anything else, and I've seen a lot of it. We've got to realize that – got too much of it, still, as a nation."

But Jimmy Williams was hardly listening. He was thinking it was good to be alone with his father in a buggy at night and good they didn't have to live in Otranto after all.

DOC MELLHORN AND THE PEARLY GATES

DOC MELLHORN had never expected to go anywhere at all when he died. So, when he found himself on the road again, it surprised him. But perhaps I'd better explain a little about Doc Mellhorn first. He was seventy-odd when he left our town; but when he came, he was as young as Bates or Filsinger or any of the boys at the hospital. Only there wasn't any hospital when he came. He came with a young man's beard and a brand-new bag and a lot of newfangled ideas about medicine that we didn't take to much. And he left, forty-odd years later, with a first-class county health record and a lot of people alive that wouldn't have been alive if he hadn't been there. Yes, a country doctor. And nobody ever called him a man in white or a death grappler that I know of, though they did think of giving him a degree at Pewauket College once. But then the board met again and decided they needed a new gymnasium, so they gave the degree to J. Prentiss Parmalee instead.

They say he was a thin young man when he first came, a thin young man with an Eastern accent who'd wanted to study in Vienna. But most of us remember him chunky and solid, with white hair and a little bald spot that always got burned bright red in the first hot weather. He had about four card tricks that he'd do for you, if you were a youngster — they were always the same ones — and now and then, if he felt like it, he'd take a silver half dollar out of the back of your neck. And that worked as well with the youngsters who were going to build rocket ships as it had with the youngsters who were going to be railway engineers. It always worked. I guess it was Doc Mellhorn more than the trick.

But there wasn't anything unusual about him, except maybe the card tricks. Or, anyway, he didn't think so. He was just a good doctor and he knew us inside out. I've heard people call him a pigheaded, obstinate old mule — that was in the fight about the water supply. And I've heard a weepy old lady call him a saint. I took the tale to him once, and he looked at me over his glasses and said, "Well, I've always respected a mule. Got ten times the sense of a — horse." Then he took a silver half dollar out of my ear.

Well, how do you describe a man like that? You don't — you call him up at three in the morning. And when he sends in his bill, you think it's a little steep.

All the same, when it came to it, there were people who drove a hundred and fifty miles to the funeral. And the Masons came down from Bluff City, and the Poles came from across the tracks, with a wreath the size of a house, and you saw cars in town that you didn't often see there. But it was after the funeral that the queer things began for Doc Mellhorn.

The last thing he remembered, he'd been lying in bed, feeling prettv sick, on the whole, but glad for the rest. And now he was driving his Model T down a long straight road between rolling, misty prairies that seemed to go from nowhere to nowhere.

It didn't seem funny to him to be driving the Model T again. That was the car he'd learned on, and he kept to it till his family made him change. And it didn't seem funny to him not to be sick any more. He hadn't had much time to be sick in his life – the patients usually attended to that. He looked around for his bag, first thing, but it was there on the seat beside him. It was the old bag, not the presentation one they'd given him at the hospital, but that was all right too. It meant he was out on a call and, if he couldn't quite recollect at the moment just where the call was, it was certain to come to him. He'd wakened up often enough in his buggy, in the old days, and found the horse was taking him home, without his doing much about it. A doctor gets used to things like that.

All the same, when he'd driven and driven for some time without raising so much as a traffic light, just the same rolling prairies on either hand, he began to get a little suspicious. He thought, for a while, of stopping the car and getting out, just to take a look around, but he'd always hated to lose time on a call. Then he noticed something else. He was driving without his glasses. And yet he hadn't driven without his glasses in fifteen years.

"H'm," said Doc Mellhorn. "I'm crazy as a June bug. Or else – Well, it might be so, I suppose."

But this time he did stop the car. He opened his bag and looked inside it, but everything seemed to be in order. He opened his wallet and looked at that, but there were his own initials, half rubbed away, and he recognized them. He took his pulse, but it felt perfectly steady.

"H'm," said Doc Mellhorn. "Well."

Then, just to prove that everything was perfectly normal, he took a silver half dollar out of the steering wheel of the car.

"Never did it smoother," said Doc Mellhorn. "Well, all the same, if this is the new highway, it's longer than I remember it."

But just then a motorcycle came roaring down the road and stopped with a flourish, the way motor cops do.

"Any trouble?" said the motor cop. Doc Mellhorn couldn't see his face for his goggles, but the goggles looked normal.

"I am a physician," said Doc Mellhorn, as he'd said a thousand times before to all sorts of people, "on my way to an urgent case." He passed his hand across his forehead. "Is this the right road?" he said.

"Straight ahead to the traffic light," said the cop. "They're expecting you, Doctor Mellhorn. Shall I give you an escort?"

"No; thanks all the same," said Doc Mellhorn, and the motor cop roared away. The Model T ground as Doc Mellhorn gassed her. "Well, they've got a new breed of traffic cop," said Doc Mellhorn, "or else — "

But when he got to the light, it was just like any light at a crossroads. He waited till it changed and the officer waved him on. There seemed to be a good deal of traffic going the other way, but he didn't get a chance to notice it much, because Lizzie bucked a little, as she usually did when you kept her waiting. Still, the sight of traffic relieved him, though he hadn't passed anybody on his own road yet.

Pretty soon he noticed the look of the country had changed. It was parkway now and very nicely landscaped. There was dogwood in bloom on the little hills, white and pink against the green; though, as Doc Mellhorn remembered it, it had been August when he left his house. And every now and then there'd be a nice little white-painted sign that said TO THE GATES.

"H'm," said Doc Mellhorn. "New State Parkway, I guess. Well, they've fixed it up pretty. But I wonder where they got the dogwood. Haven't seen it bloom like that since I was East."

Then he drove along in a sort of dream for a while, for the dogwood reminded him of the days when he was a young man in an Eastern college. He remembered the look of that college and the girls who'd come to dances, the girls who wore white gloves and had rolls of hair. They were pretty girls, too, and he wondered what had become of them. "Had babies, I guess," thought Doc Mellhorn. "Or some of them, anyway." But he liked to think of them as the way they had been when they were just pretty, and excited at being at a dance.

He remembered other things too — the hacked desks in the lecture rooms, and the trees on the campus, and the first pipe he'd ever broken in, and a fellow called Paisley Grew that he hadn't thought of in years — a rawboned fellow with a gift for tall stories and playing the jew's-harp.

"Ought to have looked up Paisley," he said. "Yes, I ought. Didn't amount to a hill of beans, I guess, but I always liked him. I wonder if he still plays the jew's-harp. Pshaw, I know he's been dead twenty years."

He was passing other cars now and other cars were passing him, but he didn't pay much attention, except when he happened to notice a license you didn't often see in the state, like Rhode Island or Mississippi. He was too full of his own thoughts. There were foot passengers, too, plenty of them – and once he passed a man driving a load of hay. He wondered what the man would do with the hay when he got to the Gates. But probably there were arrangements for that.

"Not that I believe a word of it," he said, "but it'll surprise Father Kelly. Or maybe it won't. I used to have some handsome arguments with that man, but I always knew I could count on him, in spite of me being a heretic."

Then he saw the Wall and the Gates, right across the valley. He saw them, and they reached to the top of the sky. He rubbed his eyes for a while, but they kept on being there.

"Quite a sight," said Doc Mellhorn.

No one told him just where to go or how to act, but it seemed to him that he knew. If he'd thought about it, he'd have said that you waited in line, but there wasn't any waiting in line. He just went where he was expected to go and the reception clerk knew his name right away.

"Yes, Doctor Mellhorn," he said. "And now, what would you like to do first?"

"I think I'd like to sit down," said Doc Mellhorn. So he sat, and it was a comfortable chair. He even bounced the springs of it once or twice, till he caught the reception clerk's eye on him.

"Is there anything I can get you?" said the reception clerk. He was young and brisk and neat as a pin, and you could see he aimed to give service and studied about it. Doc Mellhorn thought, "He's the kind that wipes off your windshield no matter how clean it is."

"No," said Doc Mellhorn. "You see, I don't believe this. I don't believe any of it. I'm sorry if that sounds cranky, but I don't."

"That's quite all right, sir," said the reception clerk. "It often takes a while." And he smiled as if Doc Mellhorn had done him a favor.

"Young man, I'm a physician," said Doc Mellhorn, "and do you mean to tell me — "

Then he stopped, for he suddenly saw there was no use arguing. He was either there or he wasn't. And it felt as if he were there.

"Well," said Doc Mellhorn, with a sigh, "how do I begin?"

"That's entirely at your own volition, sir," said the reception clerk briskly. "Any meetings with relatives, of course. Or if you would prefer to get yourself settled first. Or take a tour, alone or conducted. Perhaps these will offer suggestions," and he started to hand over a handful of leaflets. But Doc Mellhorn put them aside.

"Wait a minute," he said. "I want to think. Well,

naturally, there's Mother and Dad. But I couldn't see them just yet. I wouldn't believe it. And Grandma — well, now, if I saw Grandma — and me older than she is — was — used to be — well, I don't know what it would do to me. You've got to let me get my breath. Well, of course, there's Uncle Frank — he'd be easier." He paused. "Is he here?" he said.

The reception clerk looked in a file. "I am happy to say that Mr. Francis V. Mellhorn arrived July 12, 1907," he said. He smiled winningly.

"Well!" said Doc Mellhorn. "Uncle Frank! Well, I'll be — well! But it must have been a great consolation to Mother. We heard — well, never mind what we heard — I guess it wasn't so. . . . No, don't reach for that phone just yet, or whatever it is. I'm still thinking."

"We sometimes find," said the reception clerk eagerly, "that a person not a relative may be the best introduction. Even a stranger sometimes — a distinguished stranger connected with one's own profession — "

"Well, now, that's an idea," said Doc Mellhorn heartily, trying to keep his mind off how much he disliked the reception clerk. He couldn't just say why he disliked him, but he knew he did.

It reminded him of the time he'd had to have his gall bladder out in the city hospital and the young, brisk interns had come to see him and called him "Doctor" every other word.

"Yes, that's an idea," he said. He reflected. "Well, of course, I'd like to see Koch," he said. "And Semmelweiss. Not to speak of Walter Reed. But, shucks, they'd be busy men. But there is one fellow – only he lived pretty far back – "

"Hippocrates, please," said the reception clerk into the telephone or whatever it was. "*H* for horse – "

"No!" said Doc Mellhorn quite violently. "Excuse me, but you just wait a minute. I mean if you can wait. I mean, if Hippocrates wants to come, I've no objection. But I never took much of a fancy to him, in spite of his oath. It's Aesculapius I'm thinking about. George W. Oh, glory!" he said. "But he won't talk English. I forgot."

"I shall be happy to act as interpreter," said the reception clerk, smiling brilliantly.

"I haven't a doubt," said Doc Mellhorn. "But just wait a shake." In a minute, by the way the clerk was acting, he was going to be talking to Aesculapius. "And what in time am I going to say to the man?" he thought. "It's too much." He gazed wildly around the neat reception room – distempered, as he noticed, in a warm shade of golden tan. Then his eyes fell on the worn black bag at his feet and a sudden warm wave of relief flooded over him.

"Wait a minute," he said, and his voice gathered force and authority. "Where's my patient?"

"Patient?" said the reception clerk, looking puzzled for the first time.

"Patient," said Doc Mellhorn. "*P* for phlebitis." He tapped his bag.

"I'm afraid you don't quite understand, sir," said the reception clerk.

"I understand this," said Doc Mellhorn. "I was

called here. And if I wasn't called professionally, why have I got my bag?"

"But, my dear Doctor Mellhorn — " said the reception clerk.

"I'm not your dear doctor," said Doc Mellhorn. "I was called here, I tell you. I'm sorry not to give you the patient's name, but the call must have come in my absence and the girl doesn't spell very well. But in any well-regulated hospital — "

"But I tell you," said the reception clerk, and his hair wasn't slick any more, "nobody's ill here. Nobody can be ill. If they could, it wouldn't be He — "

"Humph," said Doc Mellhorn. He thought it over, and felt worse. "Then what does a fellow like Koch do?" he said. "Or Pasteur?" He raised a hand. "Oh, don't tell me," he said. "I can see they'd be busy. Yes, I guess it'd be all right for a research man. But I never was . . . Oh, well, shucks, I've published a few papers. And there's that clamp of mine — always meant to do something about it. But they've got better ones now. Mean to say there isn't so much as a case of mumps in the whole place?"

"I assure you," said the reception clerk, in a weary voice. "And now, once you see Doctor Aesculapius — "

"Funny," said Doc Mellhorn. "Lord knows there's plenty of times you'd be glad to be quit of the whole thing. And don't talk to me about the healer's art or grateful patients. Well, I've known a few . . . a few. But I've known others. All the same, it's different, being told there isn't any need for what you can do."

"*A* for Ararát," said the reception clerk into his instrument. "*E* for Eden."

"Should think you'd have a dial," said Doc Mellhorn desperately. "We've got 'em down below." He thought hard and frantically. "Wait a shake. It's coming back to me," he said. "Got anybody named Grew here? Paisley Grew?"

"*S* for serpent . . ." said the reception clerk. "What was that?"

"Fellow that called me," said Doc Mellhorn. "G-r-e-w. First name, Paisley."

"I will consult the index," said the reception clerk.

He did so, and Doc Mellhorn waited, hoping against hope.

"We have 94,183 Grews, including 83 Prescotts and one Penobscot," the reception clerk said at last. "But I fail to find Paisley Grew. Are you quite sure of the name?"

"Of course," said Doc Mellhorn briskly. "Paisley Grew. Chronic indigestion. Might be appendix – can't say – have to see. But anyhow, he's called." He picked up his bag. "Well, thanks for the information," he said, liking the reception clerk better than he had yet. "Not your fault, anyway."

"But – but where are you going?" said the reception clerk.

"Well, there's another establishment, isn't there?" said Doc Mellhorn. "Always heard there was. Call probably came from there. Crossed wires, I expect."

"But you can't go there!" said the reception clerk. "I mean – "

"Can't go?" said Doc Mellhorn. "I'm a physician. A patient's called me."

"But if you'll only wait and see Aesculapius!" said the reception clerk, running his hands wildly through his hair. "He'll be here almost any moment."

"Please give him my apologies," said Doc Mellhorn. "He's a doctor. He'll understand. And if any messages come for me, just stick them on the spike. Do I need a road map? Noticed the road I came was all one way."

"There is, I believe, a back road in rather bad repair," said the reception clerk icily. "I can call Information if you wish."

"Oh, don't bother," said Doc Mellhorn. "I'll find it. And I never saw a road beat Lizzie yet." He took a silver half dollar from the doorknob of the door. "See that?" he said. "Slick as a whistle. Well, good-by, young man."

But it wasn't till he'd cranked up Lizzie and was on his way that Doc Mellhorn really felt safe. He found the back road and it was all the reception clerk had said it was and more. But he didn't mind — in fact, after one particularly bad rut, he grinned.

"I suppose I ought to have seen the folks," he said. "Yes, I know I ought. But — not so much as a case of mumps in the whole abiding dominion! Well, it's lucky I took a chance on Paisley Grew."

After another mile or so, he grinned again.

"And I'd like to see old Aesculapius' face. Probably rang him in the middle of dinner — they always do. But shucks, it's happened to all of us."

Well, the road got worse and worse and the sky

above it darker and darker, and what with one thing and another, Doc Mellhorn was glad enough when he got to the other gates. They were pretty impressive gates, too, though of course in a different way, and reminded Doc Mellhorn a little of the furnaces outside Steeltown, where he'd practiced for a year when he was young.

This time Doc Mellhorn wasn't going to take any advice from reception clerks and he had his story all ready. All the same, he wasn't either registered or expected, so there was a little fuss. Finally they tried to scare him by saying he came at his own risk and that there were some pretty tough characters about. But Doc Mellhorn remarked that he'd practiced in Steeltown. So, after he'd told them what seemed to him a million times that he was a physician on a case, they finally let him in and directed him to Paisley Grew. Paisley was on Level 346 in Pit 68,953, and Doc Mellhorn recognized him the minute he saw him. He even had the jew's-harp, stuck in the back of his overalls.

"Well, Doc," said Paisley finally, when the first greetings were over, "you certainly are a sight for sore eyes! Though, of course, I'm sorry to see you here," and he grinned.

"Well, I can't see that it's so different from a lot of places," said Doc Mellhorn, wiping his forehead. "Warmish, though."

"It's the humidity, really," said Paisley Grew. "That's what it really is."

"Yes, I know," said Doc Mellhorn. "And now tell me, Paisley; how's that indigestion of yours?"

"Well, I'll tell you, Doc," said Paisley. "When I first came here, I thought the climate was doing it good. I did for a fact. But now I'm not so sure. I've tried all sorts of things for it – I've even tried being transferred to the boiling asphalt lakes. But it just seems to hang on, and every now and then, when I least expect it, it catches me. Take last night. I didn't have a thing to eat that I don't generally eat – well, maybe I did have one little snort of hot sulphur, but it wasn't the sulphur that did it. All the same, I woke up at four, and it was just like a knife. Now . . ."

He went on from there and it took him some time. And Doc Mellhorn listened, happy as a clam. He never thought he'd be glad to listen to a hypochondriac, but he was. And when Paisley was all through, he examined him and prescribed for him. It was just a little soda bicarb and pepsin, but Paisley said it took hold something wonderful. And they had a fine time that evening, talking over the old days.

Finally, of course, the talk got around to how Paisley liked it where he was. And Paisley was honest enough about that.

"Well, Doc," he said, "of course this isn't the place for you, and I can see you're just visiting. But I haven't many real complaints. It's hot, to be sure, and they work you, and some of the boys here are rough. But they've had some pretty interesting experiences, too, when you get them talking – yes, sir. And anyhow, it isn't Peabodyville, New Jersey," he said with vehemence. "I spent five years in Peabodyville, trying to work up in the leather business. After that I bust out, and I guess that's what landed me here. But it's an improvement on Peabodyville." He looked at Doc Mellhorn sidewise. "Say, Doc," he said, "I know this is a vacation for you, but all the same there's a couple of the boys – nothing really wrong with them of course – but – well, if you could just look them over – "

"I was thinking the office hours would be nine to one," said Doc Mellhorn.

So Paisley took him around and they found a nice little place for an office in one of the abandoned mine galleries, and Doc Mellhorn hung out his shingle. And right away patients started coming around. They didn't get many doctors there, in the first place, and the ones they did get weren't exactly the cream of the profession, so Doc Mellhorn had it all to himself. It was mostly sprains, fractures, bruises and dislocations, of course, with occasional burns and scalds – and, on the whole, it reminded Doc Mellhorn a good deal of his practice in Steeltown, especially when it came to foreign bodies in the eye. Now and then Doc Mellhorn ran into a more unusual case – for instance, there was one of the guards that got part of himself pretty badly damaged in a rock slide. Well, Doc Mellhorn had never set a tail before, but he managed it all right, and got a beautiful primary union, too, in spite of the fact that he had no X-ray facilities. He thought of writing up the case for the State Medical Journal, but then he couldn't figure out any way to send it to them, so he had to let it slide. And then there was an advanced carcinoma of the liver – a Greek named Papadoupolous or Prometheus or something. Doc Mellhorn couldn't do much for him, considering the circumstances, but he did what he could, and he and the Greek used to have long conversations. The rest was just everyday practice — run of the mine — but he enjoyed it.

Now and then it would cross his mind that he ought to get out Lizzie and run back to the other place for a visit with the folks. But that was just like going back East had been on earth — he'd think he had everything pretty well cleared up, and then a new flock of patients would come in. And it wasn't that he didn't miss his wife and children and grandchildren — he did. But there wasn't any way to get back to them, and he knew it. And there was the work in front of him and the office crowded every day. So he just went along, hardly noticing the time.

Now and then, to be sure, he'd get a suspicion that he wasn't too popular with the authorities of the place. But he was used to not being popular with authorities and he didn't pay much attention. But finally they sent an inspector around. The minute Doc Mellhorn saw him, he knew there was going to be trouble.

Not that the inspector was uncivil. In fact, he was a pretty high-up official — you could tell by his antlers. And Doc Mellhorn was just as polite, showing him around. He showed him the free dispensary and the clinic and the nurse — Scotch girl named Smith, she was — and the dental chair he'd rigged up with the help of a fellow named Ferguson, who used to be an engineer before he was sentenced. And the inspector looked them all over, and finally he came back to Doc Mellhorn's office. The girl named Smith had put up curtains in the office, and with that and a couple of potted gas plants it looked more homelike than it had. The inspector looked around it and sighed.

"I'm sorry, Doctor Mellhorn," he said at last, "but you can see for yourself, it won't do."

"What won't do?" said Doc Mellhorn, stoutly. But, all the same, he felt afraid.

"Any of it," said the inspector. "We could overlook the alleviation of minor suffering – I'd be inclined to do so myself – though these people are here to suffer, and there's no changing that. But you're playing merry Hades with the whole system."

"I'm a physician in practice," said Doc Mellhorn.

"Yes," said the inspector. "That's just the trouble. Now, take these reports you've been sending," and he took out a sheaf of papers. "What have you to say about that?"

"Well, seeing as there's no county health officer, or at least I couldn't find one – " said Doc Mellhorn.

"Precisely," said the inspector. "And what have you done? You've condemned fourteen levels of this pit as unsanitary nuisances. You've recommended 2136 lost souls for special diet, remedial exercise, hospitalization – Well – I won't go through the list."

"I'll stand back of every one of those recommendations," said Doc Mellhorn. "And now we've got the chair working, we can handle most of the dental work on the spot. Only Ferguson needs more amalgam."

"I know," said the inspector patiently, "but the money has to come from somewhere – you must realize that. We're not a rich community, in spite of what people think. And these unauthorized requests — oh, we fill them, of course, but — "

"Ferguson needs more amalgam," said Doc Mellhorn. "And that last batch wasn't standard. I wouldn't use it on a dog."

"He's always needing more amalgam!" said the inspector bitterly, making a note. "Is he going to fill every tooth in Hades? By the way, my wife tells me I need a little work done myself — but we won't go into that. We'll take just one thing — your entirely unauthorized employment of Miss Smith. Miss Smith has no business working for you. She's supposed to be gnawed by a never-dying worm every Monday, Wednesday and Friday."

"Sounds silly to me," said Doc Mellhorn.

"I don't care how silly it sounds," said the inspector. "It's regulations. And, besides, she isn't even a registered nurse."

"She's a practical one," said Doc Mellhorn. "Of course, back on earth a lot of her patients died. But that was because when she didn't like a patient, she poisoned him. Well, she can't poison anybody here and I've kind of got her out of the notion of it anyway. She's been doing A-1 work for me and I'd like to recommend her for — "

"Please!" said the inspector. "Please! And as if that wasn't enough, you've even been meddling with the staff. I've a note here on young Asmodeus — Asmodeus XIV — "

"Oh, you mean Mickey!" said Doc Mellhorn, with a

chuckle. "Short for Mickey Mouse. We call him that in the clinic. And he's a young imp if I ever saw one."

"The original Asmodeus is one of our most prominent citizens," said the inspector severely. "How do you suppose he felt when we got your report that his fourteenth great-grandson had rickets?"

"Well," said Doc Mellhorn, "I know rickets. And he had 'em. And you're going to have rickets in these youngsters as long as you keep feeding 'em low-grade coke. I put Mickey on the best Pennsylvania anthracite, and look at him now!"

"I admit the success of your treatment," said the inspector, "but, naturally – well, since then we've been deluged with demands for anthracite from as far south as Sheol. We'll have to float a new bond issue. And what will the taxpayers say?"

"He was just cutting his first horns when he came to us," said Doc Mellhorn reminiscently, "and they were coming in crooked. Now, I ask you, did you ever see a straighter pair? Of course, if I'd had cod liver oil – My gracious, you ought to have somebody here that can fill a prescription; I can't do it all."

The inspector shut his papers together with a snap. "I'm sorry, Doctor Mellhorn," he said, "but this is final. You have no right here, in the first place; no local license to practice in the second – "

"Yes, that's a little irregular," said Doc Mellhorn, "but I'm a registered member of four different medical associations – you might take that into account. And I'll take any examination that's required."

"No," said the inspector violently. "No, no, no!

You can't stay here! You've got to go away! It isn't possible!"

Doc Mellhorn drew a long breath. "Well," he said, "there wasn't any work for me at the other place. And here you won't let me practice. So what's a man to do?"

The inspector was silent.

"Tell me," said Doc Mellhorn presently. "Suppose you do throw me out? What happens to Miss Smith and Paisley and the rest of them?"

"Oh, what's done is done," said the inspector impatiently, "here as well as anywhere else. We'll have to keep on with the anthracite and the rest of it. And Hades only knows what'll happen in the future. If it's any satisfaction to you, you've started something."

"Well, I guess Smith and Ferguson between them can handle the practice," said Doc Mellhorn. "But that's got to be a promise."

"It's a promise," said the inspector.

"Then there's Mickey – I mean Asmodeus," said Doc Mellhorn. "He's a smart youngster – smart as a whip – if he is a hellion. Well, you know how a youngster gets. Well, it seems he wants to be a doctor. But I don't know what sort of training he'd get – "

"He'll get it," said the inspector feverishly. "We'll found the finest medical college you ever saw, right here in West Baal. We'll build a hospital that'll knock your eye out. You'll be satisfied. But now, if you don't mind – "

"All right," said Doc Mellhorn, and rose.

The inspector looked surprised. "But don't you want to – " he said. "I mean my instructions are we're to give you a banquet, if necessary—after all, the community appreciates—"

"Thanks," said Doc Mellhorn, with a shudder, "but if I've got to go, I'd rather get out of town. You hang around and announce your retirement, and pretty soon folks start thinking they ought to give you a testimonial. And I never did like testimonials."

All the same, before he left he took a silver half dollar out of Mickey Asmodeus' chin.

When he was back on the road again and the lights of the gates had faded into a low ruddy glow behind him, Doc Mellhorn felt alone for the first time. He'd been lonely at times during his life, but he'd never felt alone like this before. Because, as far as he could see, there was only him and Lizzie now.

"Now, maybe if I'd talked to Aesculapius—" he said. "But pshaw, I always was pigheaded."

He didn't pay much attention to the way he was driving and it seemed to him that the road wasn't quite the same. But he felt tired for a wonder—bone-tired and beaten—and he didn't much care about the road. He hadn't felt tired since he left earth, but now the loneliness tired him.

"Active—always been active," he said to himself. "I can't just lay down on the job. But what's a man to do?"

"What's a man to do?" he said. "I'm a doctor. I can't work miracles."

Then the black fit came over him and he remembered all the times he'd been wrong and all the people he couldn't do anything for. "Never was much of a doctor, I guess," he said. "Maybe, if I'd gone to Vienna. Well, the right kind of man would have gone. And about that Bigelow kid," he said. "How was I to know he'd hemorrhage? But I should have known.

"I've diagnosed walking typhoid as appendicitis. Just the once, but that's enough. And I still don't know what held me back when I was all ready to operate. I used to wake up in a sweat, six months afterward, thinking I had.

"I could have saved those premature twins, if I'd known as much then as I do now. I guess that guy Dafoe would have done it anyway — look at what he had to work with. But I didn't. And that finished the Gorhams' having children. That's a dandy doctor, isn't it? Makes you feel fine.

"I could have pulled Old Man Halsey through. And Edna Biggs. And the little Lauriat girl. No, I couldn't have done it with her. That was before insulin. I couldn't have cured Ted Allen. No, I'm clear on that. But I've never been satisfied about the Collins woman. Bates is all right — good as they come. But I knew her, inside and out — ought to, too — she was the biggest nuisance that ever came into the office. And if I hadn't been down with the flu . . .

"Then there's the flu epidemic. I didn't take my clothes off, four days and nights. But what's the good of that, when you lose them? Oh, sure, the statistics looked good. You can have the statistics.

"Should have started raising hell about the water supply two years before I did.

"Oh, yes, it makes you feel fine, pulling babies into

the world. Makes you feel you're doing something. And just fine when you see a few of them, twenty-thirty years later, not worth two toots on a cow's horn. Can't say I ever delivered a Dillinger. But there's one or two in state's prison. And more that ought to be. Don't mind even that so much as a few of the fools. Makes you wonder.

"And then, there's incurable cancer. That's a daisy. What can you do about it, Doctor? Well, Doctor, we can alleviate the pain in the last stages. Some. Ever been in a cancer ward, Doctor? Yes, Doctor, I have.

"What do you do for the common cold, Doctor? Two dozen clean linen handkerchiefs. Yes, it's a good joke – I'll laugh. And what do you do for a boy when you know he's dying, Doctor? Take a silver half dollar out of his ear. But it kept the Lane kid quiet and his fever went down that night. I took the credit, but I don't know why it went down.

"I've only got one brain. And one pair of hands.

"I could have saved. I could have done. I could have.

"Guess it's just as well you can't live forever. You make fewer mistakes. And sometimes I'd see Bates looking at me as if he wondered why I ever thought I could practice.

"Pigheaded, opinionated, ineffective old imbecile! And yet, Lord, Lord, I'd do it all over again."

He lifted his eyes from the pattern of the road in front of him. There were white markers on it now and Lizzie seemed to be bouncing down a residential street. There were trees in the street and it reminded him of town. He rubbed his eyes for a second and Lizzie rolled on by herself – she often did. It didn't seem strange to him to stop at the right house.

"Well, Mother," he said rather gruffly to the group on the lawn. "Well, Dad. . . . Well, Uncle Frank." He beheld a small, stern figure advancing, hands outstretched. "Well, Grandma," he said meekly.

Later on he was walking up and down in the grape arbor with Uncle Frank. Now and then he picked a grape and ate it. They'd always been good grapes, those Catawbas, as he remembered them.

"What beats me," he said, not for the first time, "is why I didn't notice the Gates. The second time, I mean."

"Oh, that Gate," said Uncle Frank, with the easy, unctuous roll in his voice that Doc Mellhorn so well remembered. He smoothed his handle-bar mustaches. "That Gate, my dear Edward – well, of course it has to be there in the first place. Literature, you know. And then, it's a choice," he said richly.

"I'll draw cards," said Doc Mellhorn. He ate another grape.

"Fact is," said Uncle Frank, "that Gate's for one kind of person. You pass it and then you can rest for all eternity. Just fold your hands. It suits some."

"I can see that it would," said Doc Mellhorn.

"Yes," said Uncle Frank, "but it wouldn't suit a Mellhorn. I'm happy to say that very few of our family remain permanently on that side. I spent some time there myself." He said, rather self-consciously, "Well, my last years had been somewhat stormy. So few people cared for refined impersonations of our feathered songsters, including lightning sketches. I felt that I'd earned a rest. But after a while – well, I got tired of being at liberty."

"And what happens when you get tired?" said Doc Mellhorn.

"You find out what you want to do," said Uncle Frank.

"My kind of work?" said Doc Mellhorn.

"Your kind of work," said his uncle. "Been busy, haven't you?"

"Well," said Doc Mellhorn. "But here. If there isn't so much as a case of mumps in – "

"Would it have to be mumps?" said his uncle. "Of course, if you're aching for mumps, I guess it could be arranged. But how many new souls do you suppose we get here a day?"

"Sizable lot, I expect."

"And how many of them get here in first-class condition?" said Uncle Frank triumphantly. "Why, I've seen Doctor Rush – Benjamin Rush – come back so tired from a day's round he could hardly flap one pinion against the other. Oh, if it's work you want – And then, of course, there's the earth."

"Hold on," said Doc Mellhorn. "I'm not going to appear to any young intern in wings and a harp. Not at my time of life. And anyway, he'd laugh himself sick."

" 'Tain't that," said Uncle Frank. "Look here. You've left children and grandchildren behind you, haven't you? And they're going on?"

"Yes," said Doc Mellhorn.

"Same with what you did," said Uncle Frank. "I mean the inside part of it — that stays. I don't mean any funny business — voices in your ear and all that. But haven't you ever got clean tuckered out, and been able to draw on something you didn't know was there?"

"Pshaw, any man's done that," said Doc Mellhorn. "But you take the adrenal — "

"Take anything you like," said Uncle Frank placidly. "I'm not going to argue with you. Not my department. But you'll find it isn't all adrenalin. Like it here?" he said abruptly. "Feel satisfied?"

"Why, yes," said Doc Mellhorn surprisedly, "I do." He looked around the grape arbor and suddenly realized that he felt happy.

"No, they wouldn't all arrive in first-class shape," he said to himself. "So there'd be a place." He turned to Uncle Frank. "By the way," he said diffidently, "I mean, I got back so quick — there wouldn't be a chance of my visiting the other establishment now and then? Where I just came from? Smith and Ferguson are all right, but I'd like to keep in touch."

"Well," said Uncle Frank, "you can take that up with the delegation." He arranged the handkerchief in his breast pocket. "They ought to be along any minute now," he said. "Sister's been in a stew about it all day. She says there won't be enough chairs, but she always says that."

"Delegation?" said Doc Mellhorn. "But — "

"You don't realize," said Uncle Frank, with his rich chuckle. "You're a famous man. You've broken pretty near every regulation except the fire laws, and refused the Gate first crack. They've got to do something about it."

"But — " said Doc Mellhorn, looking wildly around for a place of escape.

"Sh-h!" hissed Uncle Frank. "Hold up your head and look as though money were bid for you. It won't take long — just a welcome." He shaded his eyes with his hand. "My," he said with frank admiration, "you've certainly brought them out. There's Rush, by the way."

"Where?" said Doc Mellhorn.

"Second from the left, third row, in a wig," said Uncle Frank. "And there's — "

Then he stopped, and stepped aside. A tall grave figure was advancing down the grape arbor — a bearded man with a wise, majestic face who wore robes as if they belonged to him, not as Doc Mellhorn had seen them worn in college commencements. There was a small fillet of gold about his head and in his left hand, Doc Mellhorn noticed without astonishment, was a winged staff entwined with two fangless serpents. Behind him were many others. Doc Mellhorn stood straighter.

The bearded figure stopped in front of Doc Mellhorn. "Welcome, Brother," said Aesculapius.

"It's an honor to meet you, Doctor," said Doc Mellhorn. He shook the outstretched hand. Then he took a silver half dollar from the mouth of the left-hand snake.

III

THE STORY ABOUT THE ANTEATER

THE younger child sat bolt upright, her bedclothes wrapped around her.

"If you're going down to look at them," she whispered accusingly, "I'm coming, too! And Alice'll catch you."

"She won't catch me." Her elder sister's voice was scornful. "She's out in the pantry, helping. With the man from Gray's."

"All the same, I'm coming. I want to see if it's ice cream in little molds or just the smashed kind with strawberries. And, if Alice won't catch you, she won't catch me."

"It'll be molds," said the other, from the depths of experience, "Mother always has molds for the Whitehouses. And Mr. Whitehouse sort of clicks in his throat and talks about sweets to the sweet. You'd think he'd know that's dopey but he doesn't. And, anyhow, it isn't your turn."

"It never is my turn," mourned her junior, tugging at the bedclothes.

"All right," said the elder. "If you *want* to go! And make a noise. And then they hear us and somebody comes up — "

"Sometimes they bring you things, when they come

up," said the younger dreamily. "The man with the pink face did. And he said I was a little angel."

"Was he dopey!" said her elder, blightingly, "and anyhow, you were sick afterwards and you know what Mother said about it."

The younger child sighed, a long sigh of defeat and resignation.

"All right," she said. "But next time it *is* my turn. And you tell me if it's in molds." Her elder nodded as she stole out of the door.

At the first turn of the stairs, a small landing offered an excellent observation post, provided one could get there unperceived. Jennifer Sharp reached it soundlessly and, curling herself up into the smallest possible space, stared eagerly down and across into the dining room.

She couldn't see the whole table. But she saw at once that Mrs. Whitehouse had a thing like a silver beetle in her hair, that Colonel Crandall looked more like a police dog than ever, and that there were little silver baskets of pink and white mints. That meant that it was really a grand dinner. She made a special note of the ice cream for Joan.

Talk and laughter drifted up to her — strange phrases and incomprehensible jests from another world, to be remembered, puzzled over, and analyzed for meaning or the lack of it, when she and Joan were alone. She hugged her knees, she was having a good time. Pretty soon, Father would light the little blue flame under the mysterious glass machine that made the coffee. She liked to see him do that.

She looked at him now, appraisingly. Colonel Crandall had fought Germans in trenches and Mr. Whitehouse had a bank to keep his money in. But Father, on the whole, was nicer than either of them. She remembered, as if looking back across a vast plain, when Father and Mother had merely been Father and Mother — huge, natural phenomena, beloved but inexplicable as the weather — unique of their kind. Now she was older — she knew that other people's fathers and mothers were different. Even Joan knew that, though Joan was still a great deal of a baby. Jennifer felt very old and rather benevolent as she considered herself and her parents and the babyishness of Joan.

Mr. Whitehouse was talking, but Father wanted to talk, too — she knew that from the quick little gesture he made with his left hand. Now they all laughed and Father leaned forward.

"That reminds me," he was saying, "of one of our favorite stories — " How young and amused his face looked, suddenly!

His eldest daughter settled back in the shadow, a bored but tolerant smile on her lips. She knew what was coming.

When Terry Farrell and Roger Sharp fell in love, the war to end war was just over, bobbed hair was still an issue, the movies did not talk and women's clothes couldn't be crazier. It was also generally admitted that the younger generation was wild but probably sound at heart and that, as soon as we got a businessman in the White House, things were going to be all right.

As for Terry and Roger, they were both wild and sophisticated. They would have told you so. Terry had been kissed by several men at several dances and Roger could remember the curious, grimy incident of the girl at Fort Worth. So that showed you. They were entirely emancipated and free. But they fell in love very simply and unexpectedly — and their marriage was going to be like no other marriage, because they knew all the right answers to all the questions, and had no intention of submitting to the commonplaces of life. At first, in fact, they were going to form a free union — they had read of that, in popular books of the period. But, somehow or other, as soon as Roger started to call, both families began to get interested. They had no idea of paying the slightest attention to their families. But, when your family happens to comment favorably on the man or girl that you are in love with, that is a hard thing to fight. Before they knew it, they were formally engaged, and liking it on the whole, though both of them agreed that a formal engagement was an outworn and ridiculous social custom.

They quarreled often enough, for they were young, and a trifle ferocious in the vehemence with which they expressed the views they knew to be right. These views had to do, in general, with freedom and personality, and were often supported by quotations from *The Golden Bough*. Neither of them had read *The Golden Bough* all the way through, but both agreed that it was a great book. But the quarrels were about generalities and had no sting. And always, before and after, was the sense of discovering in each other previously unsuspected but delightful potentialities and likenesses and beliefs.

As a matter of fact, they were quite a well-suited couple – "made for each other," as the saying used to go; though they would have hooted at the idea. They had read the minor works of Havelock Ellis and knew the name of Freud. They didn't believe in people being "made for each other" – they were too advanced.

It was ten days before the date set for their marriage that their first real quarrel occurred. And then, unfortunately, it didn't stop at generalities.

They had got away for the day from the presents and their families, to take a long walk in the country, with a picnic lunch. Both, in spite of themselves, were a little solemn, a little nervous. The atmosphere of Approaching Wedding weighed on them both – when their hands touched, the current ran, but, when they looked at each other, they felt strange. Terry had been shopping the day before – she was tired, she began to wish that Roger would not walk so fast. Roger was wondering if the sixth usher – the one who had been in the marines – would really turn up. His mind also held dark suspicions as to the probable behavior of the best man, when it came to such outworn customs as rice and shoes. They were sure that they were in love, sure now, that they wanted to be married. But their conversation was curiously polite.

The lunch did something for them, so did the peace of being alone. But they had forgotten the salt and Terry had rubbed her heel. When Roger got out his pipe, there was only tobacco left for half a smoke. Still, the wind was cool and the earth pleasant and, as they sat with their backs against a gray boulder in the middle of a green field, they began to think more naturally. The current between their linked hands ran stronger — in a moment or two, they would be the selves they had always known.

It was, perhaps, unfortunate that Roger should have selected that particular moment in which to tell the anteater story.

He knocked out his pipe and smiled, suddenly, at something in his mind. Terry felt a knock at her heart, a sudden sweetness on her tongue — how young and amused he always looked when he smiled! She smiled back at him, her whole face changing.

"What is it, darling?" she said.

He laughed. "Oh nothing," he said. "I just happened to remember. Did you ever hear the story about the anteater?"

She shook her head.

"Well," he began. "Oh, you must have heard it — sure you haven't? Well, anyway, there was a little town down South . . .

"And the coon said, 'Why, lady, that ain't no anteater — that's Edward!' " he finished, triumphantly, a few moments later. He couldn't help laughing when he had finished — the silly tale always amused him, old as it was. Then he looked at Terry and saw that she was not laughing.

"Why, what's the matter?" he said, mechanically. "Are you cold, dear, or — "

Her hand, which had been slowly stiffening in his clasp, now withdrew itself entirely from his.

"No" she said, staring ahead of her, "I'm all right. Thanks."

He looked at her. There was somebody there he had never seen before.

"Well," he said, confusedly, "well." Then his mouth set, his jaw stuck out, he also regarded the landscape.

Terry stole a glance at him. It was terrible and appalling to see him sitting there, looking bleak and estranged. She wanted to speak, to throw herself at him, to say: "Oh, it's all my fault—it's all my fault!" and know the luxury of saying it. Then she remembered the anteater and her heart hardened.

It was not even, she told herself sternly, as if it were a dirty story. It wasn't—and, if it had been, weren't they always going to be frank and emancipated with each other about things like that? But it was just the kind of story she'd always hated—cruel and—yes—vulgar. Not even healthily vulgar—vulgar with no redeeming adjective. He ought to have known she hated that kind of story. He ought to have known!

If love meant anything, according to the books, it meant understanding the other person, didn't it? And, if you didn't understand them, in such a little thing, why, what was life going to be afterwards? Love was like a new silver dollar—bright, untarnished and whole. There could be no possible compromises with love.

All these confused but vehement thoughts flashed through her mind. She also knew that she was tired and wind-blown and jumpy and that the rub on her heel was a little red spot of pain. And then Roger was speaking.

"I'm sorry you found my story so unamusing," he said in stiff tones of injury and accusation. "If I'd known about the way you felt, I'd have tried to tell a funnier one – even if we did say –"

He stopped, his frozen face turned toward her. She could feel the muscles of her own face tighten and freeze in answer.

"I wasn't in the *least* shocked, I assure you," she said in the same, stilted voice. "I just didn't think it was very funny. That's all."

"I get you. Well, pardon my glove," he said, and turned to the landscape.

A little pulse of anger began to beat in her wrist. Something was being hurt, something was being broken. If he'd only been Roger and kissed her instead of saying – well, it was his fault, now.

"No, I didn't think it was funny at all," she said, in a voice whose sharpness surprised her, "if you want to know. Just sort of cruel and common and – well, the poor Negro – "

"That's right!" he said, in a voice of bitter irritation, "pity the coon! Pity everybody but the person who's trying to amuse you! I think it's a damn funny story – always have – and – "

They were both on their feet and stabbing at each other, now.

"And it's vulgar," she was saying, hotly, "plain vulgar – not even dirty enough to be funny. Anteater indeed! Why, Roger Sharp, it's – "

"Where's that sense of humor you were always talking about?" he was shouting. "My God, what's happened to you, Terry? I always thought you were – and here you – "

"Well, we both of us certainly seem to have been mistaken about each other," she could hear her strange voice, saying. Then, even more dreadfully, came his unfamiliar accents, "Well, if that's the way you feel about it, we certainly have."

They looked at each other, aghast. "Here!" she was saying, "here! Oh, Lord, why won't it come off my finger?"

"You keep that on – do you hear, you damn little fool?" he roared at her, so unexpectedly that she started, tripped, caught her shoe in a cleft of rock, fell awkwardly, and, in spite of all her resolves, burst undignifiedly and conventionally into a passion of tears.

Then there was the reconciliation. It took place, no doubt, on entirely conventional lines, and was studded with "No, it was my fault! Say it was!" but, to them it was an event unique in history.

Terry thought it over remorsefully, that evening, waiting for Roger. Roger was right. She had been a little fool. She knew the inexplicable solace of feeling that she had been a little fool.

And yet, they had said those things to each other, and meant them. He had hurt her, she had actually meant to hurt him. She stared at these facts, solemnly.

Love, the bright silver dollar. Not like the commonplace coins in other people's pockets. But something special, different — already a little, ever-so-faintly tarnished, as a pane is tarnished by breath?

She had been a little fool. But she couldn't quite forget the anteater.

Then she was in Roger's arms — and knew, with utter confidence, that she and Roger were different. They were always going to be different. Their marriage wouldn't ever be like any other marriage in the world.

The Sharps had been married for exactly six years and five hours and Terry, looking across the table at the clever, intelligent face of her affectionate and satisfactory husband, suddenly found herself most desolately alone.

It had been a mistake in the first place — going to the Lattimores for dinner on their own anniversary. Mr. Lattimore was the head of Roger's company — Mrs. Lattimore's invitation had almost the force of a royal command. They had talked it over, Roger and she, and decided, sensibly, that they couldn't get out of it. But, all the same, it had been a mistake.

They were rational, modern human beings, she assured herself ferociously. They weren't like the horrible married couples in the cartoons — the little woman asking her baffled mate if he remembered what date it was, and the rest of it. They thought better of life and love than to tie either of them to an artificial scheme of days. They were different. Nevertheless, there had been a time when they had said to each other, with foolish smiles, "We've been married a week – or a month – or a year! Just think of it!" This time now seemed to her, as she looked back on it coldly, a geologic age away.

She considered Roger with odd dispassionateness. Yes, there he was – an intelligent, rising young man in his first thirties. Not particularly handsome but indubitably attractive – charming, when he chose – a loyal friend, a good father, a husband one could take pride in. And it seemed to her that if he made that nervous little gesture with his left hand again – or told the anteater story – she would scream.

It was funny that the knowledge that you had lost everything that you had most counted upon should come to you at a formal dinner party, while you talked over the war days with a dark-haired officer whose voice had the honey of the South in it. Then she remembered that she and Roger had first discovered their love for each other, not upon a moon-swept lawn, but in the fly-specked waiting room of a minor railroad station – and the present event began to seem less funny. Life was like that. It gave, unexpectedly, abruptly, with no regard for stage setting or the properties of romance. And, as unexpectedly and abruptly, it took away.

While her mouth went on talking, a part of her mind searched numbly and painfully for the reasons which had brought this calamity about. They had loved each other in the beginning – even now, she was sure of that. They had tried to be wise, they had not broken faith, they had been frank and gay. No deep division of nature sundered them – no innate fault in either, spreading under pressure, to break the walls of their house apart. She looked for a guilty party but she could find none. There was only a progression of days; a succession of tiny events that followed in each others' footsteps without haste or rest. That was all, but that seemed to have been enough. And Roger was looking over at her – with that same odd, exploring glance she had used a moment ago.

What remained? A house with a little boy asleep in it, a custom of life, certain habits, certain memories, certain hardships lived through together. Enough for most people, perhaps? They had wanted more than that.

Something said to her, "Well and if – after all – the real thing hasn't even come?" She turned to her dinner partner, for the first time really seeing him. When you did see him, he was quite a charming person. His voice was delightful. There was nothing in him in the least like Roger Sharp.

She laughed and saw, at the laugh, something wake in his eyes. He, too, had not been really conscious of her, before. But he was, now. She was not thirty, yet – she had kept her looks. She felt old powers, old states of mind flow back to her; things she had thought forgotten, the glamor of first youth. Somewhere, on the curve of a dark lake, a boat was drifting – a man was talking to her – she could not see his face but she knew it was not Roger's –

She was roused from her waking dream by Mrs. Lattimore's voice.

"Why, I'd never have dreamt!" Mrs. Lattimore was saying "I had no idea!" She called down the table,

"George! Do you know it's these people's anniversary — so sweet of them to come — and I positively had to worm it out of Mr. Sharp!"

Terry went hot and cold all over. She was sensible, she was brokenhearted, love was a myth, but she had particularly depended on Roger not to tell anybody that this was their anniversary. And Roger had told.

She lived through the congratulations and the customary jokes about "Well, this is your seventh year beginning — and you know what they say about the seventh year!" She even lived through Mrs. Lattimore's pensive "Six years! Why, my dear, I never would have believed it! You're children — positive children!"

She could have bitten Mrs. Lattimore. "Children!" she thought, indignantly, "When I — when we — when everything's in ruins!" She tried to freeze Roger, at long distance, but he was not looking her way. And then she caught her breath, for a worse fate was in store for her.

Someone, most unhappily, had brought up the subject of pet animals. She saw a light break slowly on Roger's face — she saw him lean forward. She prayed for the roof to fall, for time to stop, for Mrs. Lattimore to explode like a Roman candle into green and purple stars. But, even as she prayed, she knew that it was no use. Roger was going to tell the anteater story.

The story no longer seemed shocking to her, or even cruel. But it epitomized all the years of her life with Roger. In the course of those years, she calculated desperately, she had heard that story at least a hundred times.

Somehow — she never knew how — she managed to

survive the hundred-and-first recital, from the hideously familiar, "Well, there was a little town down South . . ." to the jubilant "That's Edward!" at the end. She even summoned up a fixed smile to meet the tempest of laughter that followed. And then, mercifully, Mrs. Lattimore was giving the signal to rise.

The men hung behind – the anteater story had been capped by another. Terry found herself, unexpectedly, tête-à-tête with Mrs. Lattimore.

"My dear," the great lady was saying, "I'd rather have asked you another night, of course, if I'd known. But I am very glad you could come tonight. George particularly wished Mr. Colden to meet your brilliant husband. They are going into that Western project together, you know, and Tom Colden leaves tomorrow. So we both appreciate your kindness in coming."

Terry found a sudden queer pulse of warmth through the cold fog that seemed to envelop her. "Oh," she stammered, "but Roger and I have been married for years – and we were delighted to come – " She looked at the older woman. "Tell me, though," she said, with an irrepressible burst of confidence, "doesn't it ever seem to you as if you couldn't bear to hear a certain story again – not if you *died?*"

A gleam of mirth appeared in Mrs. Lattimore's eyes.

"My dear," she said "has George ever told you about his trip to Peru?"

"No."

"Well, don't let him." She reflected, "or, no – do let him," she said. "Poor George – he does get such fun out of it. And you would be a new audience. But it happened fifteen years ago, my dear, and I think I could repeat every word after him verbatim, once he's started. Even so – I often feel as if he'd never stop."

"And then what do you do?" said Terry, breathlessly – far too interested now to remember tact.

The older woman smiled. "I think of the story I am going to tell about the guide in the Uffizi gallery," she said. "George must have heard that story ten thousand times. But he's still alive."

She put her hand on the younger woman's arm.

"We're all of us alike, my dear," she said. "When I'm an old lady in a wheel chair, George will still be telling me about Peru. But then, if he didn't, I wouldn't know he was George."

She turned away, leaving Terry to ponder over the words. Her anger was not appeased – her life still lay about her in ruins. But, when the dark young officer came into the room, she noticed that his face seemed rather commonplace and his voice was merely a pleasant voice.

Mr. Colden's car dropped the Sharps at their house. The two men stayed at the gate for a moment, talking – Terry ran in to see after the boy. He was sleeping peacefully with his fists tight shut; he looked like Roger in his sleep. Suddenly, all around her were the familiar sights and sounds of home. She felt tired and as if she had come back from a long journey.

She went downstairs. Roger was just coming in. He looked tired, too, she noticed, but exultant as well.

"Colden had to run," he said at once. "Left good-by

for you – hoped you wouldn't mind – said awfully nice things. He's really a great old boy, Terry. And, as for this new Western business – "

He noticed the grave look on her face and his own grew grave.

"I *am* sorry, darling," he said. "Did you mind it a lot? Well, I did – but it couldn't be helped. You bet your life that next time – "

"Oh, next time – " she said, and kissed him. "Of course I didn't mind. We're different, aren't we?"

That intelligent matron, Mrs. Roger Sharp, now seated at the foot of her own dinner table, from time to time made the appropriate interjections – the "Really?"s and "Yes indeed"s and "That's what I always tell Roger"s – which comprised the whole duty of a hostess in Colonel Crandall's case. Colonel Crandall was singularly restful – give him these few crumbs and he could be depended upon to talk indefinitely and yet without creating a conversational desert around him. Mrs. Sharp was very grateful to him at the moment. She wanted to retire to a secret place in her mind and observe her own dinner party, for an instant, as a spectator – and Colonel Crandall was giving her the chance.

It was going very well indeed. She had hoped for it from the first, but now she was sure of it and she gave a tiny, inaudible sigh of relief. Roger was at his best – the young Durwards had recovered from their initial shyness – Mr. Whitehouse had not yet started talking politics – the soufflé had been a success. She relaxed a little and let her mind drift off upon other things.

Tomorrow, Roger must remember about the light gray suit, she must make a dental appointment for Jennifer, Mrs. Quaritch must be dealt with tactfully in the matter of the committee. It was too early to decide about camp for the girls but Roger Junior must know they were proud of his marks, and if Mother intended to give up her trip just because of poor old Miss Tompkins – well, something would have to be done. There were also the questions of the new oil furnace, the School board and the Brewster wedding. But none of these really bothered her – her life was always busy – and, at the moment, she felt an unwonted desire to look back into Time.

Over twenty years since the Armistice. Twenty years. And Roger Junior was seventeen – and she and Roger had been married since nineteen-twenty. Pretty soon they would be celebrating their twentieth anniversary. It seemed incredible but it was true.

She looked back through those years, seeing an ever-younger creature with her own face, a creature that laughed or wept for forgotten reasons, ran wildly here, sat solemn as a young judge there. She felt a pang of sympathy for that young heedlessness, a pang of humor as well. She was not old but she had been so very young.

Roger and she – the beginning – the first years – Roger Junior's birth. The house on Edgehill Road, the one with the plate rail in the dining room, and crying when they left because they'd never be so happy again, but they had, and it was an inconvenient house. Being jealous of Milly Baldwin – and how foolish! – and the awful country-club dance where Roger got drunk; and it wasn't awful any more. The queer, piled years of the boom — the crash — the bad time — Roger coming home after Tom Colden's suicide and the look on his face. Jennifer. Joan. Houses. People. Events. And always the headlines in the papers, the voices on the radio, dinning, dinning "No security — trouble —disaster — no security." And yet, out of insecurity, they had loved and made children. Out of insecurity, for the space of breath, for an hour, they had built, and now and then found peace.

No, there's no guarantee, she thought. There's no guarantee. When you're young, you think there is, but there isn't. And yet I'd do it over. Pretty soon we'll have been married twenty years.

"Yes, that's what I always tell Roger," she said, automatically. Colonel Crandall smiled and proceeded. He was still quite handsome, she thought, in his dark way, but he was getting very bald. Roger's hair had a few gray threads in it but it was still thick and unruly. She liked men to keep their hair. She remembered, a long while ago, thinking something or other about Colonel Crandall's voice, but she could not remember what she had thought.

She noticed a small white speck on the curve of the stairway but said nothing. The wrapper was warm and, if Jennifer wasn't noticed, she would creep back to bed soon enough. It was different with Joan.

Suddenly, she was alert. Mrs. Durward, at Roger's end of the table, had mentioned the Zoo. She knew what that meant — Zoo — the new buildings — the new Housing Commissioner — and Mr. Whitehouse let loose on his favorite political grievance all through the end of dinner. She caught Roger's eye for a miraculous instant. Mr. Whitehouse was already clearing his throat. But Roger had the signal. Roger would save them. She saw his left hand tapping in its little gesture – felt him suddenly draw the party together. How young and amused his face looked, under the candlelight!

"That reminds me of one of our favorite stories," he was saying. She sank back in her chair. A deep content pervaded her. He was going to tell the anteater story – and, even if some of the people had heard it, they would have to laugh, he always told it so well. She smiled in anticipation of the triumphant "That's Edward!" And, after that, if Mr. Whitehouse still threatened, she herself would tell the story about Joan and the watering pot.

Jennifer crept back into the darkened room.

"Well?" said an eager whisper from the other bed.

Jennifer drew a long breath. The memory of the lighted dinner table rose before her, varicolored, glittering, portentous – a stately omen – a thing of splendor and mystery, to be pondered upon for days. How could she ever make Joan see it as she had seen it? And Joan was such a baby, anyway.

"Oh – nobody saw me," she said, in a bored voice. "But it was in molds, that's all – oh yes – and Father told the anteater story again."

A LIFE AT ANGELO'S

I DON'T know why everybody keeps on going to Angelo's. The drinks aren't any better – in fact, they're a little worse, if anything – and the dinner never was much. I'm getting so I can hardly look a sardine in the eye any more.

Of course it's a quiet place, and they don't let in many college boys. It's generally just the old crowd from five o'clock on. Oh, people come and go naturally – the way they do in New York. If they didn't, I don't suppose Angelo could keep on running. But what I mean is, you can drop in almost any time after curfew and find somebody you know to have a quick one or a couple of quick ones with. And then, if that's your weakness, you can stay and get dinner; though I wish they'd try another brand of sardines.

Suppose everyone stopped coming, all at once? Or suppose the place closed? I don't like to think about that. I suppose it's bound to happen, sooner or later, when Angelo's made his pile – they always go back to Italy. Then there'll be all the trouble and bother of finding another place; and the crowd won't be the same. You can't keep a crowd together, once you move the place, in New York. It seems pretty safe, though, at the moment, I'm glad to say. There's never been any real trouble, you see; no one ever gets shot at Angelo's, and when the visiting firemen get too noisy, Rocco just eases them out. Rocco's the little one with the grin, and he doesn't look strong, but how he can ease a fellow out when it's necessary! He did it to me only once, and I've never held it against him. That was just after Evie and I had broken up.

No, I don't think there's any need to worry for a while yet. And when there is, I'm sure Angelo will tell me about it far enough ahead so I can make my arrangements. After all, I'm one of his oldest customers. I don't go back to the Twelfth Street place, the way Mr. Forman does, but seven years is a long time in this man's town. They're easing Mr. Forman out at 11:30 these days. It used to be all hours when I first knew him, but a man can't expect to drink like that at his age and not show it in the whites of the eyes. That's another thing I have against all this changing around. You get started going from one place to another and buying taxis and going in for general snake dancing; and before you know where you are you're on a party, and the whole next day is bad. Well, now, if you work at all, you can't afford to have the week days go bad on you. I'm not talking of Saturday night – there's a law about that. And of course those impromptu harvest homes are a lot of fun when you're young and new to the town. But when you've had a little sense knocked into you you're a fool if you don't run on schedule. Isn't that so?

Now, at Angelo's, you always know where you are. A couple of quick ones or so before dinner, and the red at dinner – or the white, if you're dining with a girl. Then a little touch after the coffee and a couple of long ones and a nightcap, and home at twelve by the old college clock. And all the time you're talking with somebody you know – about their wives, or their husbands, or religion, or the market, or what's new in the crowd – just rational conversation and maybe a little quiet singing, like "Work is the Curse of the Drinking Classes." Sometimes Mr. Forman sits down and tells one of his long stories, but generally he'd rather stand at the bar. And sometimes the whole crowd clicks, and sometimes it doesn't, and sometimes that Page girl gets started on her imitations.

But anyway, it's something you're used to, and you're doing it again, and it's warm, and you know the people, and you don't have to go home. And Angelo's there, getting a little fatter and sleeker every year, and with a little bigger white edge around his waistcoat. Now and then he'll set up some *strega* for you, if he's feeling right. I don't like *strega* myself, but it would hurt his feelings to refuse. And then, in summer, there's the little back garden, and the fat cat that always has kittens, and the pink shades on the lamps. Rocco will be telling you the fish is ver' fine – and you know it isn't, but who cares? – and you can sit and watch the lights in the skyscrapers and hear the roar of the town, going by outside. You don't have to think at all. It's restful that way.

I can remember when I used to think a lot. And wonder about the people who came to places like Angelo's, and who they were, and why they came, and what they did with the rest of their time. I used to make up stories about them, going back to the apartment with Evie, and we'd both get excited over them; and forget to turn off at our own corner, we were talking so hard. That was when everybody we met was brand-new and bound to be interesting, and it was fun going to shows together in the gallery and having pancakes afterward at Childs'. I was always going to write some of those stories down, and she helped me make notes of them. I found the start of the one about Mr. Forman the other day. Well, what was the percentage in keeping it? I've seen a good deal of this writing racket since; and I ought to know what will sell and what won't. And anyhow, I'd just made him an old soak, and he's really a pretty interesting man.

Besides, that's something you get over. Wondering, I mean. Once you're on a normal schedule, you don't have time. I used to think it was funny – meeting people the way you do and having them tell you all sorts of inside things, the way it happens, and yet not really knowing them or tying them up with anything outside. But that's stopped bothering me. You just have to let them come and go, or it breaks the charm.

Going home to dinner with Jim Hewitt was what cured me, finally. I never met a fellow I liked better at Angelo's, and we told our real names. So, when he suggested breaking the family bread one evening, I took him up. Good Lord, he lived at Scarsdale and they had three children! The baby was sounding off like a police siren as we came in, and we had one round of weak orange blossoms before the fodder. Mrs. Hewitt liked orange blossoms. Then, afterward, we sat around and played three-handed bridge and Mrs. Hewitt and Jim discussed the squeak in the car. I couldn't have stayed all night; I'd have had the mimies. Jim was sort of ritzy for a while after that, but he got all right again, finally. I guess they must have hitched up the sled dogs and moved north to White Plains or something, for I haven't seen him in I don't now how long.

Of course, now and then something comes along that you have to take notice of. People get married or divorced, and Angelo will always open a bottle of champagne, no matter which it is, if they're really old customers. I remember the party the crowd of us gave to cheer up Helen Ashland when she heard about Jake's remarriage. She certainly took it like a sport – we were thinking up funny telegrams to send the bridal couple all evening. I don't believe she really had hysterics either. That was just Bing Otis' idea. And she couldn't have meant it when she said she hated us – she'd always been the life of the crowd. Anyhow, I think she got married again last year – somebody was broadcasting about it. If she ever comes back to Angelo's, I'll have to get the low-down.

That's another thing about the crowd – the way they stick together when anything happens. I'll never forget the night Ted Harrison went out. Of course, he'd been going into reverse for quite a while, and whenever he got particularly sunk, he'd talk about doing a one-way jump through a window; but we knew Ted and just kidded him along. So when he did do it, after all, it was mean. Anyhow, he had the sense not to stage his act at Angelo's.

We went to the service afterward – those of us that could. That's what I mean by all of us sticking together. It was one of those gray winter days, and cold. There was a little boy, and he was crying. I don't see why they brought him there. I didn't know Ted had a boy. I know the rest of Ted's family sort of upstaged us. But we felt we ought to be there; though it was funny how little you could remember about Ted except parties. Well, there isn't much to those services, the way I look at it. But then we went back to Angelo's and he was fine.

Evie never took to Angelo's somehow, even at first. She felt she had to like the dinner, because it was cheap, but the atmosphere of the place never really appealed to her. She liked going to places where there was music or where somebody famous might be sitting at the next table. Of course, it was generally an out-of-town buyer or a cloak model, really, but she got just as big a kick out of pretending. We used to have dinner home a lot, too, that first year. It's wonderful how much food you can get for the money, living like that. Though, of course, it's really cheaper for me to eat at Angelo's, now I'm alone.

I've thought sometimes of getting a regular maid or one of those Japs who just come in and get dinner and clear away. There'd be money enough, for Evie never would take alimony, and now she's married again she doesn't need it anyway. But then, what would you do after dinner? You can't go to the movies every night in the week, and a man who works all day needs some relaxation.

When Evie and I were married, we used to go to all sorts of places – we even went to museums on Sundays and to those concerts they have way uptown. But there's not much point in doing that sort of thing by yourself. And if you start trotting a girl around, why, anybody knows how that finishes. You may not mean to get hooked up together at all, but some little thing happens and you're in for it, one way or the other. And if it's one way, you're bound to feel like a bum sooner or later, while if it's the other – well, I've been married to Evie, and once is enough. I'm not going to repeat at my age. This child is too wise.

Now, you can see as much of a girl as you like at Angelo's, and that's all right because you're both part of the crowd. You've got protection, if you see what I mean. And even if you should stop playing for matches, it wouldn't mean much to either of you. We're all pretty modern in the crowd and we understand about things like that. Of course, we've had some fairly wild birds at one time or another, and I don't say I agree with all the talk I hear. But there's no use being Victorian, like people were in 1910. You just have to be wise.

It's queer, though – you certainly couldn't call Evie Victorian. And yet she never genuinely fitted in with the crowd. She wasn't a gloom either, or a bluenose; she was really awfully pretty and the kind of girl that everybody likes right off. Why, Mr. Forman took a great shine to her and used to come over and sit at our table and tell her how he wished he had a daughter her age. But she just couldn't stand him. She said it was the look of his hands. Now, when anybody's been drinking for thirty semesters or so, like Mr. Forman, I think they're lucky if they have any hands at all. And if they do remind you of an alligator-skin bag, you ought to overlook it and be broad-minded. But Evie simply couldn't see it that way.

She was always wanting us to make friends with other young married people, even when they lived up by Grant's Tomb, where the climate's different. Well, that's all right, but once you go in for that sort of thing, you might as well stay in Waynesburg. That's what I kept telling her: "This is New York," I said, "this is New York." Let the Weather Bureau worry about the wide-open spaces. But all the same, after she was gone, I found a whole envelope full of real-estate ads – you know those mortgage manors with the built-in kiddie coops that all the Westchester cowboys come home to on the 5:49. Now, can you imagine that in a sensible girl?

So there it was, you see, and we didn't make a go of it. Well, it's no use crying over spilt giggle water, as they say, and a man has to take things like that in his stride. If he doesn't, he's lost in the shuffle in this man's hamlet. I can see it wasn't anybody's fault; I'm modern. Maybe if Evie had really liked the crowd – but there, I won't blame her. She's happy the way she is, I guess; and you can see the way I am. The only thing that ever hurts this little head is to think of Angelo's closing down, sardines or no sardines. But I'm sure he'll give me the eye, long enough ahead, if it does. He's always shot square with me.

Of course, occasionally you get sort of philosophic about this time in the evening, and wonder how things would have turned out if they'd been different. But I've almost quit doing that. There's no percentage in it.

I remember Mr. Forman, one of the first times Evie and I were here. She hadn't noticed his hands then, and when he got talking to us, we both thought he was a pretty quaint old character. I guess he took to us so because we both of us must have looked young and green. Anyhow, he started philosophizing. "Youth," he says. "Youth against the city; coming in every day –" Oh, he ought to have had it syndicated! "I've watched 'em come," says he, "and I've seen 'em go. And some it makes, and some it breaks, and some just dry up gradually till the whitewing sweeps 'em away. Go back to your cornfields, young people," says he – as if Waynesburg didn't have car tracks! – "Go back and raise a family of nice little mortgages, because I'm a bad old man and you're breaking my heart" – and pretty soon he's crying into his glass.

We didn't pay any attention to him. We knew we were going to lick the world. But all the same, there's something in what he said. This town is a tough spot till you get wise to it – and it's too bad to see a fine man like Mr. Forman going to pieces the way he has these last two years. But then he's got what I call too much system in his drinking. You have to have just enough so it doesn't worry you.

Take me. If I'm stepping out a little more than usual tonight, it's just because of seeing Evie again. Of course it was bound to happen sometime, the way people come to New York; but a thing like that is apt to make you a little nervous just the same. It's easier, being modern the way we are. All the same, when I stepped out of the elevator and saw her waiting where she generally used to wait . . .

She hadn't come upstairs to the office, and that was decent of her. That girl at the front desk never could see me, and it's a laugh, your ex-wife ringing you up to pass the time of day or waiting out in the reception room. Though it wouldn't have been exactly a laugh to me.

I'd thought of all sorts of things to say to her when we did meet, but I didn't say any of them. I even forgot to take off my hat. I just said, "Hello, Evie. I didn't know you were in town," and she said, "Hello, Dick. I'm just here between trains" – and then we stared at each other.

I knew her right away, and yet I didn't know her, if you can get that. She was just as pretty as ever, but we weren't married any more. And then, her face was different. It didn't have that sort of quiet look on it when we were married. Of course, she'd let her hair grow too. She always had pretty hair. It had been five years. Well, there we were.

I must have looked like something, for, when we were out on the street she touched me on the arm.

"Don't worry, Dick," she said. "Everything's all right. I just thought, as long as I was in New York, it was silly not to see each other. Do you mind?"

"Not a bit," I said. . . . Well, you have to be polite, haven't you?

"How's Mr. Barris?" I said. . . . That's Evie's husband. It's a funny name.

"Oh, he's fine . . ." she said, "just fine."

"And the children?" I said. . . . I couldn't imagine them. "I suppose they're fine too?"

"Oh, they're fine," she said.

"Well, I'm glad to hear that, Evie," I said.

I don't know why it was so hard to talk; we ought to have been used to talking to each other.

She looked at me and laughed, quite the way she used to. "We can't stand here and gape at each other, Dick," she said.

"That's right," I said, so I flagged a taxi and told him Angelo's. Then I remembered she didn't like Angelo's. But she was decent and said that it was all right.

I'll hand it to Rocco. He knew who she was, all right, but he didn't even bat an eye—just took the order. We were the only people in the little room. She said she wanted some sherry; so that was that, with a double old-fashioned for me.

When he was gone, "Was that Rocco?" she said. "He didn't remember me."

"Well," said I, "you've been away a long time."

Then we looked at each other and knew we had nothing to say. She made rings with the bottom of the sherry glass.

"Oh, Dick," she said, "it's all so different from the way I thought it would be. Tell me about yourself."

"Oh, I'm still at the old stand," I said. "Same desk, as a matter of fact. Same salary, just about."

"How about the novel?"

"Oh," I said, "I'm working at it."

But she saw through me. "It's been five years," she said.

"A good idea's worth putting time on," said I, so she gave that up. Well, I wasn't going to cry on her.

"How about yourself?" said I. "Still living in Des Moines?"

"You know Mr. Barris lives in Cleveland," she said.

"I never can keep those two towns straight," I said. I felt better now, with that old-fashioned inside me, especially as Rocco was bringing another.

"Who came from Waynesburg?" she said, trying to kid me out of it.

"Me," I said. "But you'll have to admit I've come a long way."

I don't know why that made her look as if she wanted to cry. She hardly ever did cry – that was one thing about her.

"Oh, show me the snapshots!" I said. "I know you've got them." So she did. There was the house and the children and everything, including Mr. Barris in golf pants, and the family sedan. The little girl looks like Evie. That's a break for her. I don't know what our kids would have looked like. Terrible, I suppose.

I passed the pictures back. "They're nice," I said. "It's quite a house. I suppose you've even got a garbage incinerator."

"Of course," she said. "Why?"

"It looks like a house that would have a garbage incinerator," I said. "But you'd think Barris could afford a better car now he's a family man."

"Don't talk about George," she said.

"I'm through," I said. "So you're happy, Evie?"

She looked straight at me. "I am happy," she said – and that's the hell of it; I could see she was.

"Well," I said, "skoal!" – and that was the end of that old-fashioned. I was certainly coming back to normal in grand style. I could feel it creeping all over me. Then I heard her sort of talking to herself.

"It was a mistake," she was saying. "I ought to have known, but I couldn't help it. I thought –"

"Why say that?" I said. "It's always nice to revive old times. . . . Rocco! . . . Ah, there you are, sir. And in a minute some of the crowd may blow in."

She started putting on her gloves. "I suppose they're the same too," she said.

"Who?"

"Oh, the Parsons, and that man you called the Poached Egg, and – what was her name? – Ruth something . . . and –"

"Wait a minute," I said. "You're moving too fast for me. The Parsons broke up, and they say she's up at Saranac for her lungs. I don't know whatever did happen to the Poached Egg. As for that Ruth girl – well, after Ted Harrison popped himself –"

"Ted Harrison?" she said. "Who was Ted Harrison?"

Well, there we were. We just didn't have any point of contact at all. Of course, it wasn't her fault; she'd been away, and you do get quick action in this town. But she didn't even know who Ted Harrison had been.

"Oh, well," I said, "it doesn't signify. Just wait

around a little. Some people I want you to meet will be coming in pretty soon. You'll like them; they're really awfully nice people."

"I don't think I can wait, Dick," she said. "I've got to get back to the hotel. I'm taking the night train."

"Back to Cleveland?" I said.

"Back to Cleveland," she said.

"Well," I said, "if you must, you must. And I won't tell Barris on you." I felt pretty cheery by now. She looked at me. "I'm sorry," I said.

"Oh, Dick, Dick!" she said. "Whatever are you going to do with your life? You had such a lot. I can't stand it."

"If you mean my hair," I said, "it's the barber's fault, not mine."

But she didn't pay any attention. "I didn't come back to show off," she said. "Really I didn't. I hoped – I really did – I'd come back and find you –"

"Clean and sober?" said I. "Well, I'm all of that."

"I – oh, what's the use? – I even thought you might be married."

"To some nice girl?" I said. "No, thanks. I've been."

"I held on as long as I could," she said.

"I'm not denying it," said I. "Let's leave it at that. No hard feelings."

She looked as if she wanted to say a whole lot more. Then she looked around the room and at Rocco coming in with the fresh supply. I don't know what she saw to make her look like that.

"No, it wouldn't have been," she said, sort of low

to herself. "It couldn't have been. Good-by, Dick, and thank you."

"The pleasure is all mine," said I. "Only sorry you won't have another. Just a second and I'll get you a taxi."

But when I'd settled the bill and got my hat and coat, she was gone.

I went back to the little room and sat down again. I didn't feel like thinking, but I couldn't help it. For one thing, Evie's asking about all those people who had been in the crowd – why, they'd just disappeared. And I hadn't even realized it. Come to think of it, the only two left of that particular crowd who still came to Angelo's were Mr. Forman and myself. And what was that novel about that I'd been going to write?

"Rocco!" I called.

"Right with you, mister."

"You have the right idea," I said, but when he came in, I made him stay.

"Rocco," I said, "tell me something. How do I look today?"

"Oh, mister look ver' fine; seem ver' well."

That's the trouble with Rocco. He's always so darn pleasant.

"Don't two-time me, Rocco," I said. "Do you remember when I first started coming here?"

"Oh, yes: remember ver' well. Mister ver' good customer; ver' steady customer. Wish we had all like mister."

"Leave that outside," I said. "Just tell me one thing: Do I look a lot different?"

He spread out his hands. "Sure, mister look little different. Why not? Time pass. Rocco look different too."

"You're a liar," I said. "You haven't changed that Dago grin in twenty years. . . . All right, I look different, but how old do I look?"

He spread out his hands again. "Rocco don't know. Mister maybe forty, forty-one – mister in his prime."

"You low snake," I said. "I'm thirty-two." This was serious.

"Thirty-two? That's right. That's what Rocco mean" – and he grinned. But I didn't feel so funny.

"Tell me, Rocco," I said. "You've always been a friend of mine. Now be a friend. Tell me honestly. Do you think I drink too much?"

Gosh, you couldn't get anywhere with him! He just kept on grinning.

"Mister ver' good customer," he said; "ver' old, ver' steady customer. Mister carry what he drink ver' well."

"I know that!" I said. I was getting mad by now. "But is it too much? Be sensible, Rocco. I don't put away half what Mr. Forman does."

"Nobody drink so much as Mr. Forman. Some day Mr. Forman go pop. Rocco ver' sorry then, for Mr. Forman old customer."

"Well, that's a swell way of encouraging me. How about yourself, Rocco? How's your health?"

"Fine; thanks, mister. We have new bambino only other day."

"Well, I'm certainly glad to hear that. But look here, Rocco; you take a snifter –"

"Sure. Rocco drink wine—*strega*—ver' good. But Rocco have to work. Can't drink alla time."

"I get that. But I work too."

"Sure, mister work. But Rocco work alla time. Rocco have wife, tree bambini; have to work. Work to go back to Italy, buy *trattoria,* buy farm, have more bambini, be big man in town. That work for a man. Mister have another old-fashioned?"

He wouldn't talk any more. And the next one didn't go so well, because I'd started looking at myself in the mirror.

Oh, it just shows what a state I was in. And it shows you never ought to go back on your tracks. You know, for a while there I didn't like my face a bit.

That's why I say, modern or not, things like seeing Evie again don't do you any good. Because, when Mr. Forman came in and touched me on the shoulder, I jumped a mile. And just before I jumped I caught his face in the glass right over mine. I've apologized to him since, and I guess he's forgotten it. But they all must have thought I was crazy, running out like that and leaving the money on the table. And all that week I just got crazier and crazier, getting up and taking a cold shower in the mornings, and eating at tearooms and coming right back after dinner and hunting around to see if I could find whatever became of that novel. One good thing, I did get the room pretty well cleaned up. That woman who comes in never really cleans.

But what's the use of all that when you keep getting the fidgets? And getting the fidgets makes you think too much. Anyway, one evening it was nice and warm, and

I thought, "I'll just take a walk. I can't sit here any more."

Well, I didn't have any particular direction in mind, but after a while, sure enough, there I was in front of Angelo's. Man, you should have seen the welcome they gave me. Angelo set up the drinks himself, and Rocco was grinning all over.

"Angelo think we lose our mos' steady customer," he said, "but mister come back. I know he come back."

And Mr. Forman never said a word about how I'd acted.

He wasn't a bit standoffish; in fact, Rocco had to ease him out at eleven that night.

Now, the only worry I've got is Angelo's retiring, as I say. But even if he does, maybe Rocco will keep the place on. Of course, even that would be a change, but I'd hardly mind. We've known each other a long while, and he knows I'm a good customer.

TOO EARLY SPRING

I'M writing this down because I don't ever want to forget the way it was. It doesn't seem as if I could, now, but they all tell you things change. And I guess they're right. Older people must have forgotten or they couldn't be the way they are. And that goes for even the best ones, like Dad and Mr. Grant. They try to understand but they don't seem to know how. And the others make you feel dirty or else they make you feel like a goof. Till, pretty soon, you begin to forget yourself – you begin to think, "Well, maybe they're right and it was that way." And that's the end of everything. So I've got to write this down. Because they smashed it forever – but it wasn't the way they said.

Mr. Grant always says in comp. class: "Begin at the beginning." Only I don't know quite where the beginning was. We had a good summer at Big Lake but it was just the same summer. I worked pretty hard at the practice basket I rigged up in the barn, and I learned how to do the back jackknife. I'll never dive like Kerry but you want to be as all-around as you can. And, when I took my measurements, at the end of the summer, I was 5 ft. 9¾ and I'd gained 12 lbs. 6 oz. That isn't bad for going on sixteen and the old chest expansion was O. K. You don't want to get too heavy, because basketball's a fast game, but the year before was the year when I got my height, and I was so skinny, I got tired. But this year, Kerry helped me practice, a couple of times, and he seemed to think I had a good chance for the team. So I felt pretty set up – they'd never had a Sophomore on it before. And Kerry's a natural athlete, so that means a lot from him. He's a pretty good brother too. Most Juniors at State wouldn't bother with a fellow in High.

It sounds as if I were trying to run away from what I have to write down, but I'm not. I want to remember that summer, too, because it's the last happy one I'll ever have. Oh, when I'm an old man – thirty or forty – things may be all right again. But that's a long time to wait and it won't be the same.

And yet, that summer was different, too, in a way. So it must have started then, though I didn't know it. I went around with the gang as usual and we had a good time. But, every now and then, it would strike me we were acting like awful kids. They thought I was getting the big head, but I wasn't. It just wasn't much fun – even going to the cave. It was like going on shooting marbles when you're in High.

I had sense enough not to try to tag after Kerry and his crowd. You can't do that. But when they all got out on the lake in canoes, warm evenings, and somebody brought a phonograph along, I used to go down to the Point, all by myself, and listen and listen. Maybe they'd be talking or maybe they'd be singing, but it all sounded mysterious across the water. I wasn't trying to hear what they said, you know. That's the kind of thing Tot Pickens does. I'd just listen, with my arms around my knees — and somehow it would hurt me to listen — and yet I'd rather do that than be with the gang.

I was sitting under the four pines, one night, right down by the edge of the water. There was a big moon and they were singing. It's funny how you can be unhappy and nobody know it but yourself.

I was thinking about Sheila Coe. She's Kerry's girl. They fight but they get along. She's awfully pretty and she can swim like a fool. Once Kerry sent me over with her tennis racket and we had quite a conversation. She was fine. And she didn't pull any of this big sister stuff, either, the way some girls will with a fellow's kid brother.

And when the canoe came along, by the edge of the lake, I thought for a moment it was her. I thought maybe she was looking for Kerry and maybe she'd stop and maybe she'd feel like talking to me again. I don't know why I thought that — I didn't have any reason. Then I saw it was just the Sharon kid, with a new kind of bob that made her look grown-up, and I felt sore. She didn't have any business out on the lake at her age. She was just a Sophomore in High, the same as me.

I chunked a stone in the water and it splashed right by the canoe, but she didn't squeal. She just said, "Fish," and chuckled. It struck me it was a kid's trick, trying to scare a kid.

"Hello, Helen," I said. "Where did you swipe the gunboat?"

"They don't know I've got it," she said. "Oh, hello, Chuck Peters. How's Big Lake?"

"All right," I said. "How was camp?"

"It was peachy," she said. "We had a peachy counselor, Miss Morgan. She was on the Wellesley field-hockey team."

"Well," I said, "we missed your society." Of course we hadn't, because they're across the lake and don't swim at our raft. But you ought to be polite.

"Thanks," she said. "Did you do the special reading for English? I thought it was dumb."

"It's always dumb," I said. "What canoe is that?"

"It's the old one," she said. "I'm not supposed to have it out at night. But you won't tell anybody, will you?"

"Be your age," I said. I felt generous. "I'll paddle a while, if you want," I said.

"All right," she said, so she brought it in and I got aboard. She went back in the bow and I took the paddle. I'm not strong on carting kids around, as a rule. But it was better than sitting there by myself.

"Where do you want to go?" I said.

"Oh, back towards the house," she said in a shy kind of voice. "I ought to, really. I just wanted to hear the singing."

"K. O.," I said. I didn't paddle fast, just let her slip. There was a lot of moon on the water. We kept around the edge so they wouldn't notice us. The singing sounded as if it came from a different country, a long way off.

She was a sensible kid, she didn't ask fool questions or giggle about nothing at all. Even when we went by Petters' Cove. That's where the lads from the bungalow colony go and it's pretty well populated on a warm night. You can hear them talking in low voices and now and then a laugh. Once Tot Pickens and a gang went over there with a flashlight, and a big Bohunk chased them for half a mile.

I felt funny, going by there with her. But I said, "Well, it's certainly Old Home Week" — in an offhand tone, because, after all, you've got to be sophisticated. And she said, "People are funny," in just the right sort of way. I took quite a shine to her after that and we talked. The Sharons have only been in town three years and somehow I'd never really noticed her before. Mrs. Sharon's awfully good-looking but she and Mr. Sharon fight. That's hard on a kid. And she was a quiet kid. She had a small kind of face and her eyes were sort of like a kitten's. You could see she got a great kick out of pretending to be grown-up — and yet it wasn't all pretending. A couple of times, I felt just as if I were talking to Sheila Coe. Only more comfortable, because, after all, we were the same age.

Do you know, after we put the canoe up, I walked all the way back home, around the lake? And most of the way, I ran. I felt swell too. I felt as if I could run forever and not stop. It was like finding something. I hadn't imagined anybody could ever feel the way I did about some things. And here was another person, even if it was a girl.

Kerry's door was open when I went by and he stuck his head out, and grinned.

"Well, kid," he said. "Stepping out?"

"Sure. With Greta Garbo," I said, and grinned back

to show I didn't mean it. I felt sort of lightheaded, with the run and everything.

"Look here, kid –" he said, as if he was going to say something. Then he stopped. But there was a funny look on his face.

And yet I didn't see her again till we were both back in High. Mr. Sharon's uncle died, back East, and they closed the cottage suddenly. But all the rest of the time at Big Lake, I kept remembering that night and her little face. If I'd seen her in daylight, first, it might have been different. No, it wouldn't have been.

All the same, I wasn't even thinking of her when we bumped into each other, the first day of school. It was raining and she had on a green slicker and her hair was curly under her hat. We grinned and said hello and had to run. But something happened to us, I guess.

I'll say this now – it wasn't like Tot Pickens and Mabel Palmer. It wasn't like Junior David and Betty Page – though they've been going together ever since kindergarten. It wasn't like any of those things. We didn't get sticky and sloppy. It wasn't like going with a girl.

Gosh, there'd be days and days when we'd hardly see each other, except in class. I had basketball practice almost every afternoon and sometimes evenings and she was taking music lessons four times a week. But you don't have to be always twos-ing with a person, if you feel that way about them. You seem to know the way they're thinking and feeling, the way you know yourself.

Now let me describe her. She had that little face and the eyes like a kitten's. When it rained, her hair curled all over the back of her neck. Her hair was yellow. She wasn't a tall girl but she wasn't chunky – just light and well made and quick. She was awfully alive without being nervous – she never bit her fingernails or chewed the end of her pencil, but she'd answer quicker than anyone in the class. Nearly everybody liked her, but she wasn't best friends with any particular girl, the mushy way they get. The teachers all thought a lot of her, even Miss Eagles. Well, I had to spoil that.

If we'd been like Tot and Mabel, we could have had a lot more time together, I guess. But Helen isn't a liar and I'm not a snake. It wasn't easy, going over to her house, because Mr. and Mrs. Sharon would be polite to each other in front of you and yet there'd be something wrong. And she'd have to be fair to both of them and they were always pulling at her. But we'd look at each other across the table and then it would be all right.

I don't know when it was that we knew we'd get married to each other, some time. We just started talking about it, one day, as if we always had. We were sensible, we knew it couldn't happen right off. We thought maybe when we were eighteen. That was two years but we knew we had to be educated. You don't get as good a job, if you aren't. Or that's what people say.

We weren't mushy either, like some people. We got to kissing each other good-by, sometimes, because that's what you do when you're in love. It was cool, the way she kissed you, it was like leaves. But lots of the time we wouldn't even talk about getting married, we'd just play checkers or go over the old Latin, or once in a while go to the movies with the gang. It was really a wonderful winter. I played every game after the first one and she'd sit in the gallery and watch and I'd know she was there. You could see her little green hat or her yellow hair. Those are the class colors, green and gold.

And it's a queer thing, but everybody seemed to be pleased. That's what I can't get over. They liked to see us together. The grown people, I mean. Oh, of course, we got kidded too. And old Mrs. Withers would ask me about "my little sweetheart," in that awful damp voice of hers. But, mostly, they were all right. Even Mother was all right, though she didn't like Mrs. Sharon. I did hear her say to Father, once, "Really, George, how long is this going to last? Sometimes I feel as if I just couldn't stand it."

Then Father chuckled and said to her, "Now, Mary, last year you were worried about him because he didn't take any interest in girls at all."

"Well," she said, "he still doesn't. Oh, Helen's a nice child – no credit to Eva Sharon – and thank heaven she doesn't giggle. Well, Charles is mature for *his* age too. But he acts so solemn about her. It isn't natural."

"Oh, let Charlie alone," said Father. "The boy's all right. He's just got a one-track mind."

But it wasn't so nice for us after the spring came. In our part of the state, it comes pretty late, as a rule. But it was early this year. The little kids were out with scooters when usually they'd still be having snowfights and, all of a sudden, the radiators in the classrooms smelt dry. You'd got used to that smell for months — and then, there was a day when you hated it again and everybody kept asking to open the windows. The monitors had a tough time, that first week — they always do when spring starts — but this year it was worse than ever because it came when you didn't expect it.

Usually, basketball's over by the time spring really breaks, but this year it hit us while we still had three games to play. And it certainly played hell with us as a team. After Bladesburg nearly licked us, Mr. Grant called off all practice till the day before the St. Matthew's game. He knew we were stale — and they've been state champions two years They'd have walked all over us, the way we were going.

The first thing I did was telephone Helen. Because that meant there were six extra afternoons we could have, if she could get rid of her music lessons any way. Well, she said, wasn't it wonderful, her music teacher had a cold? And that seemed just like Fate.

Well, that was a great week and we were so happy. We went to the movies five times and once Mrs. Sharon let us take her little car. She knew I didn't have a driving license but of course I've driven ever since I was thirteen and she said it was all right. She was funny — sometimes she'd be awfully kind and friendly to you and sometimes she'd be like a piece of dry ice. She was that way with Mr. Sharon too. But it was a wonderful ride. We got stuff out of the kitchen – the cook's awfully sold on Helen – and drove way out in the country. And we found an old house, with the windows gone, on top of a hill, and parked the car and took the stuff up to the house and ate it there. There weren't any chairs or tables but we pretended there were.

We pretended it was our house, after we were married. I'll never forget that. She'd even brought paper napkins and paper plates and she set two places on the floor.

"Well, Charles," she said, sitting opposite me, with her feet tucked under, "I don't suppose you remember the days we were both in school."

"Sure," I said – she was always much quicker pretending things than I was – "I remember them all right. That was before Tot Pickens got to be President." And we both laughed.

"It seems very distant in the past to me – we've been married so long," she said, as if she really believed it. She looked at me.

"Would you mind turning off the radio, dear?" she said. "This modern music always gets on my nerves."

"Have we got a radio?" I said.

"Of course, Chuck."

"With television?"

"Of course, Chuck."

"Gee, I'm glad," I said. I went and turned it off.

"Of course, if you *want* to listen to the late market reports –" she said just like Mrs. Sharon.

"Nope," I said. "The market – uh – closed firm today. Up twenty-six points."

"That's quite a long way up, isn't it?"

"Well, the country's perfectly sound at heart, in spite of this damfool Congress," I said, like Father.

She lowered her eyes a minute, just like her mother, and pushed away her plate.

"I'm not very hungry tonight," she said. "You won't mind if I go upstairs?"

"Aw, don't be like that," I said. It was too much like her mother.

"I was just seeing if I could," she said. "But I never will, Chuck."

"I'll never tell you you're nervous, either," I said. "I – oh, gosh!"

She grinned and it was all right. "Mr. Ashland and I have never had a serious dispute in our wedded lives," she said – and everybody knows who runs *that* family. "We just talk things over calmly and reach a satisfactory conclusion, usually mine."

"Say, what kind of house have we got?"

"It's a lovely house," she said. "We've got radios in every room and lots of servants. We've got a regular movie projector and a library full of good classics and there's always something in the icebox. I've got a shoe closet."

"A what?"

"A shoe closet. All my shoes are on tipped shelves, like Mother's. And all my dresses are on those padded hangers. And I say to the maid, 'Elise, Madam will wear the new French model today.' "

"What are my clothes on?" I said. "Christmas trees?"

"Well," she said. "You've got lots of clothes and

dogs. You smell of pipes and the open and something called Harrisburg tweed."

"I do not," I said. "I wish I had a dog. It's a long time since Jack."

"Oh, Chuck, I'm sorry," she said.

"Oh, that's all right," I said. "He was getting old and his ear was always bothering him. But he was a good pooch. Go ahead."

"Well," she said, "of course we give parties –"

"Cut the parties," I said.

"Chuck! They're grand ones!"

"I'm a homebody," I said. "Give me – er – my wife and my little family and – say, how many kids have we got, anyway?"

She counted on her fingers. "Seven."

"Good Lord," I said.

"Well, I always wanted seven. You can make it three, if you like."

"Oh, seven's all right, I suppose," I said. "But don't they get awfully in the way?"

"No," she said. "We have governesses and tutors and send them to boarding school."

"O. K.," I said. "But it's a strain on the old man's pocketbook, just the same."

"Chuck, will you ever talk like that? Chuck, this is when we're rich." Then suddenly, she looked sad. "Oh, Chuck, do you suppose we ever will?" she said.

"Why, sure," I said.

"I wouldn't mind if it was only a dump," she said. "I could cook for you. I keep asking Hilda how she makes things."

I felt awfully funny. I felt as if I were going to cry.

"We'll do it," I said. "Don't you worry."

"Oh, Chuck, you're a comfort," she said.

I held her for a while. It was like holding something awfully precious. It wasn't mushy or that way. I know what that's like too.

"It takes so long to get old," she said. "I wish I could grow up tomorrow. I wish we both could."

"Don't you worry," I said. "It's going to be all right."

We didn't say much, going back in the car, but we were happy enough. I thought we passed Miss Eagles at the turn. That worried me a little because of the driving license. But, after all, Mrs. Sharon had said we could take the car.

We wanted to go back again, after that, but it was too far to walk and that was the only time we had the car. Mrs. Sharon was awfully nice about it but she said, thinking it over, maybe we'd better wait till I got a license. Well, Father didn't want me to get one till I was seventeen but I thought he might come around. I didn't want to do anything that would get Helen in a jam with her family. That shows how careful I was of her. Or thought I was.

All the same, we decided we'd do something to celebrate if the team won the St. Matthew's game. We thought it would be fun if we could get a steak and cook supper out somewhere – something like that. Of course we could have done it easily enough with a gang, but we didn't want a gang. We wanted to be alone together, the way we'd been at the house. That was all we wanted. I don't see what's wrong about that. We even took home the paper plates, so as not to litter things up.

Boy, that was a game! We beat them 36-34 and it took an extra period and I thought it would never end. That two-goal lead they had looked as big as the Rocky Mountains all the first half. And they gave me the full school cheer with nine Peters when we tied them up. You don't forget things like that.

Afterwards, Mr. Grant had a kind of spread for the team at his house and a lot of people came in. Kerry had driven down from State to see the game and that made me feel pretty swell. And what made me feel better yet was his taking me aside and saying, "Listen, kid, I don't want you to get the swelled head, but you did a good job. Well, just remember this. Don't let anybody kid you out of going to State. You'll like it up there." And Mr. Grant heard him and laughed and said, "Well, Peters, I'm not proselytizing. But your brother might think about some of the Eastern colleges." It was all like the kind of dream you have when you can do anything. It was wonderful.

Only Helen wasn't there because the only girls were older girls. I'd seen her for a minute, right after the game, and she was fine, but it was only a minute. I wanted to tell her about that big St. Matthew's forward and – oh, everything. Well, you like to talk things over with your girl.

Father and Mother were swell but they had to go on to some big shindy at the country club. And Kerry was going there with Sheila Coe. But Mr. Grant said he'd run me back to the house in his car and he did. He's a great guy. He made jokes about my being the infant phenomenon of basketball, and they were good jokes too. I didn't mind them. But, all the same, when I'd said good night to him and gone into the house, I felt sort of let down.

I knew I'd be tired the next day but I didn't feel sleepy yet. I was too excited. I wanted to talk to somebody. I wandered around downstairs and wondered if Ida was still up. Well, she wasn't, but she'd left half a chocolate cake, covered over, on the kitchen table, and a note on top of it, "Congratulations to Mister Charles Peters." Well, that was awfully nice of her and I ate some. Then I turned the radio on and got the time signal – eleven – and some snappy music. But still I didn't fell like hitting the hay.

So I thought I'd call up Helen and then I thought – probably she's asleep and Hilda or Mrs. Sharon will answer the phone and be sore. And then I thought – well, anyhow, I could go over and walk around the block and look at her house. I'd get some fresh air out of it, anyway, and it would be a little like seeing her.

So I did – and it was a swell night – cool and a lot of stars – and I felt like a king, walking over. All the lower part of the Sharon house was dark but a window upstairs was lit. I knew it was her window. I went around back of the driveway and whistled once – the whistle we made up. I never expected her to hear.

But she did, and there she was at the window, smiling. She made motions that she'd come down to the side door.

Honestly, it took my breath away when I saw her. She had on a kind of yellow thing over her night clothes and she looked so pretty. Her feet were so pretty in those slippers. You almost expected her to be carrying one of those animals kids like—she looked young enough. I know I oughtn't to have gone into the house. But we didn't think anything about it—we were just glad to see each other. We hadn't had any sort of chance to talk over the game.

We sat in front of the fire in the living room and she went out to the kitchen and got us cookies and milk. I wasn't really hungry, but it was like that time at the house, eating with her. Mr. and Mrs. Sharon were at the country club, too, so we weren't disturbing them or anything. We turned off the lights because there was plenty of light from the fire and Mr. Sharon's one of those people who can't stand having extra lights burning. Dad's that way about saving string.

It was quiet and lovely and the firelight made shadows on the ceiling. We talked a lot and then we just sat, each of us knowing the other was there. And the room got quieter and quieter and I'd told her about the game and I didn't feel excited or jumpy any more—just rested and happy. And then I knew by her breathing that she was asleep and I put my arm around her for just a minute. Because it was wonderful to hear that quiet breathing and know it was hers. I was going to wake her in a minute. I didn't realize how tired I was myself.

And then we were back in that house in the country and it was our home and we ought to have been happy. But something was wrong because there still wasn't any glass in the windows and a wind kept blowing through them and we tried to shut the doors but they wouldn't shut. It drove Helen distracted and we were both running through the house, trying to shut the doors, and we were cold and afraid. Then the sun rose outside the windows, burning and yellow and so big it covered the sky. And with the sun was a horrible, weeping voice. It was Mrs. Sharon's saying, "Oh, my God, oh my God."

I didn't know what had happened, for a minute, when I woke. And then I did and it was awful. Mrs. Sharon was saying "Oh, Helen — I trusted you . . ." and looking as if she were going to faint. And Mr. Sharon looked at her for a minute and his face was horrible and he said, "Bred in the bone," and she looked as if he'd hit her. Then he said to Helen —

I don't want to think of what they said. I don't want to think of any of the things they said. Mr. Sharon is a bad man. And she is a bad woman, even if she is Helen's mother. All the same, I could stand the things he said better than hers.

I don't want to think of any of it. And it is all spoiled now. Everything is spoiled. Miss Eagles saw us going to that house in the country and she said horrible things. They made Helen sick and she hasn't been back at school. There isn't any way I can see her. And if I could, it would be spoiled. We'd be thinking about the things they said.

I don't know how many of the people know, at school. But Tot Pickens passed me a note. And, that afternoon. I caught him behind his house. I'd have broken his nose if they hadn't pulled me off. I meant to. Mother cried when she heard about it and Dad took me into his room and talked to me. He said you can't lick the whole town. But I will anybody like Tot Pickens. Dad and Mother have been all right. But they say things about Helen and that's almost worse. They're for me because I'm their son. But they don't understand.

I thought I could talk to Kerry but I can't. He was nice but he looked at me such a funny way. I don't know — sort of impressed. It wasn't the way I wanted him to look. But he's been decent. He comes down almost every weekend and we play catch in the yard.

You see, I just go to school and back now. They want me to go with the gang, the way I did, but I can't do that. Not after Tot. Of course my marks are a lot better because I've got more time to study now. But it's lucky I haven't got Miss Eagles though Dad made her apologize. I couldn't recite to her.

I think Mr. Grant knows because he asked me to his house once and we had a conversation. Not about that, though I was terribly afraid he would. He showed me a lot of his old college things and the gold football he wears on his watch chain. He's got a lot of interesting things.

Then we got talking, somehow, about history and things like that and how times had changed. Why, there were kings and queens who got married younger than Helen and me. Only now we lived longer and had a lot more to learn. So it couldn't happen now. "It's civilization," he said. "And all civilization's against nature. But I suppose we've got to have it. Only sometimes it isn't easy." Well somehow or other, that made me feel less lonely. Before that I'd been feeling that I was the only person on earth who'd ever felt that way.

I'm going to Colorado, this summer, to a ranch, and next year, I'll go East to school. Mr. Grant says he thinks I can make the basketball team, if I work hard enough, though it isn't as big a game in the East as it is with us. Well, I'd like to show them something. It would be some satisfaction. He says not to be too fresh at first, but I won't be that.

It's a boy's school and there aren't even women teachers. And, maybe, afterwards, I could be a professional basketball player or something, where you don't have to see women at all. Kerry says I'll get over that; but I won't. They all sound like Mrs. Sharon to me now, when they laugh.

They're going to send Helen to a convent – I found out that. Maybe they'll let me see her before she goes. But, if we do, it will be all wrong and in front of people and everybody pretending. I sort of wish they don't – though I want to, terribly. When her mother took her upstairs that night – she wasn't the same Helen. She looked at me as if she was afraid of me. And no matter what they do for us now, they can't fix that.

SCHOONER FAIRCHILD'S CLASS

WHEN he said good night to his son and Tom Drury and the rest of them, Lane Parrington walked down the steps of the Leaf Club and stood, for a moment, breathing in the night air. He had made the speech they'd asked him to make, and taken pains with it, too — but now he was wondering whether it wasn't the same old graduate's speech after all. He hadn't meant it to be so, but you ran into a lingo, once you started putting thoughts on paper — you began to view with alarm and talk about imperiled bulwarks and the American way of life.

And yet he'd been genuinely pleased when the invitation came — and they'd asked him three months ahead. That meant something, even to the Lane Parrington of United Investments — it was curious how old bonds held. He had been decorated by two foreign governments and had declined a ministry — there was the place in Virginia, the place on Long Island, the farm in Vermont and the big apartment on the river. There were the statements issued when sailing for Europe and the photographs and articles in news weeklies and magazines. And yet he had been pleased when they asked him to speak at the annual dinner of an undergraduate club in his own college. Of course, the Leaf was a little different, as all Leaf members knew.

When he had been a new member, as his son was now, the speech had been made by a Secretary of State.

Well, he'd done well enough, he supposed — at least Ted had come up, afterward, a little shyly, and said, "Well, Dad, you're quite an orator." But, once or twice, in the course of the speech, he had caught Ted fiddling with his coffee spoon. They were almost always too long — those speeches by graduates — he had tried to remember that. But he couldn't help running a little overtime — not after he'd got up and seen them waiting there. They were only boys, of course, but boys who would soon be men with men's responsibilities — he had even made a point of that.

One of the things about the Leaf — you got a chance of hearing what — well, what really important men thought of the state of the world and the state of the nation. They could get a lot from professors but hardly that. So, when a sensible fellow got up to explain what sensible men really thought about this business at Washington — why, damn it, nobody was going to ring a gong on him! And they'd clapped him well, at the end, and Ted's face had looked relieved. They always clapped well, at the end.

Afterward, he had rather hoped to meet Ted's friends and get in a little closer touch with them than he did at the place in Virginia or the place on Long Island or the apartment in New York. He saw them there, of course — they got in cars and out of cars, they dressed and went to dances, they played on the tennis courts and swam in the pool. They were a good crowd — a typical Leaf crowd, well-exercised and well-mannered. They were polite to Cora and polite to him. He offered them cigars now and then; during the last two years he offered them whisky and soda. They listened to what he had to say and, if he told a good story, they usually laughed at it. They played tennis with him, occasionally, and said, "Good shot, sir!" — afterward, they played harder tennis. One of them was Ted, his son, well-mannered, well-exercised, a member of the Leaf. He could talk to Ted about college athletics, the college curriculum, his allowance, the weather, the virtues of capitalism and whether to get a new beach wagon this summer. Now, to these subjects was added the Leaf and the virtues of the Leaf. He could talk to Ted about any number of things.

Nevertheless, sometimes when the annual dinner was over, there would be a little group at the Leaf around this graduate or that. He remembered one such group his senior year, around a sharp-tongued old man with hooded eyes. The ex-senator was old and broken, but they'd stayed up till two while his caustic voice made hay of accepted catchwords. Well, he had met Ted's friends and remembered most of their names. They had congratulated him on his speech and he had drunk a highball with them. It had all been in accord with the best traditions of the Leaf but it hadn't lasted very long.

For a moment, indeed, he had almost gotten into an argument with one of them — the pink-faced, incredibly youthful one with the glasses who was head of the Student Union — they hadn't had student unions in his time. He had been answering a couple of questions quite informally, using slang, and the pink-faced youth had broken in with, "But, look here, sir — I mean, that was a good speech you made from the conservative point of view and all that — but when you talk about labor's being made responsible, just what do you mean and how far do you go? Do you mean you want to scrap the Wagner Act or amend it or what?"

But then the rest of them had said, "Oh, don't mind Stu — he's our communist. Skip it, Stu — how's dialectic materialism today?" and it had passed off in kidding. Lane Parrington felt a little sorry about that — he would have enjoyed a good argument with an intelligent youngster — he was certainly broad-minded enough for that. But, instead, he'd declined another highball and said, well, he supposed he ought to be getting back to the inn. It had all been very well-mannered and in accord with the best traditions of the Leaf. He wondered how the old ex-senator had got them to talk.

Ted had offered to walk along with him, of course, and, equally, of course, he had declined. Now he stood for a moment on the sidewalk, wondering whether he ought to look in at class headquarters before going back to the inn. He ought to, he supposed — after all, it was his thirtieth reunion. It would be full of cigar smoke and voices and there would be a drunk from another class — there was always, somehow or other, a drunk from another class who insisted on leading cheers. And Schooner Fairchild, the class funny man, would be telling stories — the one about the Kickapoo chief, the one about President Dodge and the telephone. As it was in the beginning, is now and ever shall be. He didn't dislike Schooner Fairchild any more – you couldn't dislike a man who had wasted his life. But Schooner, somehow, had never seemed conscious of that.

Yes, he'd go to class headquarters – he'd go, if for no other reason than to prove that he did not dislike Schooner Fairchild. He started walking down Club Row. There were twelve of the clubhouses now – there had been only eight in his time. They all looked very much alike, even the new ones – it took an initiated eye to detect the slight enormous differences – to know that Wampum, in spite of its pretentious lanterns, was second-rate and would always be second-rate, while Abbey, small and dingy, ranked with Momus and the Leaf. Parrington stood still, reliving the moment of more than thirty years ago when he'd gotten the bid from Wampum and thought he would have to accept it. It hadn't been necessary – the Leaf messenger had knocked on his door at just three minutes to nine. But whenever he passed the Wampum house he remembered. For, for almost an hour, it had seemed as if the destined career of Lane Parrington wasn't going to turn out right after all.

The small agonies of youth – they were unimportant, of course, but they left a mark. And he'd had to succeed – he'd had to have the Leaf, just as later on, he'd had to have money – he wasn't a Schooner Fairchild, to take things as they came. You were geared like that or you weren't – if you weren't, you might as well stay in Emmetsburg and end up as a harried high school principal with sick headaches and a fine Spencerian handwriting, as his father had. But he had wanted to get out of Emmetsburg the moment he had realized there were other places to go.

He remembered a look through a microscope and a lashing, tailed thing that swam. There were only two classes of people, the wigglers and the ones who stood still — he should have made his speech on that — it would have been a better speech. And the ones who stood still didn't like the wigglers — that, too, he knew, from experience. If they saw a wiggler coming, they closed ranks and opposed their large, well-mannered inertia to the brusque, ill-mannered life. Later on, of course, they gave in gracefully, but without real liking. He had made the Leaf on his record — and a very good record it had had to be. He had even spent three painful seasons with the track squad, just to demonstrate that desirable all-aroundness that was one of the talking points. And even so, they had smelled it — they had known, instinctively, that he wasn't quite their kind. Tom Drury, for instance, had always been pleasant enough — but Tom Drury had always made him feel that he was talking a little too much and a little too loud. Tom Drury, who, even then, had looked like a magnificent sheep. But he had also been class president, and the heir to Drury and Son. And yet, they all liked Schooner Fairchild — they liked him still.

And here was the end of Club Row, and the Momus House. He stopped and took out a cigar. It was silly to fight old battles, especially when they were won. If they asked the Drurys to dinner now, the Drurys came — he'd been offered and declined a partnership in Drury and Son. But he had helped Tom out with some of their affiliates and Tom had needed help — Tom would always be impressive, of course, but it took more than impressiveness to handle certain things. And now Ted was coming along — and Ted was sound as a bell. So sound he might marry one of the Drury daughters, if he wanted — though that was Ted's business. He wondered if he wanted Ted to marry young. He had done so himself — on the whole, it had been a mistake.

Funny, how things mixed in your mind. As always, when he remembered Dorothy, there was the sharp, sweet smell of her perfume; then the stubborn, competent look of her hands on the wheel of a car. They had been too much alike to have married — lucky they'd found it out in time. She had let him keep the child — of course he would have fought for it anyway — but it was considered very modern in those days. Then the war had washed over and obliterated a great deal — afterward, he had married Cora. And that had worked out as it should — Ted was fond of her and she treated him with just the right shade of companionableness. Most things worked out in the end. He wondered if Dorothy had gotten what she wanted at last — he supposed she had, with her Texan. But she'd died in a hospital at Galveston, ten years ago, trying to have the Texan's child, so he couldn't ask her now. They had warned her about having more children — but, as soon as you warned Dorothy about anything, that was what she wanted to do. He could have told them. But the Texan was one of those handsome, chivalrous men.

Strange, that out of their two warring ambitions should have come the sound, reliable, healthy Ted. But, no, it wasn't strange — he had planned it as carefully as one could, and Cora had helped a great deal. Cora never got out of her depth and she had a fine social sense. And the very best nurses and schools from the very first — and there you were! You did it as you ran a business — picked the right people and gave them authority. He had hardly ever had to interfere himself.

There would be a great deal of money — but that could be taken care of — there were ways. There were trust funds and foundations and clever secretaries. And Ted need never realize it. There was no reason he should — no reason in the least. Ted could think he was doing it all.

He pulled hard on his cigar and started to walk away. For the door of the Momus Club had suddenly swung open, emitting a gush of light and a small, chubby, gray-haired figure with a turned-up nose and a jack-o'-lantern grin. It stood on the steps for a moment, saying good night a dozen times and laughing. Lane Parrington walked fast — but it was no use. He heard pattering footsteps behind him — a voice cried, "Ought-Eight!" with conviction, then, "Lane Parrington, b'gosh!" He stopped and turned.

"Oh, hello, Schooner," he said, unenthusiastically. "Your dinner over, too?"

"Oh, the boys'll keep it up till three," said Schooner Fairchild, mopping his pink brow. "But, after an hour and a half, I told them it was time they got some other poor devil at the piano. I'm not as young as I was." He panted, comically, and linked arms with Lane Parrington. "Class headquarters?" he said. "I shouldn't go—Minnie will scalp me. But I will."

"Well," said Lane Parrington uncomfortably—he hated having his arm held, "I suppose we ought to look in."

"Duty, Mr. Easy, always duty," said Schooner Fairchild and chuckled. "Hey, don't walk so fast—an old man can't keep up with you." He stopped and mopped his brow again. "By the way," he said, "that's a fine boy of yours, Lane."

"Oh," said Lane Parrington awkwardly. "Thanks. But I didn't know—"

"Saw something of him last summer," said Schooner Fairchild cheerfully. "Sylvia brought him around to the house. He could have a rather nice baritone, if he wanted."

"Baritone?" said Lane Parrington. "Sylvia?"

"Eldest daughter and pride of the Fairchild château," said Schooner Fairchild, slurring his words by a tiny fraction. "She collects 'em—not always—always with Father's approval. But your boy's a nice boy. Serious, of course." He chuckled again, it seemed to Lane Parrington maddeningly. "Oh, the sailor said to the admiral, and the admiral said he—" he chanted. "Remember that one, Lane?"

"No," said Lane Parrington.

"That's right," said Schooner Fairchild, amiably. "Stupid of me. I thought for a minute, you'd been in the quartet. But that was dear old Pozzy Banks. Poor Pozzy—he never could sing 'The Last Rose of Summer' properly till he was as drunk as an owl. A man of great talents. I hoped he'd be here this time but he couldn't make it. He wanted to come," he hummed, "but he didn't have the fare . . ."

"That's too bad," said Lane Parrington, seriously. "And yet, with business picking up . . ."

Schooner Fairchild looked at him queerly, for an instant. "Oh, bless you!" he said. "Pozzy never had a nickel. But he was fun." He tugged at Lane Parrington's arm, as they turned a corner and saw an electric sign — 1908 — above the door. "Well, here we go!" he said.

An hour later, Lane Parrington decided that it was just as he had expected. True, the drunk from the unidentified class had gone home. But others, from other classes, had arrived. And Schooner Fairchild was sitting at the piano.

He himself was wedged uncomfortably at the back of the room between Ed Runner and a man whose name, he thought, was either Ferguson or Whitelaw, but who, in any case, addressed him as "Lane, old boy." This made conversation difficult, for it was hard to call his neighbor either "Fergy" or "Whitey" without being sure of his name. On the other hand, conversation with Ed Runner was equally difficult, for that gentleman had embarked upon an interminable reminiscence whose point turned upon the exact location of Bill Webley's room Sophomore year. As Lane Parrington had never been in any of Bill Webley's rooms, he had very little to add to the discussion. He was also drinking beer, which never agreed with him, and the cigar smoke stung his eyes. And around the singer and the piano boiled and seethed a motley crew of graduates of all classes — the Roman togas of 1913, the convict stripes of 1935, the shorts and explorers' helmets of 1928. For the news had somehow gone around, through the various class headquarters, that Schooner Fairchild was doing his stuff — and, here and there, among the crowd, were undergraduates, who had heard from brothers and uncles about Schooner Fairchild, but had never seen him before in the flesh.

He had told the story of the Kickapoo chief, he had given the imitation of President Dodge and the telephone. Both these and other efforts, Lane Parrington noted wonderingly, had been received with tumultuous cheers. Now he played a few chords and swung around on the piano stool.

"I shall now," he said, with his cherubic face very solemn, "emit my positively last and final number — an imitation of dear old Pozzy Banks, attempting to sing 'The Last Rose of Summer' while under the influence of wine. Not all of you have been privileged to know dear old Pozzy — a man of the most varied and diverse talents — it is our great regret that he is not with us tonight. But for those of you who were not privileged to know Pozzy, may I state as an introduction that dear old Pozzy is built something on the lines of a truck, and that, when under the influence of wine, it was his custom to sing directly into his hat, which he held out before him like a card tray. We will now begin." He whirled round, struck a few lugubrious notes and began to sing.

It was, as even Lane Parrington had to admit, extremely funny. He heard himself joining in the wild, deep roar of laughter that greeted the end of the first verse — he was annoyed at himself but he could not help it. By some magic, by some trick of gesture and voice, the chubby, bald-headed figure had suddenly become a large and lugubrious young man — a young man slightly under the influence of wine but still with the very best intentions, singing sentimentally and lugubriously into his hat. It was a trick and an act and a sleight of hand not worth learning — but it did not fail in its effect. Lane Parrington found himself laughing till he ached — beside him, the man named either Ferguson or Whitelaw was whooping and gasping for breath.

"And now," said Schooner Fairchild, while they were still laughing, "let somebody play who *can* play!" And, magically crooking his finger, he summoned a dark-haired undergraduate from the crowd, pushed him down on the piano stool, and, somehow or other, slipped through the press and vanished, while they were still calling his name.

Lane Parrington, a little later, found himself strolling up and down the dejected back yard of class headquarters. They had put up a tent, some iron tables and a number of paper lanterns, but, at this hour, the effect was not particularly gay. It must be very late and he ought to go to bed. But he did not look at his watch. He was trying to think about certain things in his life and get them into a proportion. It should be a simple thing to do, as simple as making money, but it was not.

Ted — Dorothy — the Leaf — Emmetsburg — Schooner Fairchild — Tom Drury — the place in Virginia and the mean house at Emmetsburg – United Investments and a sleight-of-hand trick at a tiny piano. He shuffled the factors of the equation about; they should add up to a whole. And, if they did, he would be willing to admit it; he told himself that. Yes, even if the final sum proved him wrong for years – that had always been one of the factors of his own success, his knowing just when to cut a loss.

A shaky voice hummed behind him:

"Oh, the ship's cat said to the cabin boy,
To the cabin boy said she . . ."

He turned – it was Schooner Fairchild and, he thought at first, Schooner Fairchild was very drunk. Then he saw the man's lips were gray, caught him and helped him into one of the iron chairs.

"Sorry," wheezed Schooner Fairchild. "Must have run too fast, getting away from the gang. Damn' silly – left my medicine at the inn."

"Here – wait – " said Lane Parrington, remembering the flask of brandy in his pocket. He uncorked it and held it to the other man's lips. "Can you swallow?" he said solicitously.

An elfish, undefeated smile lit Schooner Fairchild's face. "Always could, from a child," he gasped. "Never ask a Fairchild twice." He drank and said, incredibly, it seemed to Lane Parrington, "Napoleon . . . isn't it? Sir, you spoil me." His color began to come back. "Better," he said.

"Just stay there," said Lane Parrington. He dashed back into club headquarters – deserted now, he noticed, except for the gloomy caretaker and the man called Ferguson or Whitelaw, who was ungracefully asleep on a leather couch. Efficiently, he found glasses, ice, soda, plain water and ginger ale, and returned, his hands full of these trophies, to find Schooner Fairchild sitting up in his chair and attempting to get a cigarette from the pocket of his coat.

His eyes twinkled as he saw Lane Parrington's collection of glassware. "My!" he said. "We *are* going to make a night of it. Great shock to me – never thought it of you, Lane."

"Hadn't I better get a doctor?" said Lane Parrington. "There's a telephone – "

"Not a chance," said Schooner Fairchild. "It would worry Minnie sick. She made me promise before I came up to take care. It's just the old pump – misses a little sometimes. But I'll be all right, now – right as a trivet, whatever a trivet is. Just give me another shot of Napoleon."

"Of course," said Lane Parrington, "but – "

"Brandy on beer, never fear," said Schooner Fairchild. "Fairchild's Medical Maxims, Number One. And a cigarette . . . thanks." He breathed deeply. "And there we are," he said, with a smile. "Just catches you in the short ribs, now and then. But, when it's over, it's over. You ought to try a little yourself, Lane – damn' silly performance of mine and you look tired."

"Thanks," said Lane Parrington, "I will." He made himself, neatly, an efficient brandy and soda and raised the glass to his lips. "Well – er – here's luck," he said, a little stiffly.

"Luck!" nodded Schooner Fairchild. They both drank. Lane Parrington looked at the pleasant, undefeated face.

"Listen, Schooner," said Lane Parrington, suddenly and harshly, "if you had the whole works to shoot over again — " He stopped.

"That's the hell of a question to ask a man at three o'clock in the morning," said Schooner equably. "Why?"

"Oh, I don't know," said Lane Parrington. "But that stuff at the piano you did — well, how did you do it?" His voice was oddly ingenious, for Lane Parrington.

"Genius, my boy, sheer, untrammeled genius," said Schooner Fairchild. He chuckled and sobered. "Well, somebody has to," he said reasonably. "And you wouldn't expect Tom Drury to do it, would you? — poor old Tom!"

"No," said Lane Parrington, breathing. "I wouldn't expect Tom Drury to do it."

"Oh, Tom's all right," said Schooner Fairchild. "He was just born with an ingrowing Drury and never had it operated on. But he's a fine guy, all the same. Lord," he said, "it must be a curse — to have to be a Drury, whether you like it or not. I never could have stood it — I never could have played the game. Of course," he added hastily, "I suppose it's different, if you do it all yourself, the way you have. That must be a lot of fun."

"I wouldn't exactly call it fun," said Lane Parrington earnestly. "You see, after all, Schooner, there are quite a good many things that enter into . . ." He paused, and laughed hopelessly. "Was I always a stuffed shirt?" he said. "I suppose I was."

"Oh, I wouldn't call you a stuffed shirt," said Schooner, a little quickly. "You just had to succeed – and you've done it. Gosh, we all knew you were going to, right from the first – there couldn't be any mistake about that. It must be a swell feeling." He looked at Lane Parrington and his voice trailed off. He began again. "You see, it was different with me," he said. "I couldn't help it. Why, just take a look at me – I've even got a comedy face. Well, I never wanted anything very much except – oh, to have a good time and know other people were having a good time. Oh, I tried taking the other things seriously – I tried when I was a broker, but I couldn't, it was just no go. I made money enough – everybody was making money – but every now and then, in the middle of a million-share day, I'd just think how damn silly it was for everybody to be watching the board and getting all excited over things called ATT and UGI. And that's no way for a broker to act – you've got to believe those silly initials mean something, if you want to be a broker.

"Well, I've tried a good many things since. And now and then I've been lucky, and we've gotten along. And I've spent most of Minnie's money, but she says it was worth it – and we've got the five girls and they're wonders – and I'll probably die playing the piano at some fool party, for you can't keep it up forever, but I only hope it happens before somebody says, 'There goes poor old Schooner. He used to be pretty amusing, in his time!' But, you see, I couldn't help it," he ended diffidently. "And, you know, I've tried. I've tried hard. But then I'd start laughing, and it always got in the way."

Lane Parrington looked at the man who had spent his wife's money and his own for a sleight-of-hand trick, five daughters, and the sound of friendly laughter. He looked at him without understanding, and yet with a curious longing.

"But, Schooner – " he said, "with all you can do – you ought to – "

"Oh," said Schooner, a trifle wearily, "one has one's dreams. Sure, I'd like to be Victor Boucher – he's a beautiful comedian. Or Bill Fields, for instance. Who wouldn't? But I don't kid myself. It's a parlor talent – it doesn't go over the footlights. But, Lord, what fun I've had with it! And the funny things people keep doing, forever and ever, amen. And the decent – the very decent things they keep doing, too. Well, I always thought it would be a good life, while you had it." He paused, and Lane Parrington saw the fatigue on his face. "Well, it's been a good party," he said. "I wish old Pozzy could have been here. But I guess we ought to go to bed."

"I'll phone for a cab," said Lane Parrington. "Nope – you're riding."

Lane Parrington shut the door of Schooner Fairchild's room behind him and stood, for a moment, with his hand on the knob. He had seen Schooner safely to bed – he had even insisted on the latter's taking his medicine, though Schooner had been a little petulant about it. Now, however, he still wondered about calling a doctor – if Schooner should be worse in the morning, he would have Anstey come up by plane. It was nothing to do, though not everybody could do it, and Anstey was much the best man. In any case, he would insist on Schooner's seeing Anstey this week. Then he wondered just how he was going to insist.

The old elevator just across the corridor came to a wheezing stop. Its door opened and a dark-haired girl in evening dress came out. Lane Parrington dropped his hand from the doorknob and turned away. But the girl took three quick steps after him.

"I'm sorry," she said, a little breathlessly, "but I'm Sylvia Fairchild. Is Father ill? The elevator boy said something – and I saw you coming out of his room."

"He's all right," said Lane Parrington. "It was just the slightest sort of – "

"Oh!" said the girl, "do you mind coming back for a minute? You're Ted's father, aren't you? My room's next door, but I've got a key for his, too – Mother told me to be sure – " She seemed very self-possessed. Lane Parrington waited uncomfortably in the corridor for what seemed to him a long time, while she went into her father's room. When she came out again, she seemed relieved.

"It's all right," she said, in a low voice. "He's asleep, and his color's good. And he's . . ." She paused. "Oh, damn!" she said. "We can't talk out here. Come into my room for a minute – we can leave the door open – after all, you *are* Ted's father. I'll have to tell Mother, you see – and Father will just say it wasn't anything."

She opened the door and led the way into the room.

"Here," she said. "Just throw those stockings off the chair – I'll sit on the bed. Well?"

"Well, I asked him if he wanted a doctor . . ." said Lane Parrington humbly.

When he had finished a concise, efficient report, the girl nodded, and he saw for the first time that she was pretty, with her dark, neat head and her clever, stubborn chin.

"Thank you," she said. "I mean, really. Father's a perfect lamb – but he doesn't like to worry Mother, and it worries her a lot more not to know. And sometimes it's rather difficult, getting the truth out of Father's friends. Not you," she was pleased to add. "You've been perfectly truthful. And the brandy was quite all right."

"I'm glad," said Lane Parrington. "I wish your father would see Anstey," he added, a trifle awkwardly. "I could – er – make arrangements."

"He has," said the girl. Her mouth twitched. "Oh," she said. "I shouldn't have gone to the dance. I couldn't help the Momus Club, but he might have come back afterward, if I'd been here. Only, I don't know."

"I wouldn't reproach myself," said Lane Parrington. "After all – "

"Oh, I know," said the girl. "After all! If you don't all manage to kill him, between you! Friends!" she sniffed. Then, suddenly, her face broke into lines of amusement. "I sound just like Aunt Emma," she said. "And that's pretty silly of me. Aunt Emma's almost pure poison. Of course it isn't your fault and I really do thank you. Very much. Do you know, I never expected you'd be a friend of Father's."

"After all," said Lane Parrington stiffly, "we were in the same class."

"Oh, I know," said the girl. "Father's talked about you, of course." Her mouth twitched again, but this time, it seemed to Lane Parrington, with a secret merriment. "And so has Ted, naturally," she added politely.

"I'm glad he happened to mention me," said Lane Parrington, and she grinned, frankly.

"I deserved that," she said, while Lane Parrington averted his eyes from what seemed to be a remarkably flimsy garment hung over the bottom of the bed. "But Ted has, really. He admires you quite a lot, you know, though, of course, you're different generations."

"Tell me — " said Lane Parrington. "No, I won't ask you."

"Oh, you know Ted," said the girl, rather impatiently. "It's awfully hard to get him to say things — and he will spend such a lot of time thinking he ought to be noble, poor lamb. But he's losing just a little of that, thank goodness — when he first came to Widgeon Point, he was trying so hard to be exactly like that terrible Drury boy. You see — " she said, suddenly and gravely, "he could lose quite a lot of it and still have more than most people."

Lane Parrington cleared his throat. There seemed nothing for him to say. Then he thought of something.

"His mother was — er — a remarkable person," he said. "We were not at all happy together. But she had remarkable qualities."

"Yes," said the girl. "Ted's told me. He remembers her." They looked at each other for a moment – he noted the stubborn chin, the swift and admirable hands. Then a clock on the mantel struck and the girl jumped.

"Good heavens!" she said. "It's four o'clock! Well – good night. And I do thank you, Mr Parrington."

"It wasn't anything," said Lane Parrington. "But remember me to your father. But I'll see you in the morning, of course."

The following afternoon, Lane Parrington found himself waiting for his car in the lobby of the inn. There had been a little trouble with the garage and it was late. But he did not care, particularly, though he felt glad to be going back to New York. He had said good-by to Ted an hour before – Ted was going on to a house party at the Chiltons' – they'd eventually meet on Long Island, he supposed. Meanwhile, he had had a pleasant morning, attended the commencement exercises, and had lunch with Ted and the Fairchilds at the inn. Schooner had been a little subdued and both Ted and the girl frankly sleepy, but he had enjoyed the occasion nevertheless. And somehow the fact that the president's baccalaureate address had also viewed with alarm and talked about imperiled bulwarks and the American way of life – had, in fact, repeated with solemn precision a good many of the points in his own speech – did not irk Lane Parrington as it might have the day before. After all, the boys were young and could stand it. They had stood a good deal of nonsense, even in his own time.

Now he thought once more of the equation he had

tried too earnestly to solve, in the back yard of commencement headquarters — and, for a moment, almost grinned. It was, of course, insoluble — life was not as neat as that. You did what you could, as it was given you to do — very often you did the wrong things. And if you did the wrong things, you could hardly remedy them by a sudden repentance — or, at least, he could not. There were still the wigglers and the ones who stood still — and each had his own virtues. And because he was a wiggler, he had thoughtfully and zealously done his best to make his son into the image of one of the magnificent sheep — the image of Tom Drury, who was neither hungry nor gay. He could not remedy that, but he thought he knew somebody who could remedy it, remembering the Fairchild girl's stubborn chin. And, in that case at least, the grandchildren ought to be worth watching.

"Your car, Mr. Parrington," said a bellboy. He moved toward the door. It was hard to keep from being a stuffed shirt, if you had the instinct in you, but one could try. A good deal might be done, with trying.

As he stepped out upon the steps of the inn, he noticed a figure, saluting — old Negro Mose, the campus character who remembered everybody's name.

"Hello, Mose!" said Lane Parrington. "Remember me?"

"Remember you — sho', Mr. Parrington," said Mose. He regarded Lane Parrington with beady eyes. "Let's see — you was 1906."

"Nineteen hundred and eight," said Lane Parrington, but without rancor.

Mose gave a professional chuckle. "Sho'!" he said. "I was forgettin'! Let's see – you hasn't been back fo' years, Mister Parrington – but you was in Tom Drury's class – an' Schooner Fairchild's class – "

"No," said Lane Parrington and gave the expected dollar, "not Tom Drury's class, Schooner Fairchild's class."

AMONG THOSE PRESENT

MY dear, I'm exhausted. They just wouldn't leave El Morocco, and then we went on to hear that girl sing those songs. Irish ballads, you know, and she's really a Brazilian – it gives them a quality you simply wouldn't believe. And the wonderful thing it, she learned them from a phonograph record. She can't speak a word of English otherwise. So she just sings them over and over, and everybody cheers. But everybody. Ted said he'd always been against inventing the phonograph, and now he was sure of it – but that's just the way he talks.

Well, if I do say it myself, it was rather an amusing crowd. Larry Dunn, you know – the Dunns are stuffy rich, but Larry's a darling – he does candid-camera studies that are just as good as Werbe's and you'd never know he was rich at all, except, as Ted says, when it comes to not reaching for the check. And the Necropuloffs – Russians, my dear, and so brave! Their father was actually eaten by wolves or something and they know the most ghastly stories about Stalin. And Mike Glatto – he's movies – All-American Productions – and rather unbrushed, in a way, but quite fascinating – and the Jenkinses, of course – and Jane Pierce, who does the cocktail column for *Sport and Society*. Oh, yes, and the little Lindsay girl that Ted knows – but she didn't come on to the other place. She couldn't — she works or something — so Ted dropped her and met us afterward.

Just as well, in a way. She didn't really quite fit in and she lives in some unheard-of place like Riverside Drive — Ted was hours finding us. But the rest of it — well, they're just the sort of people you can only find in New York.

I suppose it was my fault, staying quite so late. Ted growled a bit, coming home — said, wouldn't it be cheaper in the end, if we rented the house and lived in the checkroom at the Stork Club. But I think that was the guinea hen we had for dinner — guinea hen always disagrees with him, but there's a new way of basting it with brandy that Jane Pierce taught me and I couldn't resist it. And, to be utterly frank, my dear, I needed something. A little revelry. You see, I'd been to the Coles' that afternoon. And that was grim.

Oh, just a rather grim party. Hordes of people and warm Martinis. They usually give such good parties too. No, it wasn't seeing Bob and the bride — Lucille Cole phoned me they'd probably be there. And we're utterly friendly, of course — I always ask him how his work's going. I think you have to be civilized about these things. You don't scream and faint any more when you meet your ex-husband. And I'm hardly Alice Ben Bolt. But I did feel a little hurt that he hadn't told me. After all, it's still a surprise to pick up the paper and see that your former helpmeet has married somebody you've never even heard of. And in Florida, of all places! Of course, he's been painting down there. But I did send him a telegram when I married Ted.

Funny, too, I always imagined he'd pick somebody rather maternal. A nice widow or one of those hearty, earthy girls with rather flat feet. Painters are so apt. But this. . . .

Oh, that fresh, untouched type, my dear, if you happen to like it. A brave little profile, you know – a gallant little figure in sports clothes. And, I'm afraid, dancing curls. Just another Joan of Arc. They seem to produce them, nowadays. Only, I fail to see why they call her "little." She'd be quite as tall as I am if she wore heels.

No, but really an infant. Really. Twenty-one. And – oh, yes – they're going to live in the country. They were rapt about it. In fact, they've got their eye on a farmhouse. I suppose she'll raise chickens. Or doves. She's the type for doves. And Bob will turn the old stable into a studio, and they'll do it all themselves and take photographs too. It's too grim to think about, really. And she'll greet him with a flushed, happy face, when he comes home from his work, and cook little meals. Only they say she has money – so it'll probably be two very good maids. Till the children come, of course, and they have to build on the wing. . . . No, not yet, but they certainly will. Dozens of them – all Joans of Arc.

I think I'll have another cocktail, my dear, I'm a little tired. . . .

Ted? No, he was spared, though I'm sure the bride would have liked him. . . . Oh, he's very well. He liked you, my dear, by the way. . . . No, really – no, I could see. And next time it must just be ourselves and we'll have a good long talk about the old days. Ted's so funny. He's always insisted that there never could be such a place as Little Prairie. So I was delighted when you phoned. I said, "It's little Kitty Harris – the child with the bang that used to have a crush on me in school. And she's here in New York with her husband – and, my dear, they'll be babes in the wood and we must rescue them." So, you see.

Now, tell me again just what your husband does. . . . Oh, research. That's always so intelligent. And that rather lean-jawed look – very attractive, my dear. Oh, you'll have no difficulty at all. But you must begin as you mean to go on – that's the important thing. And anything I can do – well, just treat me as a mother confessor. After all, I was a mouse myself when I first came to New York – but a mouse!

The one thing is, it's so easy to get tangled up with a lot of stodgy, unimportant people. And no husband is a help about that. Why, if Ted had his way, we'd do nothing but give dinners for his partners and his Harvard classmates – not to speak of the family. And Bob was just the same about painters. He thought putting on a dress shirt meant prostituting your art. While, as a matter of fact, it's just as easy to meet the amusing people as the dull ones. All you need is the tiniest start, and perhaps a wee bit of guidance. After that, as I've often said, it just rolls like a snowball. Ted says they'll come anywhere for free liquor. Isn't it wicked of him? Well, of course, you can hardly give a party on Aunt

Emma's dandelion wine. But that's only a part of it; it needs a certain sense. Take our little party last night — well, perhaps I am supposed to have a gift for that sort of thing, but it was so simple, really. And Paul Necropuloff said it reminded him of his Great-Uncle Feodor's *dacha* in the Caucasus and nearly cried. . . .

Oh, you'll have a wonderful time. You don't really live till you're here, my dear — I assure you. I sound positively dewy-eyed, don't I? But there you are. I always knew it was going to be my town, and you'll feel the same way. Little Kitty Harris! And you'd sit reading "The Five Little Peppers" while we big girls played jacks on the porch — I can see it all so plainly. I must get some jacks; I believe they still have them in stores. We'll have a party and play them; it'll be a furor. We introduced parcheesi, you know, while I was still married to Bob, and people played it for months. . . .

Well, of course, my dear, you've kept up so much more. I do think it's so brave of you. It sometimes seems to me as if I could never have lived there at all. And Mother will send me long clippings about Hick's Garage being torn down and Willy Snamm being made head teller at the Drovers' National — as if I remembered people named Willy Snamm! . . . Oh, my dear, I'm so sorry. I didn't realize that he married your cousin. But it is a quaint name. And four children — darling, how forthright of them! That's wonderful. I suppose if I'd stayed in Little Prairie, I'd have four children myself. . . . No, we haven't. . . . Somehow, one keeps putting it off.

But when I think of what we've both escaped — at

least now you're here, too, my dear – it seems absolutely providential. I so well remember our first winter – Bob's and mine. And how discouraged he got. His work wasn't going well, though he was quite sweet about it, and he kept saying he'd like to feel the earth under his feet again. They will say the weirdest things. And I must say that, now and then, I felt pretty discouraged myself. Sometimes, when Bob was out, I'd take a bus uptown and then walk past the old Waldorf-Astoria and wonder if I'd ever know the people who went there. The Waldorf! Imagine! And I had to look up the Ritz in the telephone book to find out where it was. Why, we didn't even know a speak-easy, except the Italian place on Charlton Street, with the dollar dinner and the menu in purple ink. And then, that spring, I got my job on *Modes and Manners*. And we met the Halleys and things really began.

Though, as a matter of fact, it was Ben Christian who first took us to the Charlton Street place. . . . Oh, yes, my dear, very well. He used to sleep on our couch when they'd evict him. He was writing *Bitter Harvest* then, and I must say he'd read it aloud at the drop of a hat. Well, I did make a few suggestions – the women were simply impossible, and he knew it. Rather sensitive and sweet in those days, with untamed hair and a thin face – well, his face is still thin. He used to call me "The Kid from Little Prairie" and say we made him believe in marriage or something. And we'd sit around in the Charlton Street place and he and Bob would talk for hours. I still remember that awful wine.

There were moth balls in it, I'm sure. But we thought it was wonderful.

Well, of course, that sort of thing is all very nice when you're new. Very picturesque and all that, when you're looking back – though the ravioli always tasted of thumbs. And Ben used the place in *Bitter Harvest,* so that was all right. In fact, it got to be quite celebrated and people would come from uptown. Ben was rather rude about that – he'd call them "slummers" and say they came to watch the quaint animals perform. Of course, I'd know now that it was just an inferiority complex, because he was born on Hester Street himself – but I was a child in those days. I hadn't even read Jung.

He wasn't rude to the Halleys, exactly, but he was – well, suspicious. And the worst of it was, he made Bob suspicious too. I had quite a time getting him over that. And, really, I can't imagine why. Because, after all – and in spite of everything that's happened – the Halleys were our kind. But he used to say that the worst thing about the arts was the people who thought you could collect them like Pekingese. I'm sure I don't know what he meant by it. It must have been just a psychosis. Like washing your hands too much.

Now, I must say, I have an instinct about those things. I don't claim any credit for it; it's just in you or it's not. And I knew, when we first saw the Halleys, they were people we ought to know. It was weird, my dear – just like a premonition. Though I don't suppose I'd think that Miriam was quite so distinguished now.

She's gone off terribly, recently. And one does get tired of Halstead's imitations. He's been doing them so long. Well, I suppose you'd have to do something if you were married to Miriam.

But they were the first real New Yorkers we really knew. I don't mean people like Ben Christian, who happened to be born here, but people that counted. They took us to our first first-night, and I'll never forget it. And Miriam wore her long gold earrings and they knew the star. But, my dear, the struggle I had to get Bob into a dinner coat! I finally just had to show him that it was an investment, as, of course, it is. And even then, he would call it a tuxedo. But the Halleys just laughed and thought it was quaint and American.

They'd have asked Ben Christian, too, if they'd thought he'd come. They were always very nice about Ben, and Miriam bought dozens of copies of *Bitter Harvest* after the reviews came out. But he simply couldn't understand them—it was a blind spot. He kept on saying they were slummers and that he'd respect Halstead a lot more if he spent his money on a racing stable instead of backing bad plays and collecting worse pictures, just to please Miriam. Because, he said, there are certain people who are born to own racing stables. And there's one thing about being a horse—now and then you get a chance to kick somebody like Halstead square in the slats.

Which I think was very unfair, when Halstead had got Bob three game rooms to decorate and Miriam had started him on book jackets. Of course, it wasn't Bob's real work, but it meant he was beginning to be known.

And they'd have done just as much for Ben, if he'd let them. I used to tell him so. But he'd just grin at me and say, "Don't be fooled, kid. I know those helping hands. Remember Little Prairie!" Well, it didn't mean much, in the first place, and finally, he got to saying it all the time. And I do think that's boring.

I'm certainly the last person in the world to come between a husband and his friends. I've always been very careful about that, with both Bob and Ted. But there does come a point – you'll see. And the first big party we gave in the old studio. . . . Oh, Christian came, my dear, if you can call it coming. We were blessed with his physical presence. But he wouldn't even drink – just sat in a corner and glared. As if he wanted to get away, but didn't quite know how. And for no reason.

Of course, I didn't know as much about parties as I do now, but still it was fun. And Bob almost sold a water color because of it. I'm sure the woman would have bought it if she'd ever seen it again.

Well, we patched things up afterward, but they never were quite the same. I think it really hurt Bob – and I certainly tried to make it up to him. I even thought we might have a baby, just to take his mind off things; though where we'd have put it, I don't know. But then, thank heaven, Ben fell in love with a girl and moved to Brooklyn – and, my dear, the relief! She was years older than either of us and wore embroidered smocks – and even Bob saw there was simply no use going on.

And by that time the Charlton Street place had put in a garden and waiters, so it wasn't fun any more.

There were too many people who went there, and you'd be bothered. So we took our courage in both hands and moved uptown. Beekman Place — it hadn't really begun then. Bob never liked the light quite as well, but it looked much more like a studio when I'd fixed it up, and, after all, when you're doing game rooms, you have to do them on the spot.

And then the rush began. There's nothing like it — we simply went everywhere. Of course, I'd be a little more selective now. But I remember Halstead saying to me, "Well, little one, you two have certainly taken the town," and Halstead never exaggerates. And Bob's first show went over with a bang — they even ran a photograph of him in *Vanity Fair*. I don't know why he wasn't more pleased with it; he may have thought the pastel sketches were hasty, but everybody else thought they were divine.

Well, of course, if one critic calls your work "superficial," that's the one review you read. You ought to be glad that your husband's a scientist.

Naturally, it was prohibition then — it sounds quite prehistoric, doesn't it? But New York's always the same. We went to 42 long before it was 42. And the most amusing people were around — it's really sad to think back. That's the one sad thing about the city — the people who drop out. Of course, there are always new ones, but it isn't quite the same. Well, the Reeces, for instance — they were darlings, and had a perfect doll's house of a place. But then they started having children and now they're living in Jersey, of all places, and one never sees them any more. And Allan Lark is permanently in Hollywood and they say he drinks terribly. And Ethel Shand – my dear, you wouldn't remember her, but she made a great hit in "Welcome, Folks", and then she just dropped out of sight. The last I heard, she was doing some ghastly sort of work for a Middle Western radio station and she'd lost her looks completely. Oh, it's a casualty list. I think of it every time I go into Tony's.

One must just keep the chin up, that's all. And I've always tried. Even when Bob began drinking – and I've never quite understood that. My dear, I'm not a prude, but I can take it or leave it alone. And, as a matter of fact, it has very little effect on me. It never has. You wouldn't know I'd had a cocktail before I came here, would you? While Bob has always had a weak head. I suppose it's his shyness, partly. He needs just about two drinks to get over it and be amusing and affable. But after that you have to call in the marines.

And I certainly never tried to stop him or play the injured wife. I don't believe in that. But I did think it was a pity he should spoil things when we were having such a nice time and meeting all the right people – and I suppose he saw it. Men are so sensitive. And if I could take a cocktail or two without making a spectacle of myself, I don't see why he should feel he had to do the same. As I said, once or twice, we could just admit we were different and let it go at that. But that only seemed to make him worse. Ted says it would, but then Ted hardly knows Bob at all. And when I asked Ted what the real reason was – because men stick together so –

he only said, "Well, perhaps he felt it deadened the pain." Which doesn't make sense, my dear.

Anyhow, I noticed he was just drinking milk at the Coles'. The bride, I suppose. But it's just as artificial, I always think.

I remember one enormous party at the Nesbitts' – well, I saw how things were going and I felt simply desperate – the Nesbitts are so important. And I just couldn't get to Bob. So I was perfectly frantic – and then I looked across the room, and there was Ben Christian! In a white tie and tails, my dear – imagine! Well, he'd had his second big success. Well, any port in a storm, so I went over. And he was really quite friendly. He grinned and said, "Hello, kid! Remember Little Prairie!" And I said, "Well, how do you like it?" looking at his tie. And he grinned again and said, "It's the biggest, shiniest merry-go-round in the world. That's all right. But, gosh, what funny people they get on the horses!"

Then he asked after Bob, and I said, "He's over there," and he looked, and the queerest expression came over his face. "Why, he's tight!" he said.

"Are you telling me?" I said.

"I wouldn't have believed it," he said. "But why? Oh, well. We'd better take him home."

"If you only would," I said. "He's got his keys and the light turns on by the door. And, of course, I want to pay for the taxi."

He looked at me again, with that funny expression. "No, thanks," he said. "I can manage. Well, so long, Little Prairie!"

That's the way he is, you know—abrupt. And he did take Bob home, and everything was all right when I came in. I've always been very grateful. Of course, I meant to thank Ben when he came back to the party himself, but he didn't come back. And when I tried to phone, next day, they said at his publisher's that he'd left for the Coast.

Well, of course, that was just one time, but there were others. Really, dear, I don't know how I stood it. I couldn't have, except for my friends. They were wonderful. And most of them understood so perfectly—though I must say, I always said, "You mustn't take sides. And just treat Bob as you always have. We can't all of us succeed." I've always been like that; I try to see both sides. Though I must say it did hurt me a little, about the Halleys.

It may be very provincial of me, but I don't quite see what business it was of theirs. Though, of course, I appreciated their loyalty to Bob. I suppose that was why they did it. But, really, to hear them talk, you'd have thought I'd Led Him to the Bottle. Well, dear, you can see for yourself. And about children making a difference—why, it was pre-Victorian! When I'd told Bob in the beginning that I didn't mean to tie him down, like so many wives.

Then, finally, Halstead started on the Perils of the Big City and What New York Does to People, and it was a little too dreary. And as far as Ted was concerned—why, I'd barely met him then—though, of course, I knew who he was. But I never dreamt. Oh, well, I suppose they meant it for the best. But it rather hurt me. They didn't even offer me a cocktail — I had to stop by at Tony's afterward. And there was Bob, with the Russian friend. So that was that.

All the same, I really hated breaking up the apartment. Those things are a trifle grim. Especially when they look at you in that blond, rather appealing way. You just have to be quite sensible and talk about the furniture. Remember that, my dear. Not that I wouldn't have been glad to let Bob have it. But he meant to go South anyway — he told me so. . . .

Reno? Well, dear, it isn't New York, but it isn't bad. I met some very interesting people and let my hair grow out. That was really for Ted, and I hope he appreciated it. Of course, I never thought, at the time, we'd be anything more than very good friends. Why, he'd been a bachelor for years! But it must have been — well, predestined, for he's often said it was quite as much of a surprise to him. Don't you think that's rather sweet?

I remember how dazed he was when we drove down to City Hall for the license. . . . Oh, after I'd got back, of course — almost six months. And he hadn't even brought a ring, poor lamb; we had to stop at a jewelry store on the way. Men are such babies, aren't they, about practical things? Well, it seemed to me there was absolutely no use in putting it off, when he was supposed to go to California for the firm. He might have been out there for months, and that would have been trying for both of us. Especially as people were beginning to talk a little. You know how they are. Well, someone has to make the decisions. And, as it turned out, the business wasn't so important after all and we had a whole heavenly month at Santa Barbara. But we were glad to get back. After all, there's no place like New York.

It was quite a change, of course, but, if there's one thing I do know, it's how to make adjustments. Of course, it's rather a distinguished family, really. My dear, I should be honored, I hope you know. And a divorced woman too. Why, the family halls on the Hudson rocked to their foundations. At least, I suppose they did. But there's only Brother Eugene in New York, thank goodness. Not to speak of Sister Claudia – that's his wife. And there, my dear, is a woman. . . . Oh, you know. On the boards of schools and things, and takes an intelligent interest in politics – too tiring. And just a simple string of real pearls – the kind that look false. I asked her once if she knew the Stork Club – just to make conversation – and she said, "Was it anything like the Metropolitan?" Well, at least I've rescued Ted from people like that.

But I do what I can, and we have them at least twice a winter. I think that's only fair. When I go to see Ted's mother, I always wear my hair over my ears and knot it in the back. And we always spend two weeks with her in the summer. And that works out quite nicely – I've a definite plan for it. I just consider it a rest cure – shorts and lying around in the sun. The food's good, too – that's one comfort – and Madeira, if if you like Madeira. I'm afraid Grimes – he's the butler and positively antediluvian – was rather shocked by my shorts, at first. But he's got over that.

And Ted really has a wonderful sense of humor about it all. Because I remember asking him – oh, just amusingly – if I wasn't a little of a surprise. Though, heaven knows, I do everything I can. And he looked at me in that quizzical way he has, and said, "Well, Great-Uncle Marshall married a lady called Toots Latour, and the family stood that for fourteen years. So I guess they can stand you, darling." Wasn't it quaint of him? I simply screamed. So, now and then, I call myself the Skeleton in the Closet and he always laughs.

I asked him what happened to Toots Latour – well, the poor thing finally died and Great-Uncle Marshall married again – oh, very respectably, this time! Of course, they didn't have divorces in those days. But such interesting things happen in old families. Ted's got quite interested in the family history recently – he even found a miniature of Great-Uncle Marshall, and he's got it in his study, over his desk. He says he feels it ought to be there. Touching of him, isn't it? I asked him if he couldn't find one of Toots Latour, too, but he said he really didn't think it was necessary. . . .

Yes, I think we've adjusted very well. Of course, there's always a certain amount of weeding out to do – you'll start with a clean slate and that's such a comfort. But when Ted's partners come to dinner, I just jolly them along and pretend they're gay and amusing, even when they aren't. I feel it's the least I can do. And Judge Willoughby – he's the senior partner – and, my dear, a real old buck, with a darling little beard. I always have a wonderful time with him. Well, his wife's one of those iron-gray women with nutcracker faces, so you can hardly blame him. I do think there's so much a woman can do for her husband, if she tries. And that's the real criticism I make of women like Mrs. Willoughby. You can see that she's never tried at all. Ted says that's because she's never had to, but I can hardly agree. And, as for distinction – my dear, I don't care if she does know that stodgy set in London. We're Americans over here, I should hope, not title hunters. Why, Paul Necropuloff hardly uses his title at all – and he's really a prince!

Of course, it's meant giving up my own work. But I was willing to make the sacrifice – I told Ted so. Though I've been wondering about it just a little bit, of late. After all, we've been married almost six years – quite an age. But then, the magazines have changed so. And people are quite different, somehow, when you ask them about real jobs. I wouldn't want a full-time one, of course, with my responsibilities. But take somebody like Dorothy Thompson. She doesn't run a column every day. And after all, what did she do but live in Germany? I'm sure I've done more interesting things than that.

Naturally, I know what Ted's family would expect. But I think rather definitely not. After all, there are plenty of grandchildren, with Claudia and Eugene. It isn't that I'm afraid in the least. But one has to look at it from a sensible point of view. Even if some people do, at all ages. And as a matter of fact, Ted hasn't even brought up the subject in a long time.

And then – well, you're lucky, my dear. After all, you are quite an infant. . . . Well, that's sweet of you, but I know. There seem to be so many of them about, nowadays. Not that it really makes any difference what age you are. But I noticed the other day how gray Miriam Halley is getting. Of course, she's years older than I am, but it gave me a turn.

Then, they're so exclusive, too, the young. One just has to grab, I suppose, and I do hate grabbing. I leave that to people like the Ingram woman. But that's what I mean. She's supposed to write, I believe, and it does make things easier. And really, one should do something. It gets to be three o'clock in the afternoon so soon.

My dear, I'll tell you a secret. I've been thinking about a novel. Or even reminiscences – they're doing them earlier now. And I haven't told a soul about it – well, of course, I mentioned it to Ted – and then, Ben Christian. I thought he'd be interested and I hadn't seen him in ages. . . .

Well, he's rather hard to get nowadays, my dear – especially since they talked about him for the Nobel prize. But we got him. Just a quiet little party.

I kept it down to twelve for dinner; though, of course, people swarmed in afterward.

Well, he's improved in some ways. His dress collars fit him, for one thing. But of course one never gets a chance to really talk at a dinner party. And then he had to leave early. Just when Marcus Leigh was doing his divinely naughty songs.

So, I just called him up the next day – and, my dear, the to-do! You'd think the man was royalty. But he finally said he was free from four to five, if I cared to run in. My dear, it's the dreariest hotel and the dingiest little cocktail bar. I can't imagine why he stays there.

He's abrupt, you know – very abrupt. The same old Ben. The first thing he said was, "I like that husband of yours. Nice guy." Well, that was pleasant of him, of course. But when I started asking his advice about writing, he hardly seemed to be listening.

Finally he said to me, "Well, Myra, you know how it is. The people who are going to write novels, write them. And the ones who want to be writers just talk about it. But I'll give you a note to my agent – he's got good nerves. By the way, have you written any of it yet?"

"Well, not exactly," I said. I'm always honest.

"I thought so," he said. "And what's it going to be about, if I may ask?"

"Why, New York, of course," I said, and he just looked at me. He has the queerest way of looking at you sometimes.

"New York?" he said. "Why not Little Prairie? You knew something, then."

"Oh, Ben – do we have to be tiresome?" I said – for, really, that old joke!

"I'm not tiresome," he said. "Just surprised. After all, I was born here. And I don't pretend to know all of it. But you – "

"What do they know of England that only England know?" I said.

"Well," he said, "you do know one thing if you're

born on Hester Street. You know it's more than forty restaurants, five night clubs and a hospital."

And then he went on and talked the queerest stuff. All about little people living in the Bronx and butchers in the market, and Wall Street and corporation lawyers and the men who dig the new subways. And how it was fifty cities and you never got to the end of them, and how a man could spend his whole life looking, and still not know it all. I suppose it'll all be in his next book—it sounded like that.

"But you know it!" he said. "You know it!" and he sounded quite angry. "Forty restaurants, five night clubs and a hospital! You know it all! Well, I only hope you write the book! Can I lend you a map of the city? No, it wouldn't do any good."

Well, of course, there's no use arguing with a man in his condition, so I just thanked him for his interest, and let it go at that. He looked at me again.

"Look here, Myra. I'm going to talk to you," he said. And then he said, "No. What's the use? It's got into the bloodstream."

"I don't know what you mean," I said.

"Oh, nothing," he said. "I was just thinking aloud. Because they come every year, I suppose—ten thousand of them—the kids with a little talent and a lot of youth. And they end up thinking it's wonderful to hear a Class B heel sing dirty little songs. Or some of them. Oh, well."

"I'm glad you're so appreciative of my friends," I said.

"Oh, forget it," he said. "I was just remembering

things — it's a bad practice. But remember what I said about that husband of yours. He's a nice guy, but he looks as if he might have brains. And sometimes, you know, you can make the dose too strong."

Well, that was cryptic, I suppose — poor dear Ben, he always loved to make those mysterious remarks. But, all the same, he gave me the note to his agent. So, if I burst into print, my dear, you musn't be surprised. The only thing is, I haven't quite decided just what publisher to have. I was going to start in yesterday and rough out an outline. But, of course, one must find the time. And then, seeing Bob and the bride — well, it does give one something of a shock.

So it was such a relief — just sitting and visiting with little Kitty Harris, and hearing all about your plans. You can't imagine. . . . Well, my dear, just the barest touch and then I must fly. Your husband will think me very naughty, but I did want you to see the place. It's rather a favorite *boîte* of ours, and everybody comes here, but everybody! Bob might even bring the bride here — though, really, she might as well go to the Grand Central. They have milk bars there.

And we'll see each other very soon, shan't we? I've so enjoyed chatting about the old days. And the least little thing you want advice on — I'm right on the end of the phone. We're having a party tomorrow night, but you wouldn't be interested. Just dullish people — Harvard classmates and such — but I thought this would be a good time to work some of them off. I rather wish I'd thought of you before, though — you might have helped me out with the little Lindsay. She's rather a firm-faced child. She'll fit in all right with Ted's friends – after all, they like them young. And I needed an extra woman. But I can't think how Ted happened to think of her – he doesn't often make suggestions. And we'd just had her too. But he happened to be looking at the miniature of Great-Uncle Marshall, and out it came.

IV

THE LAST OF THE LEGIONS

THE governor wanted to have everything go off as quietly as possible, but he couldn't keep the people from the windows or off the streets. After all, the legion had been at Deva ever since there was a town to speak of, and now we were going away. I don't want to say anything against the Sixth or the Second — there are good men under all the eagles. But we're not called the Valeria Victrix for nothing, and we've had the name some few centuries. It takes a legion with men in it to hold the northwest.

I think, at first, they intended to keep the news secret, but how could you do that, in a town? There's always someone who tells his girl in strict confidence, and then there are all the peddlers and astrologers and riffraff, and the sharp-faced boys with tips on the races or the games. I tell you, they knew about it as soon as the general or the governor — not to speak of the rumors before. As a matter of fact, there had been so many rumors that, when the orders came at last, it was rather a relief. You get tired of telling women that nothing will happen to them even if the legion does go, and being stopped five times in ten minutes whenever you go into town.

All the same, I had to sit up half the night with one recruit of ours. He had a girl in the town he was mad about, and a crazy notion of deserting. I had to point out to the young imbecile that even if the legion goes, Rome stays, and describe the two men I'd happened to see flogged to death, before he changed his mind. The girl was a pretty little weak-mouthed thing — she was crying in the crowd when we marched by, and he bit his lips to keep steady. But I couldn't have him deserting out of our cohort — we haven't had a thing like that happen in twenty years.

It was queer, their not making more noise. They tried to cheer — governor's orders — when we turned the camp over to the native auxiliaries in the morning, but it wasn't much of a success. And yet, the auxiliaries looked well enough, for auxiliaries. I wouldn't give two cohorts of Egyptians for them myself, but they had their breastplates shined and kept a fairly straight front. I imagined they'd dirty up our quarters — auxiliaries always do — and that wasn't pleasant to think of. But the next legion that came to Deva — us or another — would put things straight again. And it couldn't be long.

Then we had our own march past — through the town — and, as I say, it was queer. I'm a child of the camp — I was brought up in the legion. The tale is that the first of us came with Caesar — I don't put much stock in that — and of course we've married British ever since. Still, I know what I know, and I know what a crowd sounds like, on most occasions. There's the mutter of a hostile one, and the shouts when they throw flowers, and the sharp, fierce cheering when they know you're going out to fight for them. But this was different. There wasn't any heart or pith in it – just a queer sort of sobbing wail that went with us all the way to the gates. Oh, here and there, people shouted, "Come back with their heads!" or, "Bring us a Goth for a pet!" the way they do, but not as if they believed what they were saying. Too many of them were silent, and that queer sort of sobbing wail went with us all the way.

I march with the first cohort; it wasn't so bad for me. Though here and there, I saw faces in the crowd – old Elfrida, who kept the wine shop, with the tears running down her fat cheeks, shouting like a good one, and Parmesius, the usurer, biting his nails and not saying anything at all. He might have given us a cheer; he'd had enough of our money. But he stood there, looking scared. I expect he was thinking of his money bags and wondering if somebody would slip a knife in his ribs at night. We'd kept good order in the town.

It took a long time, at the gates, for the governor had to make a speech – like all that old British stock, he tries to be more Roman than the Romans. Our general listened to him, sitting his horse like a bear. He's a new general, one of Stilicho's men, and a good one in spite of his hairiness and his Vandal accent. I don't think he cared very much for the governor's speech – it was the usual one. The glorious Twentieth, you know, and our gallant deeds, and how glad they'd be to have us back again. Well, we knew that without his telling – we could read it in the white faces along the walls. They were very still, but you could feel them, looking. The whole town must have been at the walls. Then the speech ended, and our general nodded his bear head and we marched. I don't know how long they stayed at the walls — I couldn't look back.

But my recruit got away, after all, at the second halt, and that bothered me. He was a likely looking young fellow, though I'd always thought his neck was too long. Still, he was one of the children of the camp — you wouldn't have picked him to desert. After that, half a dozen others tried it — those things are like a disease — but our general caught two and made an example, and that stopped the rest. I don't care for torture, myself — it leaves a bad taste in your mouth — but there are times when you have to use a firm hand. They were talking too much about Deva and remembering too many things. Well, I could see, myself, that if we had to be marched half across Britain to take ship at Anderida, that meant the Northmen were strong again. And I wouldn't like to hold the northwest against Northmen and Scots with nothing but auxiliaries. But that was the empire's business — it wasn't mine.

After it was over, I was having a cup of wine and chatting with Agathocles — he's a small man, but clever with the legion accounts and very proud that his father was a Greek. He has special privileges, and that's apt to get a man disliked, but I always got along well with him. If you're senior centurion, you have your own rights, and he didn't often try the nasty side of his tongue on me.

"Well, Death's-Head," I said — we call him that because of his bony face — "were you present at the ceremonies?"

"Oh, I was present," he said. He shivered a little.

"I suppose you liked hearing them squeal," he said, with his black eyes full of malice.

"Can't say that I did," I said, "but it'll keep the recruits in order."

"For a while," he said, and laughed softly. But I wasn't really thinking of the men who had been caught — I was thinking of my own recruit who'd gotten away. I could see him, you know, quite plainly, with his long neck and his bright blue Northern eyes — a tiny, running figure, hiding in ditches and traveling by night. He'd started in full marching order, too, like an idiot. Pretty soon, he'd be throwing pieces of equipment away. And what would he do when he did get back to Deva — hide on one of the outlying farms? Our farmers were a rough lot — they'd turn him over to the governor, if they didn't cut his throat for the price of his armor. It's a bad feeling, being hunted — I've had it myself. You begin to hear noises in the bracken and feel the joints in your armor where an arrow could go through. He'd scream, too, if he were caught — scream like a hare. And all for a weak-faced girl and because he felt homesick! I couldn't understand it.

"Worried about your recruit?" said Agathocles, though I hadn't said a word.

"The young fool!" I said. "He should have known better."

"Perhaps he was wiser than you think," said Agathocles. "Perhaps he's a soothsayer and reads omens."

"Soothsayer!" I said. "He'll make a pretty-looking soothsayer if the governor catches him! Though I suppose he has friends in the town."

"Why, doubtless," said Agathocles. "And, after all, why should they waste a trained man? He might even change his name and join the auxiliaries. He might have a good story, you know."

I thought, for a moment. Of course they'd be slack, now we'd left, but I couldn't believe they'd be as slack as that.

"I should hope not, I'm sure," I said, rather stiffly. "After all, the man's a deserter."

"Old Faithful," said Agathocles, laughing softly. "Always Old Faithful. You like the boy, but you'd rather see him cut to ribbons like our friends today. Now, I'm a Greek and a philosopher – I look for causes and effects."

"All Greeks are eaters of wind," I said, not insultingly, you know, but just to show him where he stood. But he didn't seem to hear me.

"Yes," he said, "I look for causes and effects. You think the man a deserter, I think him a soothsayer – that is the difference between us. Would a child of the camp have deserted the legion a century ago, or two centuries ago, Old Faithful?"

"How can I tell what anyone would do a century ago?" I said, for it was a foolish question.

"Exactly," he said. "And a century ago they would not have withdrawn the Twentieth – not from that border – not unless Rome fell." He clapped me on the back with an odious familiarity. "Do not worry about your recruit, Old Faithful," he said. "Perhaps he will even go over to the other side, and, indeed, that might be wise of him."

"Talk treason to your accounts, Greek," I growled, "and take your hand off my shoulder. I am a Roman."

He looked at me with sad eyes.

"After three hundred years in Britain," he said. "And yet he says he is a Roman. Yes, it is a very strong law. And yet we had a law and states once, too, we Greeks. Be comforted, my British Roman. I am not talking treason. After all, I, too, have spent my life with the eagles. But I look for causes and effects."

He sighed in his wine cup and, in spite of his nonsense, I could not help but feel sorry for him. He was not a healthy man and his chest troubled him at night.

"Forget them," I said, "and attend to your accounts. You'll feel better when we're really on the march."

He sighed again. "Unfortunately, I am a philosopher," he said. "It takes more than exercise to cure that. I can even hear a world cracking, when it is under my nose. But you are not a philosopher, Old Faithful – do not let it give you bad dreams."

I manage to get my sleep without dreams, as a rule, so I told him that and left him. But, all the same, some of his nonsense must have stuck in my head. For, all the way down to Anderida, I kept noticing little things. Usually, on a long march, once you get into the swing of it, you live in that swing. There's the back of the neck of the man in front of you, and the weather, fine or wet, and the hairy general, riding his horse like a bear, and the dust kicked up by the column and the business of billets for the night. The town life drops away from you like the cloak you left behind in the pawnshop and, pretty soon, you've never led any other kind of life. You have to take care of your men and see the cooks are up to their work and tell from the look on a man's face whether he's the sort of fool who rubs his feet raw before he complains. And all that's pleasant enough and so is the change in the country, and the villages you go through, likely never to see again, but there was good wine in one, and a landlord's daughter in another, and perhaps you washed your feet in a third and joked with the old girl who came down by the stream and told you you were a fine-looking soldier. It's all there, and nothing to remember, but pleasant while it lasts. And, toward the end, there's the little tightness at the back of the mind that makes you know you're coming near the fighting. But, before that, you hardly think at all.

This wasn't any different and yet I kept looking at the country. I'd been south before, as far as Londinium, but not for years, and there's no denying that it's a pleasant land. A little soft, as the people are, but very green, very smiling, between the forests. You could see they took care of their fields; you could see it was a rich place, compared to the north. There were sheep in the pastures, whole flocks of them, fat and baaing, and the baths in the towns we passed through got better all the way. And yet I kept looking for places where a cohort or two could make a stand without being cut off completely—now, why should I do that? You can say it was my business, but Mid-Britain has been safe for years. You have only to look at the villas—we've got nothing like them in the northwest. I couldn't help wondering what a crew of wild Scots or long-haired

Northmen would do to some of them. We'd have blocked up half those windows where I come from – once they start shooting fire arrows, big windows are a nuisance, even in a fortified town.

And yet, in spite of the way Agathocles rode along like a death's-head, it was reassuring too. For it showed you how solid the empire was, a big solid block of empire, green and smiling, with its magistrates and fine special ladies and theaters and country houses, all the way from Mid-Britain to Rome, and getting richer all the way. I didn't feel jealous about it or particularly proud, but there it was, and it meant civilized things. That's the difference between us and the barbarians – you may not think of it often, but, when you see it, you know. I remember a young boy, oh, eight or nine. He'd been sent down from the big house on his fat pony with his tutor, to look at the soldiers, and there he sat, perfectly safe, while his pony cropped the grass and the old man had a hand in the pony's mane. He was clean out of bowshot of the big house, and the hedges could have held a hundred men, but you could see he'd never been afraid in his life, or lived in disputed ground. Not even the old tutor was afraid – he must have been a slave, but he grinned at us like anything. Well, that shows you. I thought the worse of Agathocles, after that.

And yet, there were other things – oh, normal enough. But, naturally, you can't move a legion without people asking questions, and civilians are like hens when they start to panic. Well, we knew there was trouble in Gaul – that was all we could say. Still, they'd follow you out of the town, and that would be unpleasant. But that didn't impress me nearly as much as the one old man.

We'd halted for half an hour and he came down from his fields, a countryman and a farmer. He had a speckled straw hat on, but it takes more than a dozen years' farming to get the look out of a man's back.

"The Twentieth," he said slowly, when he saw our badge of the boar, "the Valeria Victrix. Welcome, comrade!" so I knew at once that he'd served. I gave him the regulation salute and asked him a question, and his eyes glowed.

"Marcus Hostus," he said. "Centurion of the Third Cohort of the Second, twenty years ago." He pulled his tunic aside to show me the seamed scar.

"That was fighting the Welsh tribesmen," he said. "They were good fighters. After that, they gave me my land. But I still remember the taste of black beans in a helmet," and he laughed a high old man's laugh.

"Well," I said, "I wouldn't regret them. You've got a nice little place here." For he had.

He looked around at his fields. The woman had come to the door of the hut by then, with a half-grown girl beside her, and a couple of recruits were asking her for water.

"Yes," he said, "it's a nice little place and my sons are strong. There are two of them in the upper field. Are you halting for long, Centurion? I should like them to see the eagles before I die."

"Not for long," I said. "As a matter of fact, we're

on our way to the seacoast. They seem to need us in Gaul."

"Oh," he said, "they need you in Gaul. But you'll be coming back."

"As Caesar wills it," I said. "You know what orders are, Centurion."

He looked at the eagles again.

"Yes," he said. "I know what orders are. The Valeria Victrix, the bulwark of the northwest. And you are marching to the ships — Oh, do not look at me, Centurion — I have been a centurion too. It must be a very great war that calls the Valeria Victrix from Britain."

"We have heard of such a war," I said, for he, too, had served with the eagles.

He nodded his old head once or twice. "Yes," he said, "a very great war. Even greater than the wars of Theodosius, for he did not take the Twentieth. Well, I can still use a sword."

I wanted to tell him that he would not have to use one, for there was the hut and the fields and the half-grown girl. But, looking at him, the words stuck in my throat. He nodded again.

"When the eagles go, Britain falls," he said, very quietly. "If I were twenty years younger, I would go back to the Second — that would be good fighting. Or, perhaps, to the Sixth, at Eboracum — they will not withdraw the Sixth till the last of all. As it is, I die here, with my sons." He straightened himself. "Hail, Centurion of the Valeria Victrix — and farewell," he said.

"Hail, Marcus Hostus, Centurion," I said, and they raised the eagles. I know that he watched us out of sight; though, again, I could not look back. It is true that he was an old man, and old men dream, but I was as glad that Agathocles had not heard his words.

For it seemed to me that Agathocles was always at my elbow and I grew very weary indeed of his company and his cough and what he called his philosophy. The march had done him no good—he was bonier than ever and his cheeks burned—but that did not stop his talkativeness. He was always pointing out to me little things I would hardly have noticed by myself—where a plowland had been left fallow or where a house or a barn still showed the scars of old burnings. By Hercules! As if a man couldn't plant wheat for a year without the empire's falling—but he'd point and nod his head. And then he'd keep talking—oh, about the states and the law they'd had in Greece, long before the city was founded. Well, I never argue with a man about the deeds of his ancestors—it only makes bad feeling. But I told him once, to shut him up, that I knew about Athens. A friend of mine had been stationed there once and said they had quite decent games for a provincial capital. His eyes flashed at that and he muttered something in his own tongue.

"Yes," he said. "They have decent games there. And buildings that make the sacred Forum at Rome—which I have seen, by the way, and which you have not seen—look like a child's playing with mud and rubble. That was when we had states and a law. Then we fought with each other, and it went—yes, even before the man from Macedon. And then you came and now, at last, it is your turn. Am I sorry or glad? I do not know.

Sorry, I think, for the life is out of my people — they are clever and will always be clever, but the life is out of them. And I am not philosopher enough not to grieve when an end comes."

"Oh, talk as you like, Agathocles," I said, for I was resolved he shouldn't anger me again. "But you'd better not talk like that in front of the general."

"Thank you, Old Faithful," he said, and coughed till he nearly fell from his mule. "But I do not talk like that to the general — only to persons of rare intelligence, like yourself. The general does not like me very well, as it is, but I am still useful with the accounts. Perhaps, when we get to Gaul — if we go to Gaul — he will have me flayed or impaled. I believe those are Vandal customs. Yes, that is very probable, I think, if my cough does not kill me before. But, meanwhile, I must observe — we Greeks are so curious."

"Observe all you like," I said, "but the legion's shaking down very nicely, it seems to me."

"Yes, shaking down very nicely," he said. "Do you ever think of your deserter, who went back to Deva? No, I thought not. And yet he was the first effect of the cause I seek, and there have been others since." He chuckled quite cheerfully at that and went along reciting Greek poetry to himself till the cough took him again. The poetry was all about the fall of a city called Troy — he translated some of it to me, and it sounded quite well, if you care for that sort of thing, though, as I pointed out to him, our own Vergil had covered the same subjects, as I understand it.

We had turned toward the seacoast by then — we

weren't going through Londinium after all. That disappointed our recruits, but of course the general was right about it. We'd kept excellent discipline so far, but it's a very different thing, letting the men loose in a capital. I was sorry not to see it again myself. I told the men that when they complained. This was southern country we passed through, very soft and gentle; though, on the coasts, there is danger. But, when we halted for the night, there had been no danger for years — it was a wide pocket of peace.

I remember the look of the big painted rooms of the villa, when I was summoned there. A very fine villa it was — it belonged to a rich man. They'd had Roman names so long, they'd forgotten their own stock, though the master looked British enough when you looked him full in the face. They had winged cupids painted on the walls of the dining room — they were sharpening arrows and driving little cars with doves — very pretty and bright. It must have been imported work — no Briton could paint like that. And the courtyard had orange trees in it, growing in tubs — I know what an orange tree costs, for my cousin was a gardener. A swarm of servants, too, better trained than our northern ones and sneakingly insolent, as rich men's servants are apt to be. But they were all honey to me, and sticky speeches — they knew better than to mock an officer on duty.

Well, I went into the room, and there was my general and the master of the house, both with wreaths around their heads in the old-fashioned way, and Agathocles making notes on his tablets in a corner and hiding his cough with his hand. My general had his wreath on crooked and he looked like a baited bear, though they must have had a good feed, and he liked wine. There were other people in the room – some sons and sons-in-law – all very well dressed, but a little shrill in their conversation, as that sort is apt to be, but the master of the house and my general were the ones I noticed.

My general called me in and told them who I was, while I stood at attention and Agathocles coughed. Then he said: "This is my senior centurion. . . . And how many leagues does the legion cover in a day, Centurion?"

I told him, though he knew well enough.

"Good," he said, in his thick Vandal accent. "And how many leagues would we cover in a day – let me see – accompanied by civilians, with litters and baggage?"

I told him; though, of course, he knew. It was less, of course; it made a decided difference. A legion does not march like the wind – that is not its business – but civilians slow everything up. Especially when there are women.

"As I thought," he said to the master of the villa. "As you see, it is quite impossible," and, in spite of his crooked wreath, his eyes were bleak and shrewd. Then arose a babble of talk and expostulation from the sons and the sons-in-law. I have heard such talk before – it is always the same. As I say, rich men are apt to think that all government, including the army, exists for their personal convenience. I stood at attention, waiting to be dismissed.

The master of the villa waited till the others had had their say. He was a strong man with a beaky nose, much stronger than his sons. He waited till the babble had ceased, his eyes calm, regarding our general. Then he said, in the smooth, careless voice of such men:

"The general forgets, perhaps, that I am a cousin of the legate. I merely ask protection for myself and my household. And we would be ready to move — well, within twenty-four hours. Yes, I can promise you, within twenty-four hours." There was such perfect assurance in his voice that I could have admired the man.

"I am sorry not to oblige a cousin of the legate," said my general, with his bear's eyes gleaming dully. "Unfortunately, I have my orders."

"And yet," said the master of the villa, charmingly, "a certain laxity — a certain interpretation, let us say . . ."

He left his words in the air — you could see he had done this sort of thing before, and always successfully. You could see that, all his life, he had been accustomed to rules being broken for him because of his place and name. I have liked other generals better than this general — after all, the Vandals are different from us — but I liked the way he shook his head now.

"I have my orders," he said, and lay hunched like a bear on his couch.

"Let us hope you will never regret your strict interpretation of them, General," the master of the villa said without rancor, and a cool wind blew through the room. I felt the cool wind on my own cheek, though I am a senior centurion and my appeal is to Caesar. The man was strong enough for that.

"Let us hope not," said my general gruffly, and rose. "Your hospitality has been very enjoyable." I must say, for a Vandal, he made his manners well. On the way out, the master of the villa stopped me unobtrusively.

"And what would it be worth, Centurion," he said in a low voice, "to carry a single man on your rolls who was not on your rolls before? A single man – I do not ask for more."

"It would be worth my head," I said; for though my general did not seem to be looking at me, I knew that he was looking.

The master of the villa nodded, and a curious, dazed look came over his strong face. "I thought so," he said, as if to himself. "And, after all, what then? My nephew in Gaul writes me that Gaul is not safe; my bankers in Rome write me that Rome itself is not safe. Will you tell me what place is safe if Rome is not safe any more?" he said in a stronger voice, and caught at my arm. I did not know how to answer him, so I kept silent. He looked, suddenly, very much older than he had when I entered the room.

"A king's ransom out at loan and the interest of the interest," he muttered. "And yet, how is a man to be safe? And my cousin is the legate, too – I have first-hand information. They will not bring back the legions – blood does not flow back, once it is spilt. And yet, how can I leave my house here, with everything so uncertain?"

It seemed a fine house to me, though not very defensible; but, even as he spoke, I could see the rain beating through the walls. I could see the walls fallen, and the naked people, the barbarians, huddled around a dim fire. I had not believed that possible before, but now I believed it. There was ruin in the face of that man. I could feel Agathocles tugging at my elbow and I went away—out through the courtyard where the orange trees stood in their tubs, and the bright fish played in the pool.

When we were back in our billets, Agathocles spoke to me.

"The general is pleased with you," he said. "He saw that they tried to bribe you, but you were not bribed. If you had been bribed, he would have had your head."

"Do I care for that?" I said, a little wildly. "What matters one head or another? But if Rome falls, something ends."

He nodded soberly, without coughing. "It is true," he said. "You had nothing but an arch, a road, an army and a law. And yet a man might walk from the east to the west because of it—yes, and speak the same tongue all the way. I do not admire you, but you were a great people."

"But tell me," I said, "why does it end?"

He shook his head. "I do not know," he said. "Men build and they go on building. And then the dream is shaken—it is shaken to bits by the storm. Afterwards, there follow darkness and the howling peoples. I think that will be for a long time. I meant to be a historian, when I first joined the eagles. I meant to write of the later wars of Rome as Thucydides wrote of the Greek wars. But now my ink is dry and I have nothing to say."

"But," I said, "it is there – it is solid – it will last," for I thought of the country we had marched through, and the boy, unafraid, on his pony.

"Oh," said Agathocles, "it takes time for the night to fall – that is what people forget. Yes, even the master of your villa may die in peace. But there are still the two spirits in man – the spirit of building and the spirit of destruction. And when the second drives the faster horse, then the night comes on."

"You said you had a state and a law," I said. "Could you not have kept them?"

"Why, we could," said Agathocles, "but we did not. We had Pericles, but we shamed him. And now you and I – both Romans" – and he laughed and coughed – "we follow a hairy general to an unknown battle. And, beyond that, there is nothing."

"They say it is Alaric, the Goth," I said. "They say he marches on Rome," for, till then, except in jest, we had not spoken of these wars.

"Alaric, or another, what matters?" said Agathocles. "Who was that western chieftain – he called himself Niall of the Hundred Battles, did he not? And we put him down, in the end, but there were more behind him. Always more. It is time itself we fight, and no man wins against time. How long has the legion been in Britain, Centurion?"

"Three hundred and fifty years and eight," I said, for that is something that even children know.

"Yes," said Agathocles, "the Valeria Victrix. And who remembers the legions that were lost in Parthia and Germany? Who remembers their names?"

But by then I had come back to myself and did not wish to talk to him.

"All Greeks are eaters of wind," I said. "Caw like a crow, if you like; I do not listen."

"It does not matter to me," he said, with a shrug, and a cough. "I tell you, I shall be flayed before the ending, unless my cough ends it. No sensible general would let me live, after the notes I have taken tonight. But have it your own way."

I did not mean to let him see that he had shaken me, but he had. And when, six days later, we came to Anderida and the sea, I was shaken again. The ships should have been ready for us, but they were not, though our general raged like a bear, and we had to wait four days at Anderida. That was hard, for, in four days you get to know the look of a town. They had felt the strength of the sea pirates; they were not like Mid-Britain. I thought of my man at the villa and how he might die in peace, even as Agathocles had said. But all the time, the moss would be creeping on the stone and the rain beating at the door. Till, finally, the naked people gathered there, without knowledge — they would have forgotten the use of the furnace that kept the house warm in winter and the baths that made men clean. And the fields of my veteran centurion of the

Second, would go back to witch grass and cockleburs because they were too busy with killing to plant the wheat in the field. I even thought back to my deserter and saw him living, on one side or the other, but with memory of order and law and civilized things. Then that, too, would go, and his children would not remember it, except as a tale. I wanted to ask Agathocles what a race should leave to its kind, but I did not, for I knew he would talk of Greece, and I am a Roman.

Then we sailed, on a very clear day, with little wind, but enough to get us out of harbor. It came suddenly, as those things do, and we did not have time to think. I was very busy — it was only when we were ready to embark that I thought at all. I am a child of the camp and the legion is my hearth. But I knew, as we stood there, waiting, what we were leaving — the whole green, rainy, smoky, windy island, with its seas on either hand and its deep graves in the earth. We had been there three hundred and fifty and eight — we had been the Valeria Victrix. Now we followed a hairy general to an unknown battle, over the rim of the world, and we would win fights and lose them, but our time was over.

I heard the speech for the last time — the British Latin. After that, it would only be the legion, wherever we went. Our general stood like a bear — he would take care of us as long as he could. Agathocles looked seasick already — his face was pinched and thin, and he coughed behind his hand. Before us lay the wide channel and the great darkness. And the Sixth still held Eboracum — I wished, for a moment, that I had been with the Sixth.

"Get your packs on board, you sons!" I shouted to the men.

As the crowd began to cheer, a little, I wanted to say to somebody, "Remember the Valeria Victrix! Remember our name!" But I could not have said it to anyone, and there was no time for those things.

www.ingramcontent.com/pod-product-compliance
Lightning Source LLC
Chambersburg PA
CBHW051202120726
47905CB00004B/951
9781473315860